A Twist
In The Tale

T F Grills

A Twist
In The Tale

T F Grills
Year of publication: 2020

A Twist In The Tale

ISBN: 978 -0-578-68887-9

For further information: terryfgrills@gmail.com

Acknowledgments

This book would not have been possible without the help of my wife Sue, spending many hours reading and making valued suggestions to the manuscript, editing, and formatting. Thanks to our friends Liz and Ian Plane for their help, suggestions, and encouragement. Also, thanks to Ron and Marge Jones who put considerable effort into ensuring English American phraseology was used and not my home language, South African English. A special thanks to Dave King for his considerable work in reading through various editions of the manuscript and making invaluable suggestions.

Prologue

Meet Grant Hughes, your everyday young businessman who is unexpectedly caught up in a web of conspiracy, lies and, deceit. He is being framed for murder by his family members.

   The evidence against him is overwhelming and he is left wondering to whom he can now turn and trust, it would seem only his attorney.

   An insurance investigating detective enters the scene. She discovers evidence taken from a missing boat that could turn this whole case upside-down. They become a formidable team, each with their motives and agendas.

   See how this drama twists and turns and how lies are portrayed as truths and truths as lies.

Preface

For two years the memory of my ordeal spun around in my head giving me sleepless nights and restless days. After telling my friends what happened, they said, it was such a fascinating story you should write a book.
I finally decided to put pen to paper giving me peace of mind, here it is.
A Twist In the Tale.

Route of the Yacht Skipjack

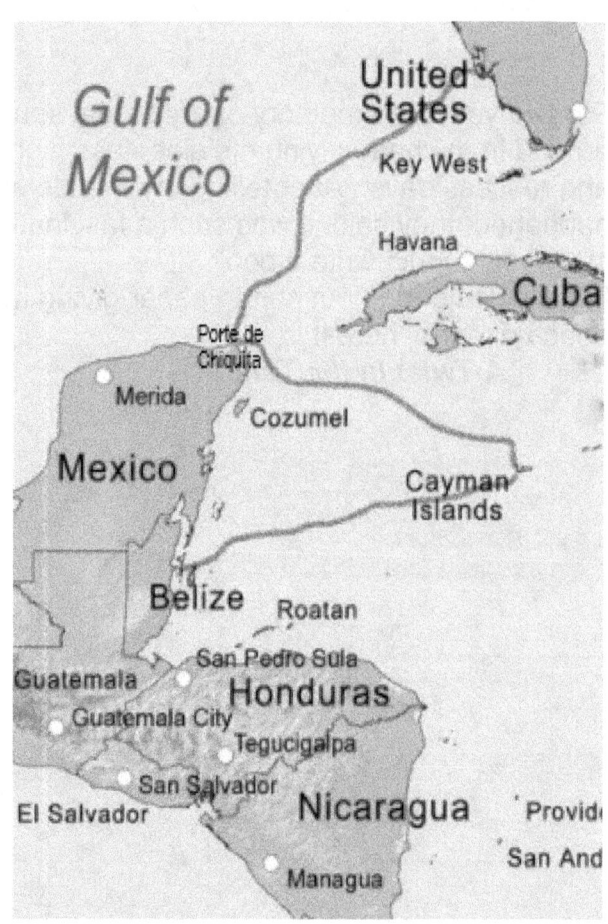

CHAPTER 1

The Saturday night flight from Philadelphia to Boston is late taking off, as a result, it will be close to 11:00 p.m. before I reach Sylvia's place in Cambridge, Massachusetts. I call the house from the plane just before take-off and tell her I'll be late. She informs me I'm sleeping in the attached studio and I have it all to myself, so I will not be disturbing anyone. What she really means is that I don't need to face Bob at 7:30 a.m. tomorrow demanding his coffee, paper, and breakfast in that order.

I'm attending the International Electrical Conference on Monday hosted by GE at the Boston Convention and Exhibition Center, being the third conference of this kind. The first one was held in Berlin, Germany, and hosted by Siemens, and the previous one was held in Paris, France, and hosted by ABB. One of the topics up for discussion at this session is (EMP) Electromagnetic Pollution and I have been asked to present a paper titled 'The health hazards associated with the long term exposure to (EMF) Electrical Magnetic Fields, produced by high voltage transmission power lines.'

The conference is for a whole week. I can't afford to be away from work for more than a day as we are right in the middle of a high-profile project worth millions. Because this year's conference is in the United States it makes it a lot easier for me to attend for one day only. Many of these conferences are an excuse for business-people to get away from the office on company expenses with the opportunity of entertaining customers and prospective clients. In a company the size of ours with a small staff of specialized people, entertainment doesn't even feature on our annual budget.

Usually, Norman Harper, the other senior partner, and I would attend these conferences, but being in the middle of a project, only one of us can afford to be away from the office. Conferences of this nature are an important networking opportunity for us to rub shoulders with some of the big shots in the industry and to meet up with colleagues from previous companies we worked with.

The flight to Logan Airport Boston was about one and a half hours. I had planned to make sure my presentation and PowerPoint were all in sync while on the plane. It has been a mad day going to work for a few hours and rushing around getting Jason to and from little league baseball, so I decided to hell with it, I'll have a scotch, sit back, and relax. I'm still chastising myself about why in hell's name I managed to get myself talked into visiting my sister-in-law Sylvia and her husband Bob. I told my wife Diane a few months ago that I had been invited to present a paper at this year's Electrical Conference in Boston. She then immediately jumped on the bandwagon suggesting we should take the opportunity, and all fly up for the weekend to visit them. Anyway, I quickly put a halt to Diane's idea. Firstly, I said, the company is not going to pay for the family to fly up to Boston and we don't have that kind of money to spend on a trip, just for a few days. Our company (GER) Global Electrical Research went public two and a half years ago and I didn't want the shareholders thinking we were squandering their profits. Secondly, I said I didn't think I could put up with Bob for more than a day at most. To keep the family peace, I agreed rather than flying Sunday night, I would go up on Saturday night, spend the

2

rest of the weekend with my sister-in-law and brother-in-law and return home after the conference on Monday afternoon. That arrangement seemed to be more acceptable to Diane. I still didn't see why Diane was making such a big issue about it, as she did not like Bob any more than I did. Sylvia visited us every six weeks or so, for a few days, when they visited their mother together. So, it isn't as if she hadn't seen her sister for some time.

It's 10:15 p.m. when I hail a cab outside Logan Airport. I give the cab driver the address in Willow Grove Lane, Cambridge. From my two years at Harvard where I completed my Ph.D., I knew where Cambridge was, it's not that far from the university. Certainly, an upscale area, not that I would have expected anything else, nothing but the best for Bob. At 11:15 p.m. the cab turns from Willow Grove Lane into their driveway, the cab's tires crunching on the long gravel driveway leading to their house.

I remember seeing pictures of the house that Sylvia had sent to Diane when they bought it two years ago. It was a typical British architecturally styled home, commonly referred to in the early 19th century as Colonial Revival. Stone steps lead up to a covered columned porch with an elaborate heavy oak door. Three dormer windows on the second floor look out over the extensive front garden that extends for two acres down to Willow Grove Lane. The old carriage shed adjoining the house had many years ago been converted into a studio, and I guessed that's where I would be sleeping for the next two nights. A new three-car garage had been built on the opposite side of the house, giving the house a long impressive frontage.

Sylvia must have seen the lights coming up the

driveway, as she is waiting at the top of the stone stairs as the cab pulls up in front of the house. I pay the driver, take my overnight bag, hook my laptop case over my shoulder and make my way up the steps to the porch. Silvia is wearing a dressing gown pulled tightly around her to ward off the chill that's present in the night air. I drop my overnight bag on the tiled floor and put my one arm around her small waist and give her a big hug and peck on the cheek.

"Hi Sylvia, sorry it's so late".

She pulls away from the embrace, looks at me for a few seconds, and says, "Hi stranger, long time no see. Come inside, it's chilly out here".

"What do you mean 'stranger,' I saw you only a couple of weeks ago down at our place?"

"Yes, but I hardly ever see you, you are always at work or traveling somewhere."

"Aww —— come on it's not that bad, where's Bob?"

"He's already in bed, dead to the world, snoring his head off."

I pick up my bag and follow her into the hallway.

Wow is this place for real, I say to myself as she closes the door behind me.

The hallway is at least ten feet wide and fifteen feet long. At the end of the hallway is the stairway, I assume goes up to the five bedrooms on the second floor. Two doors lead from either side of the hallway. The ceiling is high with a huge elaborate chandelier hanging on a gold chain. The floors are dark wooden oak. I follow Sylvia through the door on the right that leads into the dining room and then through another door into a large well-furnished and equipped kitchen.

4

"Your digs are down this way," she says pointing at a door at the end of the kitchen. I follow her through the door, down a short passage to another door opening into the studio.

"Here we are, make yourself at home, that's the bathroom over there," she says pointing to a door, "here is a closet to hang your stuff, just push some of Bob's old clothes to the side and you'll find shelves also to put stuff on. Towels are on the bed. If you want a hot drink, there's a coffee machine and a kettle on the table, cold stuff is in the mini bar fridge over there next to the TV. Help yourself to whatever you want, and we will see you in the morning. Oh! ―― Diane said I was to make sure I come and wake you, as you sleep like the dead, is that right?"

"Yes, please Sylvia, come shake me awake otherwise I won't wake up."

"Goodnight stranger see you in the morning. If you are cold there are extra blankets on the top shelf of the closet."

With those last words, she closes the door and leaves me standing in the middle of the room, looking at this king size bed and the five-star décor.

Sleep doesn't come easy and I don't know why. Normally I don't have any problem sleeping in all kinds of beds and places, having traveled extensively. I felt strange and sort of uncomfortable, maybe because I detected a bit of resentment in Sylvia's attitude because I had not agreed to bring the whole family, or was I just being too sensitive. The two sisters are remarkably close, they speak at least once a week. That's the way it has always been with them, for as long as I have been on the scene.

Diane and Sylvia, with two years difference

between them, are unalike in character and appearance. I can remember when we were all in high school together, Diane was the academic, and Sylvia was the party girl, only doing academically what was needed to get her to college. Every jock in the school wanted to date Sylvia and she could pick and choose whom she wanted, playing one against the other.

I remember one party we had at their parent's shore house down in New Jersey, where the house was right on Toms River. They had their own pier and boat. Diane and I were already dating, and we were in our senior year at high school. Sylvia was turning sixteen that year and in grade ten, but she looked twenty and had a body any woman would kill for. It was late in the evening, we had all been drinking and decided to go skinny dipping.

I can still see her, as if it were yesterday. We were all in the water except for Sylvia, she was standing on the pier next to the last mooring post with a light. I was in the water just below her and I remember saying, "Aren't you coming in?"

She gave me that impish look, removed her skimpy top revealing her beautifully formed breasts, and then pulled down her shorts and G string, winked, gave me a little sly smile, and dove over the top of me into the water. Sylvia had always been Diane's little sister to me, and I have always called her Sissy. With that image of her in my mind, I finally fell asleep.

6

CHAPTER 2

I'm dreaming I'm climbing this tall tree and the higher I climbed, the more sexually excited I became, I could feel a rhythmic muscular contraction in my pelvic region. I stretch to reach the higher branches to pull myself up the tree trying to enhance the sexual pleasure, but the branches are too far for me to reach that ultimate sexual satisfaction.

I suddenly wake up with Sissy straddled naked across my body, her lovely breasts no more than six inches from my nose.

"What the hell are you doing woman?" I exclaim.

"Well, instead of shaking you awake, I thought I'd screw you awake. Don't you agree this is a far nicer way to wake up? Hey now boy, don't you go all soft on me now you're awake."

"Christ Sylvia, where's Bob?"

"Relax, he's off playing golf in New York, left early this morning and won't be back until Monday."

"Come on Grant don't say you haven't wanted to fuck me. Every male in high school had the hots for me and you were no exception and now at last, after twenty, twenty-two years hey, you now get the chance to live out one of your fantasies. You'll never get this chance again, so lie back and enjoy it while it lasts."

She pushes her breasts against my face and says, "My tits are bigger and firmer than Diane's you must admit. Don't feel guilty Grant, it's me fucking you. Is Diane going to hear about this from you, I guess not? You know the old saying, 'what happens in Boston, stays in Boston."

I can't help myself and the more Sissy thrusts

and gyrates on top of me, and the more she oohs!
—— and aahs! —— the more the feeling I had in my
dream returns. The pleasure is mounting and I'm
back in the uppermost branches of the tree again,
but now they are within my reach. I can feel the
excitement swelling in my pelvic region and
suddenly there's this euphoric sensation as I
orgasm. Sissy must have sensed this, and she
climaxed almost at the same time, with more
sounds of pleasure.

 We lie next to each other on the bed for a short
while, not saying a thing, after all, what was there to
say anyway. Nothing would have made things
better or worse, the deed is done. Sissy leans over
the bed and removes a few tissues out of the box
on the bedside table. She bunches them together,
sticks them between her legs, and gets up from the
bed, takes her flimsy PJs, and says,

 "I'm going to have a shower and get dressed,
then I'll come down and make us a nice breakfast,
then we can go and see our boat. How does that
sound to you?" she says. just as casually as that,
one would never have guessed that she has just
fucked her sister's husband.

 "Sure, sounds perfect,"

 I lie in bed for another few minutes reflecting
on what has just happened. Feeling guilty for
having been unfaithful to Diane, moreover with her
sister. Did I have much of a choice? Well yes, one
always has choices, and I made the wrong one at
the height of passion, hopefully I will not live to
regret it someday.

 I shower, dress in a pair of shorts, a t-shirt, and
sneakers. By this time, it is already 9:40 a.m. I call
Diane to tell her I have arrived okay. I was sure
that Sissy had already called her earlier this

morning before she came and woke me in her unconventional way. The phone rings several times and then goes over to voicemail, so I leave a message. I tell Diane we are going to see the new boat, and I will call again later, and I will also try her mobile. She doesn't pick up her mobile phone either, so I leave her the same message. Maybe she is driving to her mom's place. I make the bed and hang the towels back on the drying rack and make my way to the kitchen. As soon as I open the bedroom door leading into the passage that leads to the kitchen, I know that Sissy is already there as the smell of bacon cooking comes wafting down through the passage.

"Mmmm, smells good," I say as I step into the huge gourmet kitchen.

"There's coffee in the machine, or if you prefer there's OJ in the refrigerator, help yourself. Mugs and glasses are over there in the glass cabinet to the left," as she points to a row of cabinets on the far wall.

"Coffee sounds good."

"I'm doing fried eggs, are you good with that?"

"Yep, two is just fine."

"How do you like them?"

"Over easy is fine thanks."

"Grant, push the toaster down please, it's on the counter. I thought we would eat here at the kitchen counter, are you okay with that?"

Looking through the kitchen's double casement window, I say, "Sure that's great, you have such a lovely view onto your back property from here."

"Yes, we are lucky having that big grove of trees at the back, with no neighbors directly behind us."

We sit opposite each other, not saying

9

anything until we finish eating.

"How's your coffee, need a refill?" asks Sissy.

"Yes please." She takes my mug, goes over to the coffee machine, tops up both mugs, and brings them back.

Sissy takes a sip of her coffee, looks at me, "You know Grant, I've never known anyone that can sleep as soundly as you do. When Diane told me, I would need to put a stick of dynamite under you, I thought she was joking. When I crept in and lay next to you, I expected you to wake up any minute. When you didn't, I put my hand on your leg and started to move it up towards your crotch and you just lay there on your back breathing deeply. Then I touched your manhood and began caressing it."

"Come on now Sissy, spare me all the details."

"I'm just interested to know what was going on in your mind and what you were feeling, while you were sleeping. Surely you must have been aware of some sensation otherwise you would not have got an erection. The harder you became, that's when I started to get excited. I decided to mount you and still you slept through all that, only waking up when I started to become more active and passionate, thank God! How the hell do you wake up when you are away on business trips like now for instance, if you hadn't been staying here?"

"I have a special alarm clock that produces a high-frequency sound like a smoke detector alarm. It has three settings Low, Medium, and High. When I stay at hotels, I sleep with it under my pillow set at Low and so far, it has always woken me. Believe me, even at the low setting it is very loud, and I've had a few hotel managers enquire about it."

"Okay, let's dump these few things in the dishwasher and head out to the marina and I'll take you for a spin on our new acquisition. Sorry Bob's not here, as he would have loved showing it to you himself."

"Where do you have it moored?"

"Not far, at the Riverside Boat Club, it's about fifteen minutes from here. I called down there early this morning and told them we will be coming at about this time. They'll have the boat up at the main marina, all gassed up ready to go. Do you have a warm windbreaker or something, as it can get a bit chilly out there this time of the year?"

"No, I didn't bring anything like that."

"No problem, I'm sure one of Bob's windbreakers will fit you. He has half a dozen! What about sneakers?"

"Only these I have on."

"Show me the soles."

I lift my foot and Sissy says, "Mmmm, not the best but I guess they'll be okay. I'll run upstairs, brush my teeth, get some jackets and we can be out of here."

I go back into the studio, brush my teeth, and have a pee. I come back to sit and wait for Sissy. Twenty minutes later she comes back downstairs.

"There's a nice restaurant on the front bay we frequent where one can moor the boat. I thought we could have lunch there and then I'll do something light for dinner at home if that's okay with you?"

"Sounds perfect, I'm in your capable hands Sissy, as I've already experienced," and we both laugh.

I pick up the jackets, Sissy picks up her phone from the counter, stuffs it into her small purse, and we walk out through the laundry, and through another door into the three-car garage. She presses the garage door opener on the side of the wall and the large door lifts. There are three vehicles parked there.

"We'll take the Land Cruiser, it's more practical for going down to the club."

The white Toyota Land Cruiser is parked at the far end, so we must walk around the front of the other two vehicles. The first car is a grey Lexus LS500, the other a silver Mercedes SLK convertible with the top-up. I can't see the model because it's backed in.

"I gather Bob got a cab to the airport; I ask?"

"Yes, much easier than finding parking and all that crap at the airport."

"So, you drive the Benz?"

"Yeh, sometimes, we both like driving it, but for everyday stuff, I like the Cruiser it gives me a sense of security."

I toss the jackets on the back seat of the Toyota and we drive out of the garage. Sissy closes the treble garage door behind us.

It takes us fifteen minutes to reach the club. We park, I get out and take the jackets from the back seat. We walk a short way to a small office where Sissy shows her ID and club membership to the young guy on duty, who hands her the boat keys. He points out roughly where the boat is moored. We walk along the planked wet slip with boats of all sizes moored on each side, until we stop at a white and blue boat. I imagined the boat to be about 23 Ft. long, it has the name Taimen written in fancy lettering on the front side, but I don't think that is the make.

"Well, what do you think?"

"Looks nice, but then I'm not a boat guy. What sort of boat is it? Give me some details, we engineers always want to know what makes things tick."

"I'll give you a run down as we go along, let's get this baby mobile, I'll hop in and get her running. She should already be warm from being brought up from her permanent mooring and having been gassed up. Pass me the jackets and I'll stow them in the locker. Can you loosen the bowline from the mooring cleat and push the nose out?"

I loosen the bowline and toss it on board, I hold onto the mooring post and push the nose with my foot and the bow moves away from the pier. By this time, the motor is running.

"Okay, we are up and running, untie the stern line and hop in."

I manage to do this with some grace, without losing my balance and falling on my ass. I go up to the bow, coil up the line and store it in the front hatch, then do the same with the bow fender, as well as the stern line and fender.

"Looks like you know your way around a boat," she says as she slowly maneuvers the boat out into the main river channel. By this time, I'm standing up front next to her in the cockpit.

"I've been on a few boats fishing when I was a kid with my dad, so I got the general idea of what to do, when."

Once clear of all the moorings and 'No Wake' signs, she eases the throttle forward and the boat gets up on the plane.

"I assume one needs some form of license to drive this?" I ask.

"Oh yes, you bet, I had to study and then pass a test. I have the State Boaters Education Card.

It's like your car drivers license."

"You look pretty confident handling it,"

"Thanks, I love it, I take it out whenever I have the time."

"So, tell me a bit about her?"

"Sure, as you can see, she has an inboard motor, it's a 250-hp. turbocharged, she's a 25 Ft. Sea Crest double skin fiberglass made by Stingray in New Jersey. She's only two years old, Bob picked her up for a song, paying $100k for her. Apparently from some guy who owed him a favor. You know Bob and his favors! Below there were originally two cabins sleeping four, one cabin in the forward bow and one amidships, but we had the forward cabin removed and the bow modified to give us more room down there, so now it only sleeps two. The galley is fully equipped, sink, two-burner stove, microwave, and fridge. It has a fully enclosed head/shower with a flush toilet, nice lighting, and generous storage. It also has a built-in 2.5KW 12/120V generator/alternator."

"Wow, that's quite some boat!"

As we cruise downriver, I get a chance to take in the features of the boat. From where I'm standing on the left, there is one console and directly behind me a swivel chair, then to my right the door leading below, then the console supporting the helm. Behind the helm console, there is also a swivel chair. Directly behind the two swivel chairs, plush cushioned bench seats wrap around the sides with a gap on the right-back, to give one access to the back of the boat, where there is a platform for entering the water for swimming, diving, and skiing. Here is where one presumably has access to the engine.

"Although we have plenty of power, we can't

just go speeding along, as you can see," she says. "All along the river there are yacht and boat clubs, people canoeing, kayaking, and rowing so we have to keep to a speed limit. Up ahead you can see the Charlestown Bridge, there we will have to go through the Charles Dam River Lock. Let's hope we don't have to wait too long."

There are four other boats in front of us at the lock.

"How many boats can the lock accommodate?"

"This is the small lock, it's more for pleasure craft, it's 200 ft. long, 22 Ft. wide and 17 Ft. deep. The one next to us is for commercial vessels, which is 300 Ft. long and 40 Ft. wide. The four boats in front of us and ourselves, should all fit in the small lock. Hurrah! The gates are opening, we should be in and out in about thirty minutes."

I never experienced being in a boat, in a lock, I'm surprised at how fast the water fills the lock. While we waited for the lock to fill, Sissy takes me below and gives me a tour of the accommodation, shows me all the features and the modifications they have done. Very impressive. I'm amazed at the amount of space there is below. There are windows all around giving plenty of light. One does not feel hemmed in, or claustrophobic at all.

Once we clear the locks, we head right out past East Boston on our left, out towards Boston harbor. Sissy now has the throttle full forward and we are skimming over the surface, literally flying along at 45 mph. Her long black hair is blowing in the wind behind her, she looks at me, smiles and I could see she was in her element, in control and she has the power. We pass many other pleasure craft coming and going and a few large commercial vessels. From my time here at university, I recognize many of the landmarks along the shoreline as we pass them. We race on down between Thompson and Spectacle Islands and then make a sharp right, heading towards Marina Bay. As we get closer, she throttles back, we come off the plane and slowly cruise into Safe Marina Harbor where we find a mooring. We secure the boat, take our jackets, and walk the two blocks to Bayside Bar & Grill.

By the time we get to the restaurant, it's 12:30 p.m. and the place is packed. There are no tables available, so we sit at the bar and each order a beer. We don't have too long to wait when a waitress shows us to a table with a nice view of the bay.

"That's what I want," says Sissy, pointing to a large catamaran that was cruising out to sea.

"How big would you think she is?"

"I'm not sure, but I would say looking at her from here, 35-40 Ft. There's one moored like that further up the river. I've seen it a few times when we have cruised upstream, it could even be that one, I can't see her name from here."

"I wonder what something like that would set one back?"

"For a 42 Ft. new, half million-plus. Pre-owned, say two or three years old, you could pick one up for $377 to $400K, depending on its accessories and fittings and whether it has been fitted out for long sea voyages," she says.

"Wow! I'm impressed, looks like you've done some research, Sissy."

"Oh yes, I've been doing some browsing to see what's out there. I would like to do some serious sailing one day."

"You guys ready to order?" the waitress asks.

16

"We have some specials today if you are interested."

"No, I'm okay thanks, I'll have the grilled salmon, sauté potatoes, and the house salad," Sissy says.

"Make that two, and can we have a bottle of your Giessen Sauvignon Blanc, thanks."

"Would you like some water with your meal?" the waitress asks.

"Yes please," we both reply.

"Have you done any sailing before?" I ask.

"Sure, you remember my folks had the shore house in Toms River. You guys came down there a few times. Anyway, when we were kids growing up, we'd go down in the summer and dad would enroll us in the Juniors Sailing Program. We started when we were eight years old and when we were twelve, we had to stop, as dad sold the house because of his medical condition. At the time we hated sailing, it was dad's way of keeping us off the beach. Today I'm thankful he made us do it. Now I want to do a more advanced course and get my ASA certification. I've just signed up for a course that starts next week."

"Excuse my ignorance, but what is the ASA?" I ask.

"The ASA stands for American Sailing Association."

"So how long is the course?"

"It's a four-week course, but as I said it's only the Basic ASA Bareboat Skipper Certificate and I wanted to get it under my belt before the cold weather sets in. Next year I want to take the more advanced ASA courses, eventually getting my ASA 114 Catamaran Cruising Skipper Certificate but maybe I'll do that one day, somewhere where it's tropical and nice and warm."

"You're really serious about this aren't you, what does Bob think of all this?"

"He's right there with me, as you may know, Bob has been sailing all his life, his folks had a 35 Ft. monohull until they mysteriously disappeared somewhere near the Matinicus Island in the Gulf of Maine, must be about ten years ago now I believe, so he has always been keen that we both are competent sailors."

The food arrives, the salmon is cooked perfectly. We eat in silence, each lost in our thoughts.

"Can I pour you some more wine?" I ask.

"No thanks Grant, I had better not have another glass if I'm going to get us home safe this afternoon," and we both laughed.

"Okay how about coffee then, because I could do with a cup?"

"Yes, coffee would be nice," she says.

I catch the waitress' eye, she comes over and asks, "Shall I bring the dessert tray?"

"Not for me, thanks," says Sissy, "just black coffee."

"No, I won't have any either thanks."

"Just two coffees then, one with cream and one black," I tell the waitress.

Sissy's phone rings, she apologizes and pulls it out of her purse and presses it to her ear.

"Hello Bob —— we are at the Bayside Bar & Grill —— okay, that's not a problem we can cab it – —— okay, see you sometime tomorrow."

"Bob wants me to leave the boat here. He'll pick it up tomorrow and take it for service, saving him having to come down the river and through the locks on Monday morning when they will be much busier. Hope you don't mind?"

"No, I don't mind, it would have been nice to have gone back on the boat but it's no big deal, we can catch a cab or Uber, whatever."

"What the hell, I'm not driving now, I'll have that glass of wine if there is still some in the bottle," says Sissy.

"Sure." I pour what's left in the bottle in her glass, and ask, "Where do you have the boat serviced?"

"We haven't had it serviced yet and I'm not sure where Bob is taking it. More than likely to some contact of his around here who will give him a good deal."

The coffee comes and we sip, looking out over the bay.

"Thinking about Bob and his folks, I didn't know about the accident. That must have been a terrible shock for Bob to lose both his parents like that."

"Yes, I believe he took it badly, he started drinking heavily and nearly lost the family business. Fortunately, his father's partner bought him out and helped him into a recovery program. Eventually, with the help of friends and the AA, he turned his life around," says Sissy.

"Wow —— that's quite something, I had no idea! What sort of business was his dad in?"

"His dad was in the trucking business, CC Trucking."

"Oh yes, I think I've seen Bob wearing some old t-shirts with that logo," I say.

"How did Bob end up in the brokering business?"

"You really want to know?"

"Well brokering is so far from trucking; I was just curious how he got into it."

19

"I'll tell you what, we'll call a cab now as it's going to be after five before we get back through Sunday's home going traffic. We can chat more tonight over dinner, I think we had better make sure the boat is properly moored before we leave, but I need to visit the restroom before we go."

"Okay you go and visit the restroom; I'll see if I can catch the waitress' eye and get the bill."

When she gets back, I say, "I'm still waiting for the waitress to bring the bill."

"Don't worry Mr. Hughes, it's been settled."

"You cheeky wench, I was going to pick up the tab," I say jokingly.

"Aww,——are you all upset now bro?"

She hooks her arm through mine and we walk out of the restaurant and back to the boat. Sissy climbs in, locks all the hatches, and switches off the fuel line. We make sure the bow and stern lines are secure and the fenders are at the right length.

"I don't really like leaving her here like this, but Bob said she would be quite safe and anyway the boat is fully insured.

CHAPTER 3

We call a cab but it's another thirty minutes before it arrives and around 5:30 p.m. before we arrive at the Riverside Boat Club to pick up the Land Cruiser. Little is said on the drive home, Sissy opens the garage with the remote and stops in front of the garage to let me out before she parks the Cruiser.

"Can I ask you to do me a big favor, normally Bob does it, tomorrow is trash pickup day and the trash can has to be wheeled down to the road, will you do that for me please."

"Sure, no problem," I say.

The large two-wheeled black plastic trash can is in the garage just inside the door leading into the laundry. Pulling it out of the garage and onto the driveway, now I know why Sissy didn't fancy wheeling it over the gravel, it was a pain in the ass. I leave it on the side of the road where I see other neighbors have left their trash cans. I walk back up to the house and enter through the garage, closing it after me by pressing the button near the inside door.

"Sissy I must call Diane again; she will think I'm having too good a time up here."

I take out my mobile and call the house. After three rings it's picked up and a timid little voice says, "Hello,— hello." I say, "Is that daddy's big buddy?"

"Mommy, mommy, it's daddy, when are you coming home daddy? We saw 'Grammy' today and had brownies and I got to play the piano, bye daddy, here's mommy."

"Hi, how's things in Boston, I would have expected you to have called earlier?" she says.

"I did call the house this morning but there was no answer, then I tried your mobile and it went to the message, did you check it?"

"No, I guess not. So, what have you all been up to,—— has Bob been his normal conceited self?" she asks.

"I thought maybe Sissy had spoken to you earlier this morning before I got up. My message I left you said I got in okay last night. Bob has a golf date today in New York and is staying over tonight."

"No, I haven't spoken to Sissy in a few days," she says.

"Oh okay, well we went out on the new boat, then had lunch at a nice place on the marina overlooking the bay. We left the boat at the marina because Bob will pick it up on Monday and take it for a service. We got a cab to go and get Sissy's wheels at the club and have just gotten back here a few minutes ago. Jason said you went to see your mom, how is she?"

"She's okay, memory is getting worse, Jason finds it a bit strange and can't understand why she can't remember things he tells her."

"Yes —— we knew it would be like this, anyway, do you want to speak to your sister?"

"Yes, let me have a quick word with her, I'm in the throes of putting something together for dinner, good luck with your paper tomorrow."

"Thanks, I'll hand you over to Sissy."

I call Sissy who has her head in the fridge.

"Sissy — Diane wants a word."

I hand her my mobile phone as she walks from the fridge.

"Hi, big sister what's up?"——"Umm I don't think so"——"Sister you worry too much, leave it to me, it's all under control okay, I'll speak to you next week, love you, bye."

With that, Sissy hands me back my phone. "Does Diane always sweat the small stuff?" Sissy asks.

"Oh yes, Diane is the perpetual worrier, what is it she is on about now?"

"We want to fly mom up for Thanksgiving and we are looking at all the scenarios and Diane can only see red flags; we'll sort it out next week." "Are you hungry?"

"No, not really, that was a sizable portion of fish I had for lunch."

"How does a cheese and mushroom omelet, with a green salad on the side sound?"

"Great, I'm sure that will touch the spot just right."

Sissy goes to the fridge and gets a carton of eggs, milk, butter, mushrooms and lays it all on the counter.

"What can I do?"

"You can grate the cheese if you like, there's a new block of cheese in the door of the fridge."

"Okay, where do I find the grater?"

"There's a Cuisine Automatic grater in the bottom of that cupboard over there," she says, pointing to a cupboard on the far-left wall.

I find the cheese grater and plug it into the outlet. I unwrap and cut the cheese with a large sharp kitchen knife that I find in the kitchen drawer, feeding the thick slices into the grater and in two minutes I have a bowl of grated cheese.

"Well, that didn't take too long, anything else I can do?"

"No, I don't think so, just sit here and talk to me. Oh! I've just remembered, do you know anything about guns?"

"Yes, a bit I guess, I own a few, why?"

"Bob bought me a gun, saying I should learn to use it as one never knows when one may need it. Before he left, he took it out of the safe and put it in the sideboard drawer in the dining room for me. He said I should check to see if there were still rounds in the magazine, as we had it at the range some weeks ago and he could not remember if he reloaded it. Will you check it for me, please? There have been several home intrusions around here lately and it's always better to be prepared."

"Sure,"—— I walk into the dining room and over to the large sideboard. "Which drawer did you say, Sissy?" I call out.

"I didn't, just have a look," she calls back from the kitchen.

I find the gun in the second drawer I open, together with a box of cartridges. It's a Glock G19, not really a guy's type of gun, more for a lady, but then maybe that's why he bought it for Sissy, not for himself. I pick it up, it's a nice reliable gun, the magazine holds fifteen rounds. I eject the magazine and as there were only three cartridges left, I reload it with a further twelve rounds. I slip the magazine back into the pistol, make sure the safety is on, return it to the drawer and go back into the kitchen.

"Okay I've loaded it again for you, it only had three bullets in the magazine. It now has a full magazine of fifteen rounds, the safety is on and I put it back in the second drawer on the left. Who recommended you use hollow point bullets?" I ask.

"Oh — when Bob and I went to practice at the range, one of the guys there said they had the best stopping power for short-range."

"Yeh they certainly do make a mess when

they impact, I hope you don't need to use it too soon," I say.

"Would you like to open a bottle of wine? There's white in the wine cooler there under the counter and red you'll find in the wine cabinet in the dining room, your choice. Dinner will be ready in a few minutes, is it okay if we eat here again, it's so much easier?"

"Sure, here is fine, I'll get a bottle of white." I open the wine cooler and select a bottle of Italian, Attems Pinot Grigio. Sissy has set two places opposite each other at the counter. I find two glasses and pour the wine. The omelet and salad look very good and suddenly, I'm feeling hungry.

"Looks very appetizing, cheers" and we click glasses. "Tell me, why didn't Bob ever want to be in business with his dad?"

"Bob hated trucking and wanted nothing to do with the business, he said it was degrading. He had many bad arguments about it with his folks, you know Bob, and he's a snob. It was a sore point with him as his folks said they would pay for his studies, if he came and worked with his dad, with a view to one day taking over the business. When he finished school and got his MBA at the University of Massachusetts in accounting, he told them he wanted to go into the finance business and was going to do his internship with Peel & Son Investment Brokers. Well, that was the last straw, his dad said he'd have to pay back his university tuition fees. That soured their relationship even further. As you can well imagine, this only made him more determined to succeed. Even though it left him truly short most months, he paid his dad back a set sum every month until the full amount was settled, with interest."

"Peel & Son also sponsored him for his FINRA including all the necessary series exams. He is professionally qualified and fully licensed to trade in all commodities if he wishes."

"Yes, I wouldn't doubt his qualifications for a second, he is very clever and shrewd. I just didn't know about his folks. Did they ever reconcile their differences?"

"Their accident happened long before I came on the scene, but from what I can gather, they did eventually have some relationship, and he did visit occasionally with his mom."

"When did Bob open Croning Investments?"

"That must have been four years or so before the folk's accident. After the accident he started drinking and was trying to manage both his company and his dad's old trucking company he had then inherited, resulting in both companies doing badly. His dad's partner in the business who owned 25% share, got Bob into AA and they managed to pull the trucking business back on its feet again. Bob just had no interest in the trucking business and decided to sell his 75% to his partner so he could concentrate on his investment business."

"Well, that seems to be the best thing that could have come out of that whole sad state of affairs, because he certainly seems to be doing very well for himself now."

We finish eating our omelet, stacking the dishes and pans in the dishwasher, I pick up the wine bottle which is still half full, and we go through to the living room with our wine glasses.

"You know, it still fascinates me to know how someone can sleep as soundly as you do, is it some form of sleep disorder?"

"Well yes —— it is a sleep disorder. It's part of the Parasomnia disorders, like sleepwalking, talking and such. They have categorized it under the banner of Circadian Rhythm Disorder. Mine is a particularly rare case and they don't know why I should have it. All the tests I had as a kid revealed nothing of any significance. Now I just live with it."

"The special alarm clock that gives off a high-frequency sound, very much like your smoke alarm. As I explained at breakfast it has three settings Low, Medium, and High. My mom got it for me when I was in college. I used to sleep with it under my pillow in the low setting. My freshman year at college away from home was an absolute disaster. The guys soon found out about my deep sleeping disorder. They'd come into the dorm in the early hours of the morning, lift my bed and carry me out into the main entrance or the street. Once they carried me to the women's dorms entrance. They would paint me from top to toe, put glue in my hair, tie me to my bed and leave me in the park. I got into so much trouble, I was constantly late for lectures and my grades went to hell. Eventually, my folks said, "No more", they took me out, brought me home and I finished my degree in West Chester."

"But don't you have a Ph.D.?"

"Yes, and a Masters, but that wasn't a problem because I had my own accommodation and I also worked for a few years between my master's and my Ph.D."

"You know we never knew this about you when we were kids growing up together."

"Not many people did, my mom didn't tell anyone, not even Diane knew when we were dating."

"Why not?"

"I guess I never wanted her to feel sorry for me and it was at a stage in my life when I was embarrassed, now, of course, it's no big deal."

"Ok now, enough about me, what about your first marriage, what was his name John – some guy from California, if I remember correctly?"

"John Elsworthy was his name, he turned out to be a complete asshole. You may remember when I finished my BFA degree at Columbia New York, I wanted to see if I could break into the film industry, so I moved to LA with a friend I was rooming with at college. I don't have to tell you every beautiful girl with a great body has a dream to be a movie star and there are thousands out there strutting around LA and 95% never see the front end of a movie camera, unless it's for some shitty porn movie. Most of them end up wearing hot pants, skimpy tops, and flipping burgers. It's like the old swan song of 'who you know' but in that industry, it's 'who you sleep with' and then you still need that lucky break."

"Did you have to flip burgers or shoot some porn?"

"Not quite, had plenty of offers though to get into the high-end porn industry but once you get that label, it sticks to you like shit to a wet blanket. But I did do some night-time waitressing work for an upscale restaurant to help pay the rent. My so-called day job was not an everyday job, it depended on the company's products we were shooting, when and where."

"I had a contract with a pharmaceutical company that did diet supplements, health stimulants, and stuff like that. I would be filmed in the gym doing workouts and taking the various vitamins and rubbing creams on my body. We would go to different locations like the beach, doing some shoots there and on the tennis court, me in skimpy dresses jumping for the ball. You know all that sort of stuff; you've seen it all on television a hundred times. The irony of it is, it still sells products, as corny as it may seem. The job didn't pay that well and LA is an expensive city to live in, hence I had to supplement my earnings by doing some waitressing work. It was an interesting time. I saw how unethical the pharmaceutical world is and got to hang out with a bunch of doctors and scientists."

"One female doctor, Ann Madison, and I became quite good friends. She had gone through a bad divorce and needed a shoulder to lean on, we sort of hit it off. At that time, I was between roommates and Ann had this huge home that was left to her in the divorce settlement, so I moved in with her."

"That was nice and convenient for you, I assume rent-free?"

"Yes, there was no shortage of money. She had a garden service, cleaning service, live-in maid that cooked, together with a wide circle of friends and acquaintances, all high society. It turned out Dr. Ann Madison was the society's prescription drug provider."

"How did you find that out?" I ask.

"I'd seen her write out what I thought were prescriptions a few times at parties and one day I asked her about it, and she said yes, sure she prescribes stuff for her friends when they need it. She said it's not like she's prescribing heroin, meth or coke, its pain tablets, antidepressants, and such like. If she doesn't prescribe, they'll get it from some other quack doctor that will give them bad stuff. It's no big deal, it's happening all over LA, in fact, the US."

"What did you say?"

"Nothing," I said, "I wasn't about to rock the free accommodation boat."

"It was at one of those parties that I met John; he was in the film business. Long story short we dated, fell in love, he got me into a few small parts and within six months we were married. The ceremony took place in Vegas with all his hot shot friends, Ann's friends, and a handful of my friends. You guys couldn't make it and without you, mom wasn't going to come down, so I had no family. Anyway, it was one big party for the whole week, I don't think we were sober for the entire time. The marriage lasted six months, when I found out he was screwing at least two other women."

"What did you do after that?"

"Well, obviously my career in Hollywood's film world had suddenly dived to the bottom of the Pacific Ocean. I wasn't sure who was the most pissed off, me or Ann, as it was she who introduced me to John, and she had the same experience with her ex. When she wanted to put me in touch with her attorney, I said I couldn't afford a high-profile person like that. She said not to worry about the costs, we'll sort it out later. Anyway, her attorney screwed John for an out of court settlement of two million dollars plus costs. So, I walked away with two big ones and came back to New York."

"How the hell did she manage that?"

"This lady has more connections in LA than you can count. She got the two women he was sleeping with to testify against him. He knew he would lose in court, so he made an offer and we took it," she says.

"Nice one, I never knew I had a millionaire sister-in-law."

"My glass is empty; can I top you off?"

"Just a half a glass, I need to get to bed, I have a paper to present tomorrow. But tell me before I go, how did you and Bob get hooked up, what was that now, two, three years ago? I just remember the wedding reception was at his golf club here in Boston."

"Yes, that's right, it's almost three years now. Well, when I got back to New York I was at loose ends, not quite knowing what I wanted to do with my life. I was totally disheartened by my short time in the film business and I wanted to try something else, but I didn't know what. I had that money sitting in my bank that I needed to decide about. My bank had all sorts of schemes they wanted to put me into that were interesting, but I was in no hurry. My priorities were to find a job and a place to stay. At that time, I was crashing with one of my old friends on her couch and my back was taking a beating."

"One morning I was scanning the employment page in the Times and saw an advertisement for an Event & Communications Assistant at Kissena Golf Course in Flushing New York. I immediately called them, and they told me to come and see them the next day."

"Where in New York is Flushing?" I ask.

"It's out in Queens's area, not far from the Queens College City University of New York. The next day I dressed in my best glad rags and caught a cab out to Queens. I got the job, apparently, they had been looking for a person for some months. Their employment agent hadn't come up with anyone suitable, so they decided to advertise

31

themselves. I was the first one they had seen in the two weeks since the ad had been running."

"What did you do there?"

"At that time, it was a relatively new golf course and they were doing a lot of promotions, running company tournaments, that sort of stuff. I was involved in that, as well as getting new members registered and along with the day to day running of the administration work. Sometimes it got busy when there was a tournament and I would help behind the bar in the latter part of the day. It was on one of those company-sponsored golf days that I happened to be helping behind the bar when I met Bob. He had been invited to play in a four-ball with some of his clients. His foursome was the last to tee off, as a result, they were the last to come in and everybody was already in the marquee tent for the prize-giving and speeches. Bob sat down at the bar, drank a few non-alcoholic beers, and wanted to know if I was the 'Girl Friday' as he'd seen me at the front desk, at registration, halfway house, and then at the bar."

We sat there and chatted, one thing led to another and I found out he was in the finance business, but I didn't tell him that I had money to invest. We seemed to hit it off and he asked me if he could look me up the next time, he's in New York. Well, that's how we met, and the rest is history."

"How long did you continue to work at the club?"

"For just over a year, I found a nice little apartment in Queens, very convenient and not too far from the train station. Three months before we got married, I moved up to Boston and moved into Bob's apartment."

"Did you eventually tell him about the money?"

"Oh yes, I invested it with his company not long after we were dating, it did very well for me and we were able to buy the house, which we own together."

"That's nice, I'm glad that worked out well for you."

"Oh yes, the house is now valued at over $6m. Diane and I were talking recently, and I mentioned to her how much Bob had made for me and that we had been able to put a large deposit down on the house. She asked me if he could invest some money for her and I said I'd speak to Bob if she wanted me to."

"And I suppose nothing ever came of it?"

"Oh yes," Sissy said, "Diane invested fifty grand with him a few months ago, don't tell me you didn't know?"

"Strange, Diane would normally tell me about things like that."

"Oops, maybe I've let the cat out the bag."

"No big deal, she must have had her reasons."

"You're not going to blast her about it are you, because then she'll know I told you."

"No of course I won't mention it, I just hope Bob makes a bundle for her. I really must hit the sack now otherwise I'm going to be a blithering idiot on the podium tomorrow."

"What time do you want me to wake you in the morning and I promise not to fuck you awake again, that's unless you want me to?" she says grinning.

"Thanks, but let's keep it at once only. Let's see, I need to be at the conference center by 8:30 a.m., from here I suppose it will take a cab an hour at that time of day to get into town?"

"Yes, and we should order your cab now for

7:15 a.m. tomorrow, and what time do you want me to wake you?"

"6:30 should be fine thanks."

"I'll call our regular cab company; they know us and are very reliable. What can I get you for breakfast tomorrow morning?"

"Just coffee will be fine thanks, I'll get a sandwich at the Center, they will have stuff all over the place to eat. I'm the second speaker, so I have some time, but I need to get there early to get the technician to set up my PowerPoint and sound stuff."

"Okay then, you go and hit the sack, I'll call and book the cab, good night."

With that Sissy gets up from the couch and walks to where her phone is on the kitchen counter. I get up and walk back to the studio.

CHAPTER 4

At 6:30 a.m. Monday morning October 16, Sissy shakes me awake.

"Come on sleepyhead, time to rise and shine or whatever you do in the mornings."

I blink, rub my eyes and sit up,—

"Thanks, I'll be through for coffee in thirty minutes, what do you want me to do with the linen and the used towels?"

"Don't worry about the bed, I'll strip it when you've gone, just leave the towels in the bathtub."

I shower, shave and dress in my grey suit, white shirt, and red and blue striped tie that Diane had put out for me to wear as she thought I looked particularly smart wearing it. I pack my bag, leave it on the bed with my laptop in its carry bag, and go through to the kitchen.

"Coffee's just brewed, help yourself, mugs are in the cabinet above the coffee maker and cream is in the door of the fridge if you want. Ooh —— I've a few small things for Diane and Jason, can I squeeze them into your bag, and do you have room?"

"I'm sure you'll find some space, I travel light. My bag is on the bed." Sissy picks up a bulging plastic bag from the counter and takes it back to the studio. I pour myself some coffee and look over the sports page of the Times while sipping my coffee.

"Okay I found some space in your bag and stuffed it in," she says as she comes from the studio.

"Good, glad you got it in. I see the Red Socks have lost the last two games, that won't make Bob happy."

Sissy and I made small talk while we waited for

the cab. At 7:22 the cab honks outside. I had already collected my bag and laptop and placed them next to the door.

"Well, I guess it's goodbye until who knows when. Hey, hope your conference goes well," she says.

"Do me a favor on your way out and drop this plastic trash bag in the trash can you kindly wheeled down to the curb for me. It's old salad stuff and the empty wine bottle, be careful, it's a bit messy so don't tip it up."

"Ok no problem, say hi to Bob, sorry I missed him, when does he get back?"

"Sometime tomorrow, remember he's got to take the boat for service. I'm not coming out, so cheers." She gives me a hug and pecks on the cheek. I tell the cab driver to stop at the end of the driveway and I quickly hop out and deposit the plastic trash bag into the trash can. Although it was only eleven miles to the Boston Convention Center, it takes close to an hour to get there through the morning traffic. There are two lanes of cabs at the entrance, so we must wait another five minutes before I can get out. It is already 8:40 a.m. by the time I get to the Ballroom reception on the third floor. I register, get my name tag, and access card into the restricted area, as well as a free beverage and sandwich coupon. A technician comes and escorts me to the back of the stage to where things were being set up.

"Where can I leave my overnight bag?" I ask.

"There are some change rooms down the back with some lockers, I'll show you where as soon as we have you all set up here."

The stage is set with two large overhead screens, one on the left and one on the right, with two podiums, also one on each side. The first speaker of the day is busy setting up his presentation on the right and I would follow immediately after his talk on the left podium at 10:15 a.m. They have allocated me 40 minutes for my presentation and 10 minutes for discussion time. The technician and I run through a couple of slides to check that everything is working fine. He then takes me down to the change rooms, I find a locker with a key, lock my bag inside and go and find something to eat.

At 10 a.m. I return to the backstage, get my notes together, speak to the technician to see if everything is okay, and check to see that my laser pointer is working. Peeping through the curtains to see what sort of audience we have; I see close to four or five hundred people. I have spoken to large audiences before, but this was an exception and quite daunting.

The Presenter and Master of Ceremonies is Donald Morgan, ex-radio news broadcaster. The applause for the speaker before me is still reverberating in the room when he starts his next announcement.

"Ladies and gentlemen, our second guest speaker for this morning is Dr. Grant Hughes. Dr. Hughes has a BS in Heavy Current Electrical engineering, a master's degree in Transmission and Conversion, as well as a Ph.D. in Electrical Engineering Science. His paper today is entitled

'The health hazards associated with long-term exposure to the EMF, produced by high voltage transmission power lines.'"

I step out from behind the curtains and take my place at the podium.

"Good morning ladies and gentlemen. When I

heard Donald's introduction, it made me feel like my old university professor, so I hope I'm not going to bore you with too much technician detail. The subject of EMF's (Electromagnetic Fields) has been with us ever since electricity was discovered. The concerns that the exposure to these magnetic fields may cause some health risk, has also been the subject of many papers and discussions over the past decades.

So why then am I bringing up a subject that has already been kicked around this magnetic field (excuse the pun) for so long, without any real conclusion as to its defined health hazards?

The results of new tests and studies conducted in this last decade, when viewed over long term exposure, show, and give different results that are quite alarming.

Now here we are talking mainly of the EMFs from high and ultra-high voltage power transmission lines. As you may be aware the higher the voltage, the higher the EMF will be and as we enter a new decade of ultra-high voltage, the bigger this risk will get.

We have been conducting intensive studies with our partners in Japan and if you look at this slide here you can see the increase in the EMF is proportional to……. and this slide here shows that the findings could be interpreted to reflect linear increases in risk, a threshold effect that ………

Ladies and gentlemen, as I have illustrated here today there is an increased risk due to long term exposure to EMFs on high and more so from ultra-high voltage power transmission lines. The question is, what are we going to do about it? Perhaps more so, what are the power and transmission companies going to do about it, or indeed what are they prepared to do about it?

Yes, we have solutions, but they cost money and in the long run, we the people will ultimately end up footing the bill with higher electricity costs. The problem is we can continue to stick our heads in the sand and pretend it does not exist. I believe we have done just that for the past half-century and continue having those health risks I pointed out in my slides, exactly like we did with cigarettes. Remember we kept telling ourselves, 'NO, THERE IS NO HEALTH RISK' with smoking and look where we are today, spending billions on health issues related to smoking.

Just like with the tobacco industry, nothing will be done until the government says so. There is just too much money at risk here. The Power and Transmission companies will have their lobbyists queuing in Washington to fight any bill to alter the status quo. I know this paper is highly controversial and will no doubt create even more discussions and debates. Those opposed to this will bring expertise that will argue against what I have presented here today. Thank you for your interest. I'll hand you back to our presenter Donald Morgan."

"Well ladies and gentlemen, I'm sure you found Dr. Hughes's paper very interesting, although I must admit most of the technical jargon was above my IQ. I found it quite alarming that we are still debating things like this, instead of doing something about it. Are there any questions, we have time for a few before our next speaker this morning? You know the drill, please give your name and company or association you represent."

"Yes sir, gentlemen on the side there with your hand raised, press the microphone button that's blinking green on your desk and speak up please."

"Frank Burns from 'The Electrical Engineering and Research Journal'. Dr. Hughes, you mentioned there was a solution to this problem, but it was costly. What is the solution and how costly?"

"The solution is to shroud the individual power lines with an aluminum meshed cage. Like a sieve in the shape of a long sock with the conductor passing through the center and three nylon support struts holding the conductor away from the meshing every meter. Estimated costs at this stage per meter for the 200 mm diameter cage would be in the region of $45. This sounds costly I know, but I'm sure once competition comes into it and the volumes increase, the cost will decrease dramatically."

"Is that cost installed?"

"Yes, that's what they estimate."

"Dr. Hughes there are trillions of kilometers of power conductors running throughout the US, let alone the world. Can you imagine what this will cost the country?"

"Yes, I have imagined that, but essentially one needs to concentrate the efforts in the areas where these power lines run through populated regions."

"Ladies and Gentlemen, I'm afraid we have run out of time. I would like to thank Dr. Hughes for his most interesting and might I say, thought-provoking paper. Please give him a warm hand of appreciation." Said Donald Morgan.

I close my laptop, slide it back into its case, sling the strap over my shoulder and make my way to the back of the stage. I thank the technician for his help. I look at my watch. It is now 11:15 a.m. and I can hear Donald Morgan introducing the next speaker. My flight back to Philly is only at 2:30 p.m. so I have plenty of time to kill before I must be at the airport. I decided to go downstairs and have a look at some of the electrical exhibitions on show.

As I come out of the Ballroom and into the lobby, I'm confronted by a group of people who have been waiting for me. A young lady I guess in her late twenties, wearing a short black skirt approaches me.

"Dr. Hughes, I'm Mary Jones from the Daily Mail. I'm wondering if I could ask you a few questions regarding your paper you just delivered."

"Sure, what is it you want to know?"

"The images of those deformed poor monkeys and chimps that have been exposed to EMF testing, have you not considered the inhumane aspect of this research? Have you not heard that there is a worldwide outcry to ban experiments on macaques, marmosets, and other monkeys?"

"Yes, I'm as horrified as anyone about these tests, but what would you have us do? Force families to live under high voltage power lines as they do in China and then monitor the growth and IQs of these families' kids? Do you think that's humane? If we had the media back in the fifties we have today, we could have shown the world what tobacco did to the lungs of chimpanzees, tobacco would have been banned fifty years ago, and we would have saved the world trillions of dollars."

"Mr. Hughes I also have a quick question."

This question comes from a slightly built man of dark skin with a grey beard and mustache, he's wearing a dark brown suit with a Pagari on his head.

"My name is Ranzu Mataji. Did you also write a paper about the impact large hydroelectric dams were having on the environment?"

"Yes, I did, it was a paper I presented for my

Ph.D. some years ago."

"Did you also grant permission for this paper to appear in the Punjab Tribune in the English language and also in the Jalandhar edition?"

"No, I'm sorry, I had nothing to do with that. The copyrights of the paper belong to the university."

"Well let me tell you Mr.— Dr — that paper, just like this paper you just presented, is full of fabrication and untruths. Because of that paper, the Dongari Dam is not going to be built in Pakistan, as well as the hydroelectric plant, and millions of my people will be unable to benefit from this project."

"I'm sorry that you feel this way. I would love to stand here and discuss the impacts that large dams are having on our environment and that is why more than one thousand four hundred dams have been removed in the US since 1912. In 2014 alone, we removed seventy-eight dams in twenty-one of our states. Maybe you should switch your power option to wind or solar. You have a lot of sunshine in that area. I'm sure it would be a viable and feasible alternative. Look, I would like to discuss this with you, but I've got a plane to catch," and I start to walk away.

He pushes in front of me and sticks his finger in my chest and says, "You people don't understand how the rest of the world lives, that's why people like you don't deserve to live."

He then backs away and walks down towards the escalator. I just stand there for a few seconds wondering if that was a threat I just heard?

Somebody else wanted to ask a question, I say "sorry, I have no further comments," and walk down to the escalators.

I'm just about to step onto the escalator when two guys step up from behind me and take me by my elbows.

CHAPTER 5

"Mr. Hughes, we need to have a word with you."

"I'm sorry guys as I've said, I have a plane to catch and I have no further comment."

"Mr. Hughes, we're from the Cambridge Precinct and we would like you to come with us to answer a few questions."

They both flashed their badges at me, "It shouldn't take too long."

"Is there a problem?"

"I'm afraid yes Mr. Hughes, there has been an accident and your brother-in-law is dead. Sorry, we must be the ones to bring you the bad news."

"What do you mean he's dead, how, where is he, how's my sister-in-law? How did you find me?"

"Sorry, Mr. Hughes, we were just told to come and pick you up. We would like you to come down to the precinct, they have all the details down there."

"Okay, I will need to collect my overnight bag from the locker room if that's okay, as I don't want to have come back here again to collect it before I go to the airport."

"Sure thing, where's the locker room?"

"Down that way"

"OK, we'll tag along."

We pick up my bag and the one officer insists on carrying it for me. We go down the escalator and out front to where their Black Ford Explorer patrol car is parked, with the 'Cambridge Police Department' written on the side panel. They put my bag in the trunk even though I say I can have it in the back seat with me, they say that protocol calls for it to be stored in the back caged section.

I sit in the back; my head is spinning. What in the world could have happened to Bob and why hasn't Sissy or anyone else called me? I turned my mobile phone off some time before my talk and I can't remember switching it back on again. I fish it out of my pocket and check, —— no damn it, I had forgotten to. I turn it on, and a bunch of messages and emails pop up with a lot of notification sounds.

The officer in the passenger seat turns to me and says, "Sorry sir you can't use your mobile in the car, we need to have that please," and he stretches out his hand to take it from me.

"I'm not going to make a call; I just want to check my messages and emails. My phone has been off for several hours and that's most probably why I didn't know about the accident." I say.

"Sorry sir, protocol, please give me the phone, I don't want to have to stop the car and take it from you."

"Okay, okay, here take the damn thing," I say, agitated that they could be so fucking pissy.

We park in front of a red brick and glass building with double glass doors and a sign saying Robert W. Healy Public Safety Facility. We walk in through the front glass doors to security check, which is the same procedure as that at airports and all other government facilities. My bag, laptop, and cell phone go through the scanner, with my belt, shoes, and wallet. I then walk through the screening machine with no peeps and collect my belt, shoes, and wallet from the container. My cell phone, laptop, and bag have already been picked up by the two accompanying officers.

"Follow us please."

We walk to the escalator and take it to the second floor, past a lot of open-plan offices to a glass partitioned office, where I can see two people, one sitting behind a desk and one standing. As we approached the office door, the guy behind the desk indicated for the officers to enter.

"Ah Mr. Hughes, thanks for coming in, much appreciated."

I think to myself, 'did I have much of an option?'

"Thank you, guys, for picking up Mr. Hughes. Are those his things there?"

"Yes Sir."

"Has it's been with you guys all the time?"

"Yes Sir."

"Okay, you can put it on the table over there, thank you, officers, that will be all. Stay in the building, I may need you later."

With that, the two officers leave the room.

"Sorry, Mr. Hughes. I'm Superintendent Mike Ross from the criminal investigation division and this is Detective Alan Burns."

Ross must have been in his late fifties, if not sixty, lean, and his suit sort of hung on him as if it were a size too big. Burns was much younger in his mid-forties, puffy red face, blotched eyes, and a paunch that hung over his belt, his suit looked like he had slept in it.

"What's this all about? I'm in the complete dark here, I heard that there has been an accident and my brother-in-law is dead. That's all I've been told. I can't make a call, I can't look at my cell phone, what the hell's going on, am I under arrest or something?" I say.

"Calm down Mr. Hughes, have a seat."

I take a seat in front of his desk.

"Okay, so now tell me what's going on?" I say.

"Mr. Hughes, the sad news is that your brother-in-law was murdered sometime last night, your sister-in-law was molested, beaten, and is in the hospital suffering from smoke inhalation. She was lucky, somebody saw the smoke and alerted the fire department. We found your sister-in-law's mobile phone and one of the emergency numbers listed was yours, but there was no answer, the other was that of your wife. When we managed to contact your wife, she told us that you had spent the weekend at the house and then you were presenting a paper at the convention center and that's how we located you."

"That's impossible, —— I spent the weekend at my sister-in-law's house, my brother-in-law was away in New York playing golf and was only due to be back home sometime today. I left the house this morning around 7:30 a.m. and my sister-in-law and I had coffee together before I left."

"Unfortunately, Mr. Hughes we are going to have to hold you in remand until we can get a statement from Mrs. Croning in the hospital."

"Are you arresting me, do I need a lawyer?"

"No, we aren't arresting you. Why do you think you need a lawyer?"

"I don't know, this whole thing seems like a fucking mistake, something's not right here."

"We need to take you downstairs to a holding cell, I'm sure this whole thing will be cleared up as soon as we can get a statement from Mrs. Croning. We also need to ask you a few more questions, get your fingerprints and a mouth swab for DNA."

"Jees —— this is just bullshit; I haven't done a fucking thing and now you want my fingerprints and DNA stuff."

"Mr. Hughes, take it easy, it's standard practice."

47

"Yeh, yeh standard practice, protocol, and all that BS. Can I at least call my wife and tell her I won't be home?"

"Okay, you will have to do it here, as they may not let you use the phone downstairs, you can use this phone here."

"Why can't I use my mobile?"

"Sorry, you can't use your mobile in the station."

"Okay, okay, I know —— it's the protocol and all that crap."

"Look, Mr. Hughes, we are doing you a favor letting you use this phone, we don't make the rules and regs, we just apply them."

"Sorry —— I'm just so damn upset."

"Detective Burns and I are going to go get us some coffee from the machine while you make your call."

Burns steps out of the office and Ross hands me the phone from his desk and follows Burns. I dial our home number, I'm thinking, please let Diane answer the phone for a change. The phone rang five times and then she answered.

"Hello — hello, who's this?"

"Doll it's me —— (silence), Diane it's me, Grant, can you hear me?"

"Yes, I — can — hear — you."

"Diane are you okay, you sound half asleep?"

"I was —— resting."

A new voice came on the line, "Hello who's this I'm talking to?"

"Emma, is that you?" I ask.

"Grant where are you, everybody's looking for you?"

"Emma yes it's me, what's going on with Diane, she sounds like she's had too much to drink?"

"Grant she's taken some sedatives and it's knocked her loopy. Listen, the cops are looking for you, what the hell's going on up there?"

"Look, I'm in custody at the moment in Cambridge Precinct and I think I may need a lawyer at some time, so please get the name of our attorney from Diane when she is compos mentis and get him up here ASAP. I'm sorry I don't have time to explain, the cops will be back in the office in a minute, tell her I love her and hugs for Jason."

I hang up, thank heavens Emma was there. Emma and Jim are our close friends who live in West Chester, about thirty minutes from our house.

Ross and Burns come back into the office.

"Okay Mr. Hughes you made your call, let's go."

They picked up my bag, phone, and laptop and marched me out of the office and back the way we came, to the elevator. This time we are going down to the basement level. We exit the elevator and proceed down a passage, stop at a door, and go inside. I immediately recognize it from the movies as an interrogation room, the typical large window, and the starkness of the furniture in the room. Burns pulls out one of the plastic chairs and tells me to sit at the table on the opposite side facing the window. I do as I'm told. I can't see through the window; I expect it's a one-way mirror. He puts my things on the table, pulls up a chair, and sits down facing me.

"Superintendent Ross has gone to arrange the lab guys to come and fingerprint you and to take a mouth swab," he says.

We sit in silence for about ten minutes, then Ross comes in with a female and male, both in white coats, carrying plastic cases the size of a briefcase.

"Okay Mr. Hughes let's do the mouth swab first as that takes two seconds," says the female technician.

She opens her case, puts on a pair of gloves, takes out a test tube, and unwraps what looks like an elongated Q-tip which she runs under my tongue. She puts the tip back into the test tube which has its own seal halfway up the shaft. She then takes out a small printer and asks me for my details which I give her. She prints out a label, sticks it on the test tube, and then packs up her stuff and leaves.

The fingerprints and palm prints take a lot longer. I must do them several times until the technician is satisfied, he has good images of my hands and fingers. He gives me some cream and a paper towel to clean my hands. I look at my watch. It's now 2:45 p.m. and my flight has gone anyway. By the looks of things, it doesn't look like I'm going anywhere today, but to a holding cell.

"Alan go with the technician and do a quick check on the prints on those items you brought back from the house this morning. That will confirm whether Mr. Hughes was there or not."

"I already told you I was there,"

"Mr. Hughes. I must inform you although you have not been charged, you are being held in custody and anything you may say can be used as evidence against you at any later stage, you do understand that don't you?"

"Yes, I understand that, but as I said, I spent the weekend there so my fingerprints will be all over the house."

"Ah yes! They will be, but will they be found in

the victim's bedroom?"

"No, they won't, because I was never in their bedroom."

"Well then you see Mr. Hughes, that's a good thing in your favor, not so?"

Nothing else was said for at least thirty minutes. I just realized that the last time I had anything to drink was the quick glass of orange juice I had when I got something to eat for breakfast at the conference center.

"It's been over 4 hours since I had anything to drink, is there a chance I can get a cup of coffee or some water?"

"Nah I don't think so, not down here, it's just me and you. I can't leave you, so we will have to wait until Burns gets back, then I'll ask him to get you something."

"Thanks."

Twenty minutes later Burns sticks his head through the door, nothing is said, and Ross gets up and leaves me there. I know they can see me through the one-way mirror so there was no point in me trying to do anything, not that I want to anyway. A few minutes later the two of them come back and Burns has a white plastic bag in his hand.

"Alan before you sit down, could you please get Mr. Hughes some water from the drinking fountain,— here you can give me the bag, I'll hang on to it."

Burns turns ungraciously and goes out, returning a few minutes later with a plastic cup of water.

"Okay Mr. Hughes, we have some good news, you were correct, we did not find any of your fingerprints in the victim's bedroom, but then with all that water they could have been washed away," said Ross.

"Is this your overnight bag?" asks Ross, pointing to my bag on the table. I assume it has been with you ever since you left the house early this morning?"

"Well, yes,—— except for the hour or so when it was locked away in the locker in the change rooms at the Convention Center, then you guys had it in your sight ever since you picked me up."

"Right," said Ross.

"Do you mind if we have a look in your bag? We could go and get a search warrant, but that's only going to delay things here and if you have nothing to hide, maybe you don't mind? Would that be okay?"

"As you said, you are going to do it anyway, so do it now. I have nothing in there to hide, so go ahead."

They open the bag and begin to unpack my stuff and place it in a pile on the table. Then they come to the plastic bag that Sissy had put there for Diane and Jason. They remove the bag and ask me what's in it?

"I don't know, it's stuff that my sister-in-law packed for my wife and my son, she said it was something for them and I never asked what it was specifically. Open it if you like," I say.

They open the bag and pull out a T-shirt and packed inside the shirt are wads of crisp one-hundred-dollar bills tied with elastic bands.

"Mr. Hughes, how much is here?" asks Ross.

"I don't know, I've never seen it before."

"Nice present for your wife and kid I'd say. Alan, I want you to count the cash for the records. The camera is rolling isn't it?"

"Yes Sir, it's been on all afternoon."

"Look I have no idea what's going on here, I told you that package was put into my bag by my sister-in-law."

"Sure, you did Mr. Hughes, we're not saying you didn't."

"Okay Alan, let's have a tally for the record."

I didn't need any more water, what I needed now was a double scotch and my lawyer to walk through the door, but that was not going to happen today. Ten minutes later Burns had tallied up the bundles into seven piles.

"We have sixty-five grand here boss."

"Wow! That's a tidy sum for a present. Now for our next surprise."

They push my stuff off the table and onto the floor. A black plastic bag is put down in front of me on the table.

"Take a guess what's in the plastic bag, Mr. Hughes?" Ross asks.

"I have no idea."

"Open it up Alan, see if Mr. Hughes recognizes it."

Burns opens the black plastic bag and pulls out another clear plastic bag with a gun in it. He holds up the bag so I can see it more clearly.

"Do you know what this is Mr. Hughes?" asks Burns.

"Yes, I'd say it's a gun."

"Any idea what type of gun it is?"

"It looks like a Glock 19."

"And would you like to take a stab at whose gun this belongs to?"

"No, I wouldn't," but in my mind, I had a bad feeling I knew whose gun it was.

"Well let me tell you, it is registered to no other than your sister-in-law, guess where we found it?"

"I'm sure you are going to tell me," I say, as I am slowly getting tired of their games.

"We found it in a plastic bag, together with an empty bottle of wine and some other trash, in the trash can in front of the premises of the late Mr. Croning."

"The other amazing thing is that the ballistics we dug out of the back of the bed, match those fired from this handgun here, and guess whose fingerprints are all over this weapon?" says Burns.

Now I was worried, I knew I had handled that gun and reloaded it for Sissy the night before, so my fingerprints had to be on the gun.

"Mine," I say, "and I can explain why they are there."

"Sure, you can, but save that story for the jury."

"Hang on Alan —— let's not get carried away, no one has charged anyone with anything yet,"

"Um umm, we'll soon see about that."

Just then the door of the interrogation room opens, and someone sticks his head in and says, "Detective there's a call for you."

"I'll be right back," says Burns and he steps out of the room.

A few minutes later he sticks his head back in the door.

"We need to go, boss, she has gained consciousness."

I'm taken to a holding cell and sit there contemplating my dilemma. Two hours later the superintendent Mike Ross and Detective Alan Burns march into my cell with a warrant for my arrest.

"Mr. Hughes, we are hereby officially charging you with first-degree murder of Mr. Robert Archer Croning and the rape and aggravated assault of

Mrs. Sylvia Rebeca Croning, together with the theft and robbery of sixty-five thousand US dollars from the safe in their home at 44 Willow Grove Lane, Cambridge, Massachusetts, as well as calculatingly setting ablaze the said premises, to cover all evidence. You will appear at the Cambridge District Court tomorrow at 10 am." Burns is reading this from the docket he is holding.

"You don't have to plead or say anything. The criminal justice department guys will come and collect you shortly to take you to your new digs for the night, and we will see you in court tomorrow morning," says Ross. With that, they turn and leave.

I shout after them, "I need to speak to my lawyer," but they had no intention of even acknowledging they heard me.

I sit trying to piece together what the hell is happening, how is it that I'm being framed for murder. Why me? What have I done to Sylvia to deserve this? How can Bob be dead when he wasn't even supposed to be at home? What is Sylvia doing? She must have told the cops it was me who shot Bob, then beat her and raped her. What the fuck,— why would she do that? She knows full well I didn't do it. What the hell is going on here? Why is she trying to frame me for this? The more I think about it, the less it makes sense.

CHAPTER 6

Around 5:30 p.m. two cops come in, handcuff, and lead me down some passages, through doors and more passages, finally into another room where I'm stripped, photographed, and given a brown jumpsuit. I'm then taken to a cell where there are three other inmates. The cell is small with four bunk beds, a washbasin, and a toilet. Two of the inmates are young black guys in their early twenties I would imagine, and one middle-aged white man, say in his fifties.

"So, what do they nab you for?" asked one of the black guys.

"First-degree murder."

"Wow! That some heavy shit they frowin at yo, I guess you never done it hey?"

"You're a hundred and one percent correct."

"And what are you in for?"

"We, me in ma partner here, we get caught with some drugs man, dey say we was dealing, no way was we dealing, hey bro?"

"No way we are dealing," says the other black.

The white guy is lying on one of the bunks, he looks disdainfully at me and says.

"So, should I be worried that I'm going to get bumped off in my sleep tonight?"

"I don't think so, unless you have a gun I can borrow;"

That seems to get more of his attention, and he sits up on the side of the bunk and says, "Hi I'm Carl Edson and you are?"

"Grant Hughes," and we shake hands. I notice he has a Band-Aid over his knuckles.

"So, what are you in for Carl"?

"Aggravated assault, I hit my neighbor and he

filed an assault charge against me. No big deal, I get to sleep one night in the slammer, and tomorrow my lawyer gets me out. It was worth it."

"What provoked you to hit him?" I ask.

"It's been an ongoing saga with his dog coming and shitting on my grass. I've asked him a hundred times to keep the dog on his property. I told him to put up a fence, and if he didn't want a fence, put in an invisible fence. No, —— he's too fucking mean to lay out a few bucks for that. He'd rather let me be aggravated. The other day there was a bunch of dog poop on my grass again. I scoop it up into a large envelope, address it to his mutt, and put it in his mailbox."

"Well one of his kids, she's eight years old, a nice kid, takes the mail inside and opens the mutt's letter on the kitchen table. All hell breaks loose as you can imagine. The father knows full well who put the envelope in the mailbox, and he comes storming over to my place banging on my front door. One thing leads to another and I eventually lose it and punch him in the mouth. He goes flying ass over the tea kettle backward, down the three front steps, and lands on his back on the walkway. I suppose I'm lucky he didn't break anything."

"I was wondering why you had the Band-Aid on your hand."

"So, Grant what's your story?" he asks.

"Mine is a bit more complicated and a lot more drawn out."

"Well I don't think we are going anywhere tonight, so why not sit down here and tell me."

So that's what I do. After relating the story, he looks at me and says, "You know that's just too damn far-fetched not to be true."

The two black kids look at me and one shakes

his head, "Man that bitch she sure did screw you over."

"Yeah, literally and figuratively, that's the way it looks to me, but I haven't figured out why or for what reason."

They fed us at 6 pm, only then did I realize that I hadn't eaten since breakfast that morning and although the food wasn't very appetizing, I ate most of it and drank the water. As Carl had already taken the bottom bunk, I climbed up onto the top one. At 7 p.m. the lights went out. It wasn't completely dark as the light came in through the open bars from the passage lights and you could still see the clock on the wall in the passage. I wasn't sure if I should undress or sleep in the jumpsuit, I ended up just lying on top of the bed. So many thoughts were going through my mind there was no way I was going to get any sleep.

I started to wonder about Diane, what had she been told, what did she know? Was she in on this? No, no, I said to myself, take that thought right out of your mind Mr. Hughes, she would not be part of something like this, not my Diane, she is too timid and kindhearted, she could never hurt a fly. But what must she be thinking of me now? — Her husband up for the murder of her brother-in-law and rape and assault of her sister. Who is this man I'm married to for ten years?

Would she now just abandon me in my time of need, and not get me a lawyer? Did Emma get in touch with our attorney before Sylvia came out of the coma accusing me of murder and rape? I can only hope so. It was a depressing and daunting thought. I have no idea how this was going to play out. If my wife is against me, then who have I to turn to except my folks and my business partner,

58

but is Norman going to be very sympathetic? He must look after the interests of the company and his own family; he can't be seen to be allying with me in any way. Have my parents been informed and if so, what must they be thinking? These thoughts are running through my mind like an express train. I feel so at the end of my tether, I want to cry.

I must have fallen asleep sometime in the night, as I'm being shaken awake by Carl.

"Christ you really do sleep soundly, it's time to get up, the lights have been on since six this morning."

I wonder if we will get any breakfast for what it may be worth. I desperately need to pee, so hop down from the bunk, use the toilet, wash my face in the basin with cold water and dry it on some toilet paper.

Sometime later they bring us breakfast, scrambled eggs that look grey, and a slice of dry brown bread. I don't eat mine, neither does Carl, but the two black kids ate theirs and ours as well. The clock in the passage shows eight o-clock when the guards come and collect us for our transport to the courthouse. We are handcuffed and chained together and marched out to a waiting police van. I have never felt so humiliated. But I soon would get used to it.

CHAPTER 7

Arriving at Cambridge District Court we are taken to a holding cell in the courthouse and there we wait until we are called. I estimate the time to be close to nine as they have already just taken Carl and he told me his arraignment with the judge was at 9 a.m. The guard comes and tells me I have a visitor in the visitor's room. So again, I'm cuffed, and this time put in leg irons, also chained to the cuffs. I shuffle along down the passage to where the interview room is situated. I have no idea who I'm supposed to be meeting. The guard opens the door and sort of shoves me inside. There is nobody there, I just stand there waiting with the guard watching over me. A few minutes pass and the door opens and a tall guy in a light blue suit enters carrying a briefcase.

"Hi Mr. Hughes," he says, stretching his hand out to shake my cuffed hands.

"I'm Adrian Mink from Brook Attorney Associates. Your attorney in Philadelphia contacted me early this morning. Guard, do you think we can dispose of the cuffs."

The guard took out a bunch of keys and unlocked my cuffs.

"That's better let's take a seat. Guard, I think we can be left alone."

"He's a murder suspect and a dangerous criminal."

"That's fine guard, I'll take my chances, you can stand outside the door and I'll shout if I'm in danger."

He shrugs his shoulders and goes out.

"Right Mr. Hughes, what have you been getting yourself mixed up in?" he asks as he opens his briefcase and pulls out a document.

"Looking at the docket, they are throwing the book at you. First, what we need to establish is, do you want me to represent you? But I must first inform you of our fees. In criminal cases like this, we would charge an hourly rate of $600.00 and require a retainer of $10,000.00. If you agree on those figures and you want us to represent you, then I will need you to sign here for me please before we can go any further."

"Gee I'm so sorry, what can I say, only that I didn't bring my checkbook along with me to jail today, what did you say your name was again, Mr.– – Brink?"

"It's Mink."

"Where the fuck am I supposed to get $10,000.00 sitting in the slammer?"

"Relax Mr. Hughes, all I need from you is the okay that you will honor your commitment, we don't expect you to write us a check today."

"Okay I'm sorry, this has all been a terrible shock to me. I don't know what the fuck is going on."

"I understand Mr. Hughes, so if you're happy to take on our services, sign here and let's see if we can get to the bottom of this mess."

I scan through the document briefly and as I'm reading; Adrian explains the terms of the agreement and what my liabilities are, etc. After I sign the document, he put it in his briefcase.

"Now this is what's going to happen when we go into court, the judge will read the charges against you. He will make sure that you understand the charges brought against you. The judge will then ask you to enter a plea. You can enter a plea of 'guilty' or 'not guilty,' do you understand?"

"I've read the charge sheet and spoken to one of the cops that I'm friendly with at Robert Healy Precinct and apparently you have created quite a furor. The mayor in this town has gotten the crime rate down by 20% in the last two years and there have been no homicides. Now you come along from out of state, commit a homicide in his town, and upset the whole apple cart. You'll get truly little sympathy from the prosecution. So, they have assigned your case to the district attorney himself. They want no mess up in this case. The judge is Kenneth Gould, a badass judge. I've been up against him before, so don't expect any favors."

"We are then going to ask the judge for bail and you can bet your bottom dollar in this case, the DA is going to be there to ensure you don't get bail, or that it is at least set damn high. They will want to keep you close at hand, they won't want you flying back to Philly if they can help it, believe me. I know these guys."

"Unfortunately, we don't have time to discuss your case now as they are going to call us any time now. We will have plenty of time to go over your case after the booking procedure."

Just then the door to the interview room opens and the guard comes back in and announces that we are due in court.

My attorney picks up his briefcase and says, "Okay Mr. Hughes, I'll see you in court shortly."

I'm again cuffed and chained to my leg irons, I hobble along after the guard down several passages to the elevator, and eventually arrive at the courtroom.

I see my attorney sitting at a table to the left of the judge's bench. I'm led to a cubicle directly behind and to the left of my attorney, where my leg irons are locked to a shackle that is bolted into the floor. I sit and look around, there is another table about twelve feet to the right of where my attorney is sitting. This is where I assumed the prosecutor is to be sitting. I recognize Ross the superintendent and Detective Burns who are standing to the side of that table, talking in low voices to a tall lean guy in a dark grey suit. The bailiff walks over to Ross and Burns, speaks to them and they immediately go and sit in the public area. The grey suit guy sits down at the table.

The bailiff goes back to his table next to the judge's bench and announces, "All rise for the honorable presiding judge Kenneth Gould."

We all stand up. The judge comes in and looks around the courtroom. He must be in his sixties, not very tall, say five' eight," a bit overweight, grey hair slightly balding in front, he's wearing thin-rimmed glasses.

"Please be seated," he says.

We all take our seats again. The clerk of the Court hands him the docket. He reads it, looks up over the rim of his glasses at me and then at my counsel. He glances over at the bailiff and sort of nods.

The bailiff says, "Will the Defendant Grant Hughes please rise."

I stand up and so does my attorney.

The judge looks at my attorney and says.

"Is your name Grant Hughes?"

"No, your honor I'm his counsel."

"Well, unless you also want to be charged, sit down."

"Yes, your honor, thank you." And he sits down again.

"Mr. Hughes, I'm going to read to you the charges brought against you. I will then ask you if you understand these charges, not whether you agree with them or disagree with them, only that you understand them, is that clear."

"Yes, your honor."

"I will then ask you how you plead, and you can make your choice. Guilty or not guilty. Is that quite clear?"

"Yes, your honor."

With that, he adjusts his glasses on his nose, picks up the docket, and begins to read the charges.

"*Mr. Hughes, we are hereby officially charging you with first-degree murder of Mr. Robert Archer Croning, the rape and aggravated assault of Mrs. Sylvia Rebecca Croning, the theft and robbery of sixty-five thousand US dollars from the safe in their home at 44 Willow Grove Lane, Cambridge Massachusetts, as well as calculatingly setting ablaze the said premises to cover all evidence.*"

"Mr. Hughes, do you understand the charges brought before you?"

"Yes, your honor."

"Mr. Hughes, how do you plead, guilty, or not guilty?"

"Not guilty, your honor."

The judge removes his glasses and looks at me and says, "Mr. Hughes, do you have an attorney?"

"Yes, your honor, he is sitting over there," and I indicate where Adrian is sitting.

"Now's your chance to rise, counsel for the defense," says the judge.

My attorney stands up.

"Counsel for the defense, do you wish to post

bail?"

"Yes, your honor."

Before the judge can utter another word, the prosecutor is on his feet shouting, "objection your honor."

"On what grounds, counselor?"

"Your honor, this has been a malicious and brutal crime. The defendant is remarkably familiar with international travel, has contacts worldwide, and is quite capable of fleeing to another country where we have no jurisdiction or rights of extradition. I believe he is a flight risk and should be held in custody until trial."

"Counsel, I fully agree, bail denied."

"Your honor," protests my attorney. "The Supreme Court has indicated that pretrial detention based on a person being dangerous or a flight risk, is not per se unconstitutional, and I state the case of United States v——"

"Mr. Mink let me stop you right there, you can protest as much as you like. The only thing it's going to get you is contempt and you can spend the night with your client in his cell. You, of all people Mr. Mink, should know better than to question my judgment. If you want to protest, take it up with the State Supreme Court."

"Counselors, I'll see you both in my chambers."

He looks at the bailiff and the bailiff says, "All stand," while the honorable Judge Kenneth Gould leaves the bench.

My attorney comes over to me and says, "I'm sorry but I did warn you."

"So, what happens to me now?" I ask.

"Well, you will now go to jail, pending a trial date. I think that's what the judge wants to discuss with us, so I had better get back there, I can't afford to piss him off any more than I already have. I'll try to get to see you as soon as I have more information."

With that, he disappears through one of the court-side doors. The guard comes in and unlocks me from the bolt in the floor and takes me back to a holding cell in the court, until they can arrange secure transport for me to the jail, back at the Robert W. Healy Public Safety Facility.

For three days now I've been cooling my heels so to speak, in solitary confinement. I'm now in a two-person cell I assume because there are two bunks, but there has been no other person here with me in the cell for the past three days. I have a plastic chair, a heavy metal table bolted to the wall, a washbasin, and a toilet with no seat. I suppose being a high-profile criminal who's been charged with murder, they put one in a cell on his own. I've tried to reason with myself what the hell is going on and for the love of me, I can't think of one plausible reason why I'm sitting here in jail. The jailer won't speak to me when I get my food. I get an hour outside in an enclosed courtyard to exercise, where all I can see is four walls, a door, and the sky. The sun never gets to me at that time of the day.

The jailer opens the cell door and informs me that my attorney is here to see me. I get the handcuffs but fortunately no leg irons and chains, I suppose that's reserved for the court in case I try to make a run for it — like bloody hell, I'm going to run, where to with cops all around.

Adrian Mink is sitting at the table behind a caged section of this visitor's room. The jailer indicates for me to sit in the chair facing him.

"You have ten minutes," says the jailer.

"Hell, can't you make that twenty?" asks

Adrian.

"Look Mr.——, I don't make the rules here, I just enforce them, so take it or leave it, your choice." With that, he turns, goes out, and locks the door.

"Okay Mr. Hughes, or can I call you Grant, you can call me Adrian. We're going to be working together for some time, so we may as well cut with all the bullshit formalities."

"First thing, I have been talking to your wife. She is terribly upset as you can well imagine, and she is making out okay and your son is fine. She has told him you are away on business, but your name is going to be in the paper soon and that's going to be a problem, so she is thinking of moving down to her aunt's place in Florida. Secondly, she has arranged the payment of the retainer and so that's all settled. Third and most important, the judge wants this trial set and over with before Christmas, or should I say the mayor wants it that way. The date has been set for four weeks from today and jury selection starts in two weeks, so it does not give us a lot of time to prepare our defense. I need you to take this pad and pen to write down for me exactly, in every detail, what you did from the day you left your home in Philadelphia. I'll get it from you at our next meeting."

"These guys aren't going to allow us much time for discussion. In the meantime, I will go and see the district attorney and request that he allow us more visiting time, because this is unconstitutional. I'll also find out what evidence they have against you."

"Look I don't know how things work here, but do you think you could organize some toiletries, and do you think you can call my dad. This is his number —," and he writes it down. "Tell him I'm okay and he's not to worry, it's all a mistake, just do your best to appease him. Please, until I can get a chance to speak to my folks."

"Okay, I'll see what I can do."

Just then the door to the visiting room opens and the jailer comes back in.

"Time is up," and with that, he hooks his Billy club under my arm and jerks me up out of the seat. I'm marched out of the room, hardly having a chance to pick up the pen and pad Adrian has pushed under the railings to me.

Well, at least now I have something to do and I sit on the plastic chair at the table, starting to write in my best longhand scrawl. Unfortunately, it doesn't take me that long and I'm finished. I read it repeatedly and end up rewriting it three times until I'm satisfied, I have not missed anything.

Two days pass before I see my attorney again. This time the attitude of the jailer is a little more pleasant. We immediately get down to business.

"I see you brought the note pad back, I gather that's your story."

"Look Adrian let's get this straight right now. This whole thing is bullshit, and this here is NOT A STORY, it's factual." I almost shout in frustration as I push the pad over to him under the railings separating us.

"Okay, okay, hold your horses. It was just a figure of speech, don't get so touchy, we've got a long way to go before this is all over, one way or the other, so just calm down. Here is a copy of the report on what they have on you so far and the written statement of your sister-in-law. I'll read through your account of the events leading up to your arrest and you can read her statement. Then we can discuss the two, okay."

"How much time do we have?" I ask.

"No don't worry about it, I fixed that with the district attorney's office yesterday, we have plenty of time."

"How did you manage that?"

"I just went in there and told him if he didn't authorize me with enough time to see my client and seeing that the trial date was so soon, I would file for a mistrial as soon as we go to court. This morning I made an appointment to see you, and when I got here, I asked the officer on duty how long I had and he told me we have as long as we needed, but not to push it."

"By the way, I got hold of your old man and we had a long chat. He says and I quote, 'I don't believe a fucking word those assholes print in their papers, most of it's all bullshit and if there's anything you need, you must shout - he's quite a character."

"Thanks, Adrian I appreciate that, yes he's quite a character, one of the old school, a spade is a shovel with him."

Ten minutes later I've read the report and sit and wait for Adrian to finish reading my report, he reads it a second time and makes some notes in the margin.

"Is it true, do you really sleep that soundly?"

"Yes, I'm afraid I do."

"So, she fucked you while you were asleep. Christ that's one for the records. If it wasn't so out of the norm, I wouldn't have believed it, but who's going to make up a story like that."

"Yes, I know it's hard to believe, but that's what happened. I have a rare sleep disorder like sleepwalking and talking, it falls within the

Parasomnias," I say.

"Okay,— I have never heard of it before, but I'm sure you have some medical records to back this up,— not so?"

"Well, I would think so, my mother had me tested by various doctors and specialists when I was young. They could not establish anything abnormal, so we just left it at that. I'm sure she has those records somewhere, as she keeps everything." I say.

"Okay that's good, we may have to access them at some stage."

"Now we have to try and figure out what Sylvia's motive is for literally and figuratively screwing you, excuse the pun," he says. "Okay we know what you did, now let's take a look at her statement and see what she alleges."

Statement: Sylvia Rebecca Croning
Dated: 10/16/2020
Place: Greys Hospital, Boston East
Taken by: Detective Alan Burns

On Sunday, October 15 at around 7:30 p.m., the three of us, myself, my husband, and my brother-in-law Grant Hughes, all had dinner together in the dining room. A fair amount was drunk. Grant became a little hostile and agitated about an investment of fifty-thousand dollars that his wife Diane had placed with Bob some time ago. Bob had promised to double her money and Grant was upset because Bob hadn't shown any significant investment return to date. Grant said we are driving around in flashy cars, we have this fancy house and stuff, but what has happened to the fifty-thousand

dollars Diane had invested with Bob. He was getting more and more agitated. Grant wanted to know if the money Diane had given to Bob to invest, paid for the booze we were drinking. He then got up from the table, threw his napkin down, and stormed off to his room in the studio. We cleared up, put the dishes in the dishwasher, and retired to our bedroom on the second floor.

Sometime in the early hours of the morning, Grant came upstairs into our bedroom and switched on the light. I woke up. He had a gun in his right hand and a kitchen knife in his left hand. Bob sat up in bed and asked him what the fuck he was doing in our bedroom. He told Bob to shut the fuck up, open the safe and give him the fifty grand Diane had given him, plus interest. Bob protested he didn't have that sort of money in the house. Grant said he was a lying bastard and he came around to Bob's side of the bed, took a pillow, pushed it over Bob's head, held the gun against the pillow, and shot him three or four times, I think. He then came over to my side of the bed and asked me if I wanted some of that too, and I said no. He said I was to open the fucking safe. So, I went to the safe in the closet and opened it. He told me to take out all the cash and count it. I did and it totaled sixty-five thousand dollars. He told me to find a bag for the money. I found an old Macy's plastic bag in the closet and put the money in that. He then told me to pull the top sheet off the bed and hold it, then he took the knife and cut strips from it. He used the strips to tie me to the bed, beat me about the face, and raped me.

Before leaving, he stuffed my pajama panties in my mouth and tied them with a strip of sheeting. I remember hearing this loud bang, like an explosion and then there was a lot of smoke. I think I must have blanked out and the next thing I woke up in the hospital.

This is a true statement.

Signature: _____ Witness:

_____

"Wow, quite some statement huh, Grant you are a very bad, bad person."

"I see here in the report I tried to burn the house down."

"You only partially succeeded in burning it down, the fire was started in the garage, destroying the three motor vehicles, then spread to the rest of the house. The fire department got there before it reached the main bedroom where your sister-in-law and her dead husband were, so the firemen managed to get them out before the fire reached that section. I saw a picture in the paper, it looks like a complete write off. The water damage alone has made such a mess. It looks like it was a very nice place."

"I see they found a large kitchen knife under the bed in the main bedroom and it has your fingerprints all over it and nobody else's, do you remember having used a large kitchen knife while you were there, because I don't see it mentioned in your report?"

"Hell, no I don't remember — wait a minute, yes, I grated some cheese, and I cut it with a knife to feed it into the automatic grater!"

"You see Grant, we have to be extremely thorough here, that's why I said I need to know every detail, even when you went for a piss, I want to know about it and when. So, take it back, have a second and third go at it, don't leave a stone uncovered. I'll pick it up tomorrow and have it typed up. I must go, I have another appointment in half an hour."

"Oh, by the way, you were also mentioned in the two local papers who published the story of the fire, murder, and the rape. They must have got some inside information as they had quite a lot of details and the report said it looked like an open and shut case. I'll see if they will let me bring you a copy."

Back in my cell, I sit down with my notes and meticulously go through them again. This time I take a new sheet, draw a margin, and start with a timeline in the margin and try to think back as to what I was doing, when. The six pages I had written previously, had now grown to ten pages. I was amazed at what I had left out.

The next day we are back in the interview room again, and I hand the newly written pages over to Adrian.

"Okay, I see you have drawn up a timeline of events, that's good, I'll have this typed up and give you a copy. I'll keep your original for safekeeping."

"I just heard your sister-in-law has been kicking up a bit of a fuss downstairs, she wants her husband's body released so she can arrange the funeral for him."

"So why don't they release the body?"

"The DA said he wanted to have an autopsy done."

"What for?" I ask.

"Exactly my thought, but here's the good part. Apparently, this story is all over the office downstairs. Your illustrious sister-in-law storms into the DA's office unannounced and screams at him, so half the general office can hear. From all accounts, this is what she shouted at him and I quote."

'You want to perform an autopsy on my dead husband, to see why he died? I'll tell you how he fucking died, he was lying in bed next to me, and he was shot point fucking blank three times in the face, his whole fucking face is blown away. That's exactly how he died. Do you want to cut him up to see what he had to eat the night before? I can tell you that too if you like and in detail, because I prepared the fucking meal. So, if you don't mind Mr. DA, I would like to bury my poor husband and get this whole sordid business behind me.'

"I believe she turned around, slammed the glass door so hard it rattled and stormed out the main office."

"Yes, I can well believe that. I'm slowly starting to get a picture that she is capable of anything."

"So, by now Grant, you must have come up with at least a few scenarios of why she is trying to set you up for the murder of her husband and all the other accusations?"

"Look,— Bob, her husband was a real dickhead, he was in and out of rehab for booze and drugs from an early stage of his life. Don't get me wrong he was bright, but he only applied himself when it was absolutely necessary. I know he slapped her because she told my wife and of course I got to hear about it. I never told any of the family this, but when I heard they were going to get married, I did a bit of digging and he had done a few shady deals in his life and had been arrested a few times on suspicion of fraud, but they had to let him go because of lack of evidence."

"I don't know, the only reasonable conclusion I can come up with is, Sylvia got tired of his aggression and bullying, maybe she found out he was having an affair. He's away from home enough to have the opportunity and maybe she finds out about it and decides to do away with him. Her first husband didn't work out, he was having it off with a couple of women and when she found out, she divorced him. She got a two-million-dollar payout from him. My coming up to the conference was an excellent time and provided the perfect setup. She's been in the film industry, so she knows how to act and set the stage."

"That's all very well, but we can't prove it, remember it's you that's on trial, not her. Our best bet will be to cast doubt in the jury's mind that she may have murdered her husband for whatever reason. All we need is one or two jurors that don't buy her story and then we have a hung jury."

"What does that mean?" I ask.

"Well it means it's a mistrial, but that doesn't necessarily mean you walk. The judge could tell the jury to resume deliberation, but he can only do that twice, without getting into trouble with the Supreme Court."

"Then what happens if they still can't agree?"

"You're in for a new trial, a new date, and a new jury."

"And I sit in jail?"

"Yes, I'm afraid so."

"What's the advantage of a mistrial for me?"

"Well, the prosecutor knows that getting a conviction at a second trial could be a tough job because we already know his case and strategy and we can be more prepared."

"That's still a long shot isn't it?"

"Yes, but at the moment it's our only shot."

"First, we must try and figure out her motive, was it revenge, financial motivation, jealousy, was he having an affair, or was she in fear for her life? We don't know. We do know it was planned, so that takes care of that aspect."

"Look, it's Friday, I have to take the family out later so I can't be late. I need to get back to the office and get your notes typed up and make some calls before the end of the day. Let's work on that scenario of yours, I'm sure there is a motive somewhere there, we just need to find it. I'll get the office guys to start digging around and see what they can discover from her financial records, friends, and look for some motivation. Hey, I almost forgot —," he says and opens his briefcase.

"I've brought you yesterday's papers, you didn't feature in today, so you see you're not that important, ha-ha."

"How did you get it past security?"

"They were in my briefcase and they said nothing, so you take them, if they confiscate them, so be it, I tried. I'll see you again Tuesday afternoon. Monday I'm in court all day."

The guard checks the papers and gives them back to me without saying a word, at least I have something to read over the weekend.

CHAPTER 8

Back in the cell, I can't get the thought of Diane out of my head, what she must be thinking of me, how could I do something like this to her sister and brother-in-law? How does she take sides between her husband and her sister Sylvia? What are my parents thinking? What's going on with my business, how is Norman managing with all this, he hasn't tried to contact me as far I know. These are some of the questions that are constantly running around in my head. Being locked up here is so frustrating and demoralizing, not being able to get hold of anyone to find out what is going on. At times I get quite emotional and I've only been locked up for five days. What the hell is it going to be like for months or years, maybe even for life? Well feeling sorry for myself isn't going to get me out of jail, I need to put my mind into figuring out Sissy's motive for framing me.

I sit on the side of my bed and open one of the newspapers, the Daily Telegraph, and turn to page two. Yes, there it is, with the heading *'Executive Director Commits murder for $65K,'* with a picture of me taken at the convention center. I read the article and feel sick in my stomach as they have all mine and my family's details, as well as my company's details. A pretty grim and sordid picture has been painted of the whole affair. The article indicates an inside source stating the evidence against me is overwhelming and this, together with the statement from Mrs. Croning, once the case is started, will be over in a few days. This is not very assuring for me to read at the beginning of the weekend, locked up in jail. I don't even bother reading the other newspaper.

Tuesday afternoon couldn't come soon enough for me, the last three days having been exasperating, tiresome with phases of despair.

The first thing I ask Adrian when I see him is, "Why am I still being held in solitary confinement? I can hardly hear people in other cells, I don't see anyone except the jailer. He brings me my food, doesn't say a damn thing, even if I ask him something. I get to speak to no one; it drives me insane and I've only been in here for a week."

"Well good afternoon to you too Mr. Hughes!"

"Sorry, Adrian, hi how are you, — how was your weekend?"

"Fine, — you don't have to ask me about my weekend, but it was good thank you. Okay, I'll speak to the DA's office and find out their reason for keeping you in solitary. But you may want to reconsider going into a general cell, there are some badass characters in there that may take a liking to your white ass and I'm not joking. So, think about it."

"Maybe you could get me some books to read. I read the article in the paper, it's not good huh?"

"Well, that's what the press does best, they print stuff that sells to make money, don't take too much notice of what they say."

"It's not so much what they say about the case will be all over in a couple of days, it's the fact that my name, my family, and company's details are all out there. That's what's so worrying."

"Well, Grant it was going to come out sooner or later, so you better get used to it, as it's only going to get worse when the trial begins."

"Okay let me try and find out why they have you in solitary and I'll see if they will allow you some reading matter."

"Has my wife contacted you?"

"No, I haven't heard from her again, and I gather you're not surprised that she hasn't tried to see you? She must be in a terrible frame of mind, torn between her sister and you. Your business partner has contacted me. He has been trying to get an appointment to see you, but the DA is not allowing any visitors other than direct family and your counsel. He wants to know if he can get your laptop back that they have. I said I would ask, which I did, and they told me no way, they are holding it as evidence."

"What —— as evidence, that's my company laptop. It has absolutely nothing to do with this whole thing. Do they think I used it to batter her with it or something? It's got all our company's information and files on it. There's stuff on there that I've been working on that Norman doesn't have. Jees they are so full of BS, I can't believe they'd do this sort of thing."

"You better believe it, they are capable of much worse than that, and the party has only just begun. Oh, by the way, your illustrious sister-in-law got her late husband's body released from the morgue on Friday and the funeral has been announced for tomorrow. The announcement was in the paper over the weekend. That girl won't let the grass grow under her dancing feet."

"I wonder if Diane will fly up for the funeral, and will she come and see me?" I say.

"We are going to have a few of our people at the funeral just to see who Sylvia's close friends are, as we may need to tap into one or two of them to get some information. If your wife appears, we'll let you know."

79

"Here's the typed copy of your report on what you say happened. Read it through and check to see if that's what you wrote to your knowledge. You don't have your notes to check what you wrote, but I'm sure by now you almost know it all by heart."

"I'm sure it's OK, but I'll read it through."

"I need to get back to the office, I'll check with the DA on those two issues. He may move you, if so then you will have access to the library, if not I'll get some reading matter over to you, anything in particular?"

"Historical, mystery — crime would be good ha! ha! Anything but romance, thanks."

"Next week is jury selection and it's been scheduled for Wednesday. Unless something important comes up, I won't see you until after jury selection, then I'll come to see you and we can discuss the jury. Hopefully, we can get more men on the jury than women, but I know that SOB of a DA, he'll push for a large percentage of female jurors, because they will be more sympathetic to her situation."

Late Thursday afternoon the jailer arrives at my cell holding an open shoebox with four books in it, with a folded paper tucked in the top book. He puts the box down on the table and goes out without saying a word, but now I'm used to him not saying anything. I pull the folded sheet of paper out, and it's a note from Adrian saying he is sorry he took so long, but the DA was away and nobody else would give him authority to get me the books. He says he eventually got to see him, and the DA says it's his right to have you locked up wherever he thinks it's the safest. After the trial when I'm sentenced and no longer on his watch, he doesn't give a fuck where they send me, but the worse the place the better, as far as he's concerned. He says my wife was at the funeral.

Would Sylvia now try and convince Diane that I did the things I'm being accused of? Even though Sylvia was the younger sister, she has always been the more domineering of the two. She could lead her older sister by the nose so easily at times. It's funny to see the two of them together, they are like chalk and cheese, in looks and character, but as the saying goes, joined at the hip. I am worried that Sissy will talk her around to seeing things her way. She was an actress and a convincing one at that.

I don't see Adrian until the Monday morning after the jury selection. Back in the visitor's room, Adrian gives me the news.

"It took us a full two and a half days to do the selection. The judge was being a complete asshole, virtually everyone I picked that the DA challenged, the judge granted the challenge. The only fact in our favor as we were running out of jurors, he knew time was running out and the DA had promised his buddy the mayor he'd have this case all wrapped up before Christmas, and there was no time left to organize for another batch of jurors. We managed to do okay under the circumstances. The good news is we have managed to get five male jurors, three are black. Bad news we have seven females, again three are black, one Hispanic and three are white," he says.

"Trial date is set for next Monday at 10 am. I must make sure that the DA's office is keeping me informed of their witnesses and what other incriminating evidence they may have. I see they are going to call your wife as a witness and the examining doctor at the hospital. Then there is the normal investigating team, the forensic people, and maybe the pathologist, depending on what he or she did, or didn't do to the body. There seem to be no surprises at this stage, but my office will keep tabs on them daily."

"Discovery rules require us to also disclose any evidence or witnesses to the prosecution, so we have your sister-in-law's statement. The only statement they have from you is the one they took at your arrest, the recording they made while interviewing you, and searching your bag. That's when they found the money, and I have a copy of that recording. There is no other statement that you made to the cops on file is there, that you know of?"

"No, I never made any other statements, other than the one they took from me when they read me my rights."

"So far, we haven't had any luck tracking down any of your sister-in-law's friends who may know anything shady on her or her husband, not even that he was abusive. It seems the only person she confided in was your wife and we don't know what she will say. Do you think she will perjure herself to protect her sister?"

"I don't know for sure, but my gut tells me, yes she will, those two are as close as two halves of a clothespin."

"There is not much we can prepare for, other than to pull their evidence to pieces, and throw doubt on her story. Mrs. Croning will take the stand so I will cross-examine her left, right, and center until she doesn't know what's hit her. Let's see how good an actress she is. I will also be very blunt with your wife when I get my chance to cross-examine her. I don't want you to be upset with me for asking her pertinent and awkward questions if I have to."

"Okay I understand, I know it will be difficult but if you think it's necessary, then we have to do it."

"I take it you were wearing a suit when they arrested you?"

"Yes, they presumably have it with all my other belongings."

"Ok I will get it released seeing they haven't listed it as evidence in any way, I'll get it cleaned, your shirt and briefs laundered, and shoes cleaned. I'll get them over to you hopefully by Friday afternoon, if not, it will be Monday morning. Unless something comes up, I'm not going to see you again until trial."

"This procedure is different from the arraignment hearing. We will be in the main courtroom. As before you will be in a holding cell somewhere in the courthouse. Once everyone in the courtroom, including spectators and the jury, are seated, the courtroom clerk will call the case and instruct the bailiff to get you. The bailiff will escort you into the courtroom and you will be seated next to me at the defense table, facing the bench, to the left. The prosecutor and his aide, if any, will be seated at a table to the right of our table, closest to the jury box and the witness stand," he explains.

"Any questions?"

"No, I don't think so."

"Well, then I'm going to leave you now and I'll see you in court on Monday week. Sorry I can't shake your hand, but it's too narrow to get one's hand through the bars and no physical contact is allowed anyway. So, let me say this, I've taken on a lot of criminal cases in my career as an attorney of law and I have won eighty percent of them. Out of those eighty percent, I only believed that twenty percent of them were innocent. In your case I know you're innocent and I will fight to the very end to get you free. Go relax and read some books. I'll see you in court. "

CHAPTER 9

As promised my suit, shirt, tie, underwear, socks, and polished shoes are brought to my cell on Friday. On Monday morning it is so nice to put on my old familiar clothes, normally I loathe wearing a suit, but this suit feels like home to me. The guard comes to cuff me around 8 a.m. and takes me down to the basement garage, where I'm put in the back of a patrol car. There's a cop next to me and one upfront with the driver. Although it is only five miles to the district courthouse, looking at the clock on the dashboard it takes us close to thirty minutes to get there, because of the morning rush-hour traffic.

At the courthouse, I'm taken to a holding cell. It's quite a while before the bailiff and the court officer arrive to get me. My mind is racing back and forth with so many unanswered questions and I know I may never know the answers. Why me, why me Sylvia, what have I ever done to you to deserve this? I just could not get it out of my mind.

Well, there is no more time to delve on my self-pity, I now must face a jury who will decide my future.

"Mr. Hughes, please come with us."

I'm escorted down the passage accompanied by a police officer and the bailiff. We come out through a side door into the main courtroom and I'm directed to a chair at a table next to Adrian.

"Hi – how are you holding out?" he whispers.

"Okay, under the circumstances I suppose," I whisper back.

I looked around the courtroom and there were maybe thirty spectators. Not as many as I had expected, it seems the case has not yet caught the attention of the public.

"I see the district attorney has brought his sidekick assistant District Attorney Kevin Moore to the party," Adrian whispers and indicates with his eyes to the two people sitting at the table to the right of us."

The bailiff gets up and says, "All rise for the honorable Judge Kenneth Gould, now presiding in the First District Court of Cambridge. This court is now in session."

The judge comes in, looks around, and says, "Good morning ladies and gentlemen, please be seated," and with that, he sits down, and we do the same.

The clerk hands the judge a sheet of paper and sits down again.

The judge looks up and says, "Calling the case of the People of the State of Massachusetts versus Grant Hughes. Are you ready?"

The district attorney gets up and says, "Ready for the people your honor."

Adrian gets up and says, "Ready for the defense your honor."

The judge addressed the clerk, "Please swear in the jury."

"Will the jury please rise."

He waits until they have all risen and it allows me to get a good look at them.

"Please all raise your right hand and each of you swear that you will fairly try the case that's going to be set before you in this court and that you will return a verdict in accordance with the evidence and instructions of this court, so help you, God. Please say — I do."

They all mumbled "I do" and the clerk tells them to be seated.

The judge looks over at the DA's table and asks, "Does the prosecution wish to make an opening statement?"

The district attorney gets up and says, "Yes your honor."

"Then please proceed, let's keep it short and to the point."

"Thank you, your honor."

The DA walks over in front of the jury box,

"Ladies and gentlemen of the jury. The defendant you see to the left of the defense counsel is Mr. Hughes," and he points to where I'm sitting, "who looks from all accounts, to be your normal all American gentlemen that you and I would invite over for Sunday dinner, or to stay for the weekend. But ladies and gentlemen, don't be fooled by this man's clean-cut, neat dress and intellectual character. Lurking deep down inside that subtle mind is a vindictive murderer, rapist, and arsonist. We will show that in the early hours of the morning of October 16, he left the room downstairs in the house where he was a guest, going upstairs to the main bedroom where his sister-in-law Mrs. Sylvia Croning and her husband Robert Croning were sound asleep. There, he went to the side of the bed and point-blank shot Mr. Croning three times in the face. He forced Mrs. Croning to open the safe, where he stole sixty-five thousand dollars, before raping and battering her. After tying her to the bed and gagging her, he then left in a cab to go and present his paper at a convention. But before he left, he set fire to the house, hoping to destroy all evidence. The evidence we will present will prove to you beyond any reasonable doubt, that he is guilty as charged. Thank you."

He turned around and walked back to his table

staring at me.

His statement caused some stirring and discussion from the spectators. The judge rapped his gavel on his bench.

"Quiet, quiet, there will be no discussion in my court, or I'll have it cleared, do you understand?"

"Does the defense counsel wish to make an opening statement?"

"Thank you, your honor."

Adrian gets up from the table and walks to a position in front of the jury box.

"Ladies and gentlemen of the jury, the prosecution has paid many fine attributes to my client's character. Well, dressed, clean-cut and of intellectual character, the sort of person you and I would graciously invite into our homes for dinner or to stay for the weekend. The only thing I could find wrong with his character reference was the part of having a vindictive mind. My client is an upstanding citizen of the United States, doesn't even have a traffic offense. He served his country in the Gulf war and was discharged with honors. He is married with a six-year-old son. The so-called proof that the prosecution is referring to is at most circumstantial. My client's conference in Boston gave his sister-in-law the perfect opportunity to stage the murder of her abusive husband and put the blame on Mr. Hughes. Ladies and gentlemen of the jury, by the time you have heard all the witnesses and seen the evidence, I'm convinced you will find my client not guilty. Thank you."

The judge looks sort of annoyed at the prosecution desk and says,

"The prosecution may call their first witness."

The assistant district attorney gets up.

"The people call the Cambridge Taxicab Company driver, Mr. Aduri Kumar."

The bailiff brings in the witness and places him in the witness stand.

The clerk addresses him and instructs him to raise his right hand.

"Do you swear that the testimony you are about to give in front of this court shall be the truth, the whole truth and nothing but the truth, so help you, God?"

The cabbie raises his hand and swears "I do."

I can't help thinking to myself if this guy is a Muslim, swearing to our God means absolutely nothing to him.

"For the record, please state your first and last names."

"Aduri Kumar," he says.

"You can put your hand down now Mr. Kumar."

"Oh, thank you."

I could see the poor guy was nervous, he must have been in his fifties and I don't remember him. Was he the one that picked me up at the airport, or the one that picked me up at the house in the morning to take me to the convention center? Well, I will soon find out.

The assistant district attorney walks over to the witness stand and addresses him.

"Mr. Kumar, have you picked up people from number 44 Willow Grove Lane, Cambridge before?"

"Yes, I have, I've picked up Mr. Croning there at his home a lot of times."

"So, you knew Mr. Croning?"

"Yes, and I also pick up his wife sometimes."

"Mr. Kumar please cast your mind back to the morning of October 16. Did you come and collect someone from that same address at around 7:20 a.m.?"

"Yes, I did."

"Your honor, will you please instruct the accused to stand and face the witness."

The judge looks at me and says," Mr. Hughes, please rise and face the witness."

This I do.

"Mr. Kumar, is this the man that you collected at Mr. and Mrs. Cronings's home on the morning of October 16 at around 7:20 a.m.?"

"Yes, that be him, sir."

"Your honor, may the court reflect that Mr. Kumar has identified Mr. Hughes as the person he collected at those premises on that day."

"Mr. Hughes, you may sit," said the judge.

"Mr. Kumar, did something unusual happen after you picked Mr. Hughes up at the front steps of the house that morning?"

"Yes, he asked me to stop at the end of the driveway, just before you get to the street, saying he wanted to throw a plastic bag in the rubbish can that was on the sidewalk."

"You mean he threw a plastic bag like this here" and he holds up a white bag tied with a bag tie, "into the trash can?"

"Yes, that's right, he got out of the car and threw it in the trash can."

"Thank you, Mr. Kumar. I have no further questions."

The judge looks down at Adrian and says.

"Does the defense have any questions?"

"No, not at this time your honor."

"Then the witness is excused," he says.

The judge waits for the cabbie to walk out of the court and says, "The prosecution can call their next witness."

The assistant district attorney gets up and says, "The people call Detective Officer Alan Burns."

We go through the same swearing-in process, name, rank, etc., and the assistant district attorney starts his questioning.

"From the records I have here, I see that you were called to a fire scene at 44 Willow Grove Lane, Cambridge on October 16 at 8:47 a.m.?"

"Yes, that is correct, I was in the area and got the call."

"Were you alone?"

"Yes, I was, my partner is a diabetic and he had to see the doctor that day, so I was on my own."

"I see, can you tell the jury what you found at the scene of the fire when you got there."

"There were several fire trucks already on the scene and the fire was raging. It had already consumed the left side of the dwelling where the garages were, and it was now burning through the roof of the second story. The fire department had half a dozen or more hoses on the blaze trying desperately to douse the flames. A few minutes before I arrived, the fire department had bravely managed to rescue two people from the main bedroom on the upper floor. Unfortunately, the male person was deceased, the female was semi-conscious. The ambulance was busy getting ready to take them to the hospital."

"Did you perhaps manage to talk to the female person or examine the deceased male?"

"The female as I said, was semi-conscious, the paramedics already had a breathing apparatus attached to her, and the male was in a body bag. I did unzip it and his face had been blown away completely, there were no recognizable features left."

"What conclusion did you come to at that stage of what may have caused his death?"

"Well, that is very difficult to explain, as I said, it looked like his face had been blown away and I was trying to think at that time what could have done that in the fire, because it looked more like a blast of some sort, but I was unable to come up with any conclusion."

"What happened then detective, did you leave the scene?"

"No, I didn't, I was curious as to what could have caused such an injury to a person and I decided to wait until the fire was completely dowsed and it was safe to enter the top floor section that had not been completely burnt. The fire chief and I went up to the second-floor bedroom where they had found the bodies in bed."

"What did you find there?"

"Well, at first it was difficult to see as there was so much water damage and black soot everywhere. Then I found one of the pillows and although it was sopping wet, it was covered in blood and there was a hole in the non-blood-stained side, which looked very suspicious to me. As it looked like a bullet hole, I called my superintendent and we got the forensic people to investigate the scene."

"Then what happened?"

"Within forty-five minutes we had the place cordoned off as a possible crime scene. We had already established the two occupants were Mr. and Mrs. Croning. Among the things we found was a mobile phone in the bedside drawer that had miraculously escaped most of the water and was still functional. From the phone records, we managed to contact Mrs. Corning's sister who informed us that the defendant had been staying there the night before and was presenting a paper at the Boston Convention Centre that morning."

"What happened then detective, did you just go and arrest the defendant?"

"No, we had no grounds on which to arrest him. We dispatched two officers to the Convention Center and had him picked up for questioning."

"What time was that?"

"I believe they picked him up at around 11:30 a.m. and brought him to the Cambridge Police Department. We held him in remand and proceeded to get all his details, fingerprints, and mouth swabs for the records. In the meantime, our forensic team was analyzing all the material they had collected at the scene of the fire."

"What happened then?"

"Mid-afternoon the forensic lab informs me that they had something to show me. I went to see what it was and shortly after came back to the interrogation room with a black plastic bag, which I placed on the table."

"Did you show the defendant what was in the bag?"

"No, not immediately, we wanted to see what he had in his overnight-bag."

"What were you looking for?"

"We weren't sure, we wanted to see what else was in his bag that may be of interest."

"I gather he allowed you to search his bag without a search warrant?"

"Yes, he said we could search it as there was nothing in his bag that was incriminating, as far as he was concerned."

"Did you find anything incriminating in his overnight-bag?"

"Well, we found a package in a plastic shopping bag among his clothes and when we asked him what was in the package, he said it was a present from his sister-in-law to his wife and son."

"Did you open it?"

"Yes, I opened it and it contained sixty-five thousand dollars, in crisp new hundred-dollar bills."

"Did I hear you correctly, detective — sixty-five thousand dollars?" and with that, he walks up to the witness stand and says, "That's an awful lot of cash for a present don't you think detective?"

He then turns and while walking back to face the witness he asks, "What did he say when you showed him the money?"

"Nothing, he just stared at it like he wasn't really seeing it."

"What did you do then?"

"I opened the plastic bag, brought up from Forensic, and took out a clear plastic bag, containing a gun. I showed it to the defendant and asked him if he perhaps knew what type of weapon it was, and he identified it correctly as a Glock 19. I asked him if he knew whose gun it could be, and he said he had no idea. I then asked him if he knew where we found the weapon and again, he said he did not know."

"Did you inform the defendant whose gun it was and where it had been found?"

"Yes, I informed him that the gun had been found by our Forensic team wrapped in a dishcloth, placed in a white plastic bag with an empty wine bottle and some other vegetable trash."

"Did you also inform him where the white plastic bag was found?"

"Yes, I did, the white plastic bag had been found in a large trash can on the street outside number 44 Willow Grove Lane."

"I suppose the defendant was surprised that the municipal trash collectors hadn't collected the trash yet?" remarked the assistant DA.

Adrian immediately jumps up and says, "Objection your honor, pure speculation, the prosecution is suggesting that the defendant knew the weapon was in the trash."

"Sustained counsel, no games in my court, is that understood?"

"Yes, your honor."

"Detective, what else did you ask the defendant?"

"I asked him if he knew who's gun it was."

"What was his response?"

"He said, I don't know, but I'm sure you are going to tell me."

"Did you inform the defendant whose gun it was?"

"Yes, we told him the weapon was registered in the name of his sister-in-law, Sylvia R. Croning."

"I also asked if he knew whose fingerprints were all over the weapon," said the detective.

"What was his response"?

"He said they were his fingerprints and he could explain why they were on the gun."

"Did the defendant explain why his prints were on the weapon?"

"No, I told him he could explain that to the jury because the three spent shells dug out of the back of the bed matched those having been fired from that weapon."

"Did you then formally arrest the defendant?"

"No, at that stage we wanted to get a

statement from Mrs. Croning, and we were waiting to hear from the hospital, as to when we could interview her."

"Did you eventually interview Mrs. Croning and get her statement?" asked the assistant DA.

"Yes, Superintendent Ross and I went to the hospital and took a statement from her."

"Is that a copy of the statement you have there with you?"

"Yes, it is."

"Will you please read it to the jury, loud and clear?"

"Witness Statement dated: October 16 ...... "

"Detective, you can skip the formalities, just read the statement please."

"Sorry, yes certainly."

On Sunday, October 15 at around 7:30 p.m., the three of us, myself, my husband, and my brother-in-law Grant Hughes, all had dinner together in the dining room. A fair amount was drunk. Grant became a little hostile and agitated about an investment of fifty-thousand Dollars that his wife Diane had placed with Bob some time ago. Bob had promised to double her money and Grant was upset because Bob hadn't shown any significant investment return to date. Grant said we are driving around in flashy cars, we have this fancy house and stuff, but what has happened to the fifty-thousand dollars Diane had invested with Bob. He was getting more and more agitated. Grant wanted to know if the money Diane had given to Bob to invest, paid for the booze we were drinking. He then got up from the table, threw his napkin down, and stormed off to his room in the studio. We cleared up, put the dishes in the dishwasher, and retired to our bedroom on the second floor.

Sometime in the early hours of the morning, Grant came upstairs into our bedroom and switched on the light. I woke up. He had a gun in his right hand and a kitchen knife in his left hand. Bob sat up in bed and asked him what the fuck he was doing in our bedroom. He told Bob to shut the fuck up, open the safe and give him the fifty grand Diane had given him, plus interest. Bob protested he didn't have that sort of money in the house. Grant said he was a lying bastard and he came around to Bob's side of the bed, took a pillow, pushed it over Bob's head, put the gun against the pillow, and shot him three or four times, I think. He then came over to my side of the bed and asked me if I wanted some of that too, and I said no. He said I was to open the fucking safe. So, I went to the safe in the closet and opened it. He told me to take out all the cash and count it. I did and it totaled sixty-five thousand dollars. He told me to find a bag for the money. I found an old Macy's plastic bag in the closet and put the money in that. He then told me to pull the top sheet off the bed and hold it, then he took the knife and cut strips from it. He used the strips to tie me to the bed, beat me about the face, and raped me. Before leaving, he stuffed my pajama panties in my mouth and tied them with a strip of sheeting. I remember hearing this loud bang, like an explosion and then there was a lot of smoke. I think I must have blanked out and the next thing I woke up in the hospital.

This is a true an —— "

"Yes detective, thank you, you can skip with the formalities."

"So detective, after you got this incriminating statement, you arrested the defendant?"

"Yes, we arrested him and officially charged him with first-degree murder of Mr. Robert Archer Croning, together with the rape and aggravated assault of Mrs. Sylvia Rebecca Croning. Also, we charged him with the theft and robbery of sixty-five thousand dollars from the safe in their home at 44 Willow Grove Lane Cambridge Massachusetts, as well as intentionally setting ablaze the said premises to cover all evidence."

"Your honor, I would like to present a copy of Mrs.Croning's statement as part of the prosecution's evidence."

The assistant district attorney took the statement from the detective and handed it to the court clerk.

"Your honor, with your permission, we would at this stage also like to present to evidence the weapon and the knife referred to in Mrs. Croning's statement."

The judge looks at his watch and says, "Ladies and gentlemen it's been a long first morning, it is now 12:10 p.m. I suggest we recess for lunch and be back in court at 1:15 p.m. sharp."

The bailiff gets up and says, "All rise," as the honorable Judge Kenneth Gould leaves the court.

"What now?" I say to Adrian as we are standing, and the people are leaving the court. "What do you think?"

"Well, nothing has changed, nothing has come up that we didn't know about, it all depends on how the jury sees it."

"Are you going to question the detective?"

"Yes, I think so. Look I'm going to get a bite to eat and make some calls to the office and see if they've had any luck in finding anyone with info on our Sylvia. They are going to lock you up again while we have a lunch break, but I can get you something if you like?"

"Man, a hamburger and fries would taste good right now, if that's possible."

"Okay, let me see what I can do, here comes the bailiff to get you."

Adrian, sometime later but good to his word, has a hamburger, fries, and can of Coke delivered to me. I don't normally like fizzy drinks, but the Coke went down like a scotch on ice and it was the best hamburger I'd ever eaten. I scarcely had time to finish my fries when the jailer arrived to escort me back to the court.

We are all back in court and the detective is again in the witness stand. The judge has reminded him he is still under oath.

The assistant district attorney gets up and says, "Your honor, the people wish to bring in addition to the evidence that has already been lodged, a new piece of evidence that has just this hour, come to our notice."

Adrian jumps up.

"Objection your honor, the defense has not had time to examine this so-called new piece of evidence."

"Counselors, both of you, approach the bench."

Adrian and the assistant district attorney walk up to the left side of the bench. The judge is bent over the front of the bench and I could hear him say in a quiet voice.

"What's this new evidence, Mr. Moore?"

"Your honor, ever since we arrested the defendant, we have been pouring over his computer looking for any evidence that will tie him to this crime and we believe we have found it."

"Yes, and what is it?" asks the judge.

"It's detailed plans on how to construct a remote-controlled trigger device for a bomb or incinerating device. These plans were more than likely taken from the Dark Web. This will show how he managed to set fire to the house while he was miles away."

"Your honor," protests Adrian, "there is no way that having plans of a piece of electronic gadgetry on his PC proves that my client set fire to the house. He's an electrical engineer, for God's sake, he could have that sort of stuff on his PC all the time."

"Mr. Mink, watch your mouth, I'll have no blasphemy in my court, do you understand?" His normally quiet voice went up a notch or two.

"Sorry, your honor."

"Your objection is overruled."

"How do you propose presenting this evidence, Mr. Moore?"

"Your honor we propose that tomorrow we have the court's TV monitors display the images from the computer. We will have it all rigged up before the court is in session."

"Fine, let's get on with what we have at the moment, you may return to your tables."

"Thank you, your honor."

When counsels are back at their respective tables, the judge announces,

"New evidence will be brought before the court tomorrow morning and will be displayed on the overhead television monitors at the appropriate time."

"The prosecution can continue with the witness."

The assistant district attorney walks over to the clerk's table and picks up a see-through plastic bag with a large black-handled kitchen knife inside. He walks back and takes up his position in front of the jury box again.

"Detective Burns," he says, holding up the plastic bag, "this large knife I believe was found under Mrs. Croning's bed, where she was tied, battered and raped, is that correct?"

"Yes, that is correct."

"Whose fingerprints were on this knife?"

"The defendant's fingerprints were all over the handle of the knife."

The assistant DA walks back to the clerk, puts the plastic bag with the knife back down on the table and picks up the plastic see-through bag with the gun, and comes back in front of the jury box.

"Detective, is this the gun that was found in the trash can on the sidewalk outside the premises of Mr. and Mrs. Croning's home?"

"Yes, that is the weapon we found in the trash can."

"When you inspected it, how many rounds were left in the magazine?"

"There were twelve rounds left in the mag."

"What type of gun is this detective?" he said, holding the bag for the jury to see.

"It's a Glock 19 and it can hold fifteen rounds."

"What type of rounds, bullets were still loaded into the magazine?"

"The type of rounds loaded in the mag are commonly known in the industry as dum-dum bullets, hollow-point, or soft-point bullets."

"Detective, what is the difference between this type of ammunition, and a standard bullet that doesn't have these features?"

"The so-called dum-dum bullet is designed to expand on impact, thus preventing over-penetration, causing a large wound, making it a more lethal bullet."

"Were the spent bullets dug out of the back of the bed in which the deceased was sleeping, a match to those that you are describing?"

"Yes, they are a complete match."

"Your honor, at this time the people would like to display on the overhead monitors, a picture of the head of a pig that was shot point-blank with this firearm, using this same sort of dum-dum bullet. This is very graphic and may be upsetting for some of the jury and spectators, I do apologize."

Adrian immediately objects but the judge overrules him, and he sits down and looks at me and shrugs his shoulders.

The assistant district attorney continues.

"Detective, we see from this enlarged photograph displayed on the monitors that unless one knew it was a pig's head, one would not recognize it as such. Most of the snout and both the eyes and cheeks have been shredded."

"Thank you we can switch it off now."

"Detective, those tests were conducted by the Forensic department to simulate what would happen if the same thing were done to a human head, am I correct?"

"Yes, that is correct, although the skin and tissue of the pig is harder and slightly denser than that of the human."

"Well, then detective, could one therefore reason that the damage to a human's face would be more severe?"

"Yes, I think that is a fair observation."

The assistant district attorney walks over to the

clerk's table and picks up a clear folder with a picture.

"Your honor, the people wish to show the jury this picture of the deceased's blown-away face."

Again, Adrian is on his feet.

"Your honor I must object, the prosecution is now playing the sensation game, seeking the sympathy of the jury. There is no reason for the jury to see this picture."

"Mr. Moore, may I have a look at the picture," asks the judge.

The assistant district attorney gives it to the clerk who hands it to the judge. He looks at it for a few seconds and hands it back to the clerk.

"What is the prosecution's reason for wanting to show it to the jury?"

"Your honor, the people wish to assure the jury that what they saw happen to the face of the pig, is also possible to happen to the face of a human."

"I will allow it."

Immediately Adrian jumps up and says, "Your honor I must"— but he didn't get to finish his sentence.

"Mr. Mink, sit down, I have ruled, I don't want to speak to you again."

Adrian sits down with a sigh, shakes his head, and whispers to me, "We are farting against thunder here."

The picture gets passed around the jury, I could see some of them shaking their heads. The women just glanced at it and passed it on, and it ended up back at the clerk's desk.

The assistant district attorney continues. "Detective, you said the defendant admitted that the fingerprints on the weapon were his?"

"Yes, he did, we checked his prints and they

were all over the weapon."

The assistant district attorney walks to the clerk's table and picks up a brown paper bag and removes several strips of sheeting. He holds them up and says, "Detective, are these the strips of sheeting that were used to restrain the victim, Mrs. Croning, to her bed while she was brutally beaten and raped?"

"Yes, those are the strips of sheeting we removed from the crime scene."

"Your honor, we would like to display these items as evidence."

He stuffs the strips back in the bag and hands the bag to the clerk.

"Detective, where did you find these strips of sheeting?"

"They were tied to the slats of the headboard and the same at the foot of the victim's bed."

"Then am I correct in saying that had the Fireman not freed Mrs. Croning from these restraints, she would have died?"

Immediately Adrian is on his feet objecting.

"Your honor, with due respect, the detective is in no way skilled in making such a conclusion."

"I agree. Detective, you will ignore that question." Says the judge.

"Thank you, detective, I have no further questions at this time."

The judge looks over the rim of his glasses at our table and asks, "Does the counsel for the defense wish to cross-examine the witness?"

Adrian stands up and says, "Yes, thank you, your honor."

He walks over in front of the witness stand and looks at the detective for a few seconds before asking, "Detective, you say the weapon was covered with the defendant's fingerprints. Were there no other fingerprints on the weapon?"

"Yes, that's correct, and there were no other fingerprints on the weapon."

"Detective, you mentioned that the defendant acknowledged that his prints were on the weapon, but you never let him explain why they were on the weapon, did you not ask him that question?"

"No, I did not."

"So, am I to believe that you still have no idea why my client's fingerprints were on the weapon?"

"We didn't need to ask him, because we already knew why they were there."

"And what was that conclusion?"

"Well, that he had shot the deceased Robert Croning."

"I see, and when did you come to that conclusion detective?"

"As soon as we got the testimony from Mrs. Croning."

"But didn't you already make that conclusion before you interviewed Mrs. Croning?"

"No, I don't think so."

"Sorry detective, I beg to differ. In the interrogation room you said, and I quote, let me see now," —— and Adrian looks through his notes in his hand.

"Yes, here it is —— you say, 'the ballistics we dug out of the back of the bed, match those fired from this handgun here, and guess whose fingerprints are all over this weapon?'"

"And my client said," 'Mine and I can explain why.'

"You said," 'Sure you can, but save that story for the jury.'

"Then your superintendent says," 'Hang on

Alan, let's not get carried away, nobody has been charged with anything yet.'

"And you reply," 'Um umm, we'll soon see about that.'

"Now it looks to me, detective, that you had already made up your mind that my client was guilty long before you got a statement from Mrs. Croning, is that not so?"

"No, I don't think I actually said he was guilty."

"No detective, not in those words, but I think you implied that he was guilty, but let's leave that for the moment."

"Detective, in all the years that you have been in the force, how many criminals have you interviewed and cross-examined, one hundred, two hundred?"

The assistant district attorney was upon his feet.—— "Objection your honor, what has this got to do with this case in hand?"

"Mr. Mink please explain," the judge asks.

"Your honor I'm trying to establish the detective's experience in similar cases."

"I see, we'll keep it brief. Objection overruled," says the judge.

"Well then, detective, how many would you say?"

"I don't know a hundred and fifty, two hundred it's hard to say."

"Okay let's say hundred and fifty. Now can you recall in any of those interrogations that any of those one hundred and fifty suspects ever admitted that their fingerprints were on a piece of evidence?"

"No, I don't think I ever had one that I can recall."

"So, detective did you not think it strange that my client should admit to his prints being all over a weapon that could have been used in a murder?"

"I never really thought about it at the time."

"So, you decided to let the jury hear his reason, you weren't very interested. As far as you were concerned, this was an open and shut case and you went straight ahead and had my client charged with the crime. Don't you think it would have been prudent of the department to hear what my client had to say? It may have put you on another track that could possibly have prevented this whole case." "No, I don't think it was prudent, we have strong evidence convicting the accused." "I'm just making an observation, let's carry on."

"Did you not find it strange that there were no other fingerprints on the gun seeing the gun belonged to Mrs. Croning?"

"No, not really, she could have cleaned it before putting it away."

"Yes, maybe that's a good reason, knowing full well someone else would be putting their fingerprints all over it at a later stage."

Up jumps the prosecution. "Objection your honor, allows for speculation."

"Sustained, the jury will ignore that remark."

"Detective, before your Forensic guys shot up the pig's head, did they perhaps check to see if there were any fingerprints on the twelve remaining dum-dum bullets that were left in the magazine?"

"Yes, they did."

"And whose fingerprints were all over those bullets?"

"The defendants."

"I see, because you never mentioned that."

"Did you ask Mrs. Croning where she left her gun?"

"Yes, she said she kept it in the drawer of the

sideboard."

"Did you ask her what type of bullets she had loaded in the gun?"

"She said she didn't know, as her husband always loaded it for her."

"Did you perhaps ask her if her husband always loaded the gun, how come my client's fingerprints were on the remaining bullets?"

"No, I never asked her."

"Why not?" asks Adrian.

"We didn't think it was relevant."

"Did she give any explanation as to how my client would have known where to find her gun in the sideboard's drawer?"

"Yes, she said she remembers the defendant asking her at dinner the night before the incident, if she wasn't scared when her husband was away so often and she told him she kept her gun handy in the sideboard drawer."

"Did you inspect the sideboard?"

"Yes, we did, but it was badly burnt in the fire and not much was left to examine."

"Did you find any traces of ammunition in the drawers?"

"No, as I said the sideboard was badly burnt, it would have been difficult to find traces of ammunition having been there."

"Detective, did you find any other empty shell casings, or bullets in the house, if the bullets fired due to the heat the empty brass casings would still be there?"

"No, we found no other shells in the house."

"All right detective, so we have several scenarios here."

"First scenario — the defendant shoots the husband with the dum-dum bullets that were already loaded in the gun by her husband. He removes the magazine, takes out the remaining twelve bullets, wipes them clean, then puts his fingerprints all over them, reloads them into the magazine, wraps the gun in a dishcloth, and puts it in the trash."

"Are you with me here detective?"

"Yes, I think so"

" Good, —— the second scenario, the defendant brings his own dum-dum bullets with his fingerprints all over them and loads them into the gun, takes the old bullets that were in the gun and throws them away. He goes upstairs and shoots the husband, comes downstairs, wraps the gun in the dishcloth, and dumps it in the trash."

"So detective, which one of these two scenarios do you think it is?"

"I don't know, maybe none of them."

"Well, you are the detective. I'm sure the jury would like to know your theory on how my client's fingerprints got on all the bullets."

"Our Forensic department is still working on that explanation."

"That's good to know, because I'm going to ask you again later in this trial what explanation they have come up with."

"Detective, the strips of sheeting you say were used to restrain the victim, did you find any of my client's fingerprints on the strips?"

"No counselor, you should know fingerprints don't stick to the cloth."

"Oh yes silly of me to forget that, well then, what about hair, skin, bits of his clothes, any of that?"

"No, none."

"Did you not find that unusual, with all the

handling of the strips and yet no trace of any of my client's hair, skin, or bits of his clothing."

"No, not really, he could have been wearing gloves."

"Did you ask Mrs. Croning if her attacker was wearing gloves?"   "No, I did not."

"No further questions, your honor, but I reserve the right to recall this witness if necessary."

Adrian walks back to his desk and sits down.

The judge looks at his watch and says.

"The witness may step down. Ladies and gentlemen, at this stage of the questioning, I propose we adjourn for the day and meet back here at 10 a.m. sharp tomorrow. Jury, you are being accommodated at one of our local hotels I'm told. There is no need to remind you that you should not discuss this case with anyone outside of this court."

The bailiff gets up and says,

"All rise," as the honorable Judge Kenneth Gould leaves the court.

Adrian looks at me and says,

"Phew, well that's the first day behind us! How do you feel?"

"Much like you I imagine, drained. I listened to every word the prosecutor said and tried to analyze every line."

"Well, tomorrow they are going to show that detonation device they found on your laptop, any ideas about that?" he says as he looks at me skeptically.

"Christ don't give me that look, I have no idea where it came from, I don't even know how to get into the fucking Dark Web, or whatever it's called."

"Well, then somebody was on your pc and put it there."

"Look they are coming to get you and they

110

won't take you back to the Police department in Cambridge, you'll spend the night here. I'll get some clean clothes over to you early tomorrow."

CHAPTER 10

The next morning just before 10 a.m., the bailiff escorts me into court and I look around at the spectators to see if Diane is there, and my heart sort of skips a beat. I don't know if I'm happy to see Diane sitting in court, but I'm happy to see her. She's sitting close to a couple I had noticed the day before in the same spot, the woman is small and attractive, and the guy looks like her overweight grandfather. I look up towards Diane and smile, but she continues to look down and never acknowledges that she has seen me.

"Morning Grant, I see you got the clean clothes we sent over to you?"

"Morning, Adrian, —— yes thanks. Sorry I was looking at the gallery, I see my wife is there."

"Where?" he says.

"She's sitting on the second row of benches from the back on the left side, near that fat old guy and the young woman next to him."

He turns his head slightly and says, "Okay I see her."

The bailiff announces the judge and we all stand up.

The judge comes in saying,

"Good morning ladies and gentlemen," and takes his seat behind the bench and says, "please be seated." He looks over at the jury and addresses them.

"Members of the jury, I take it your accommodation was adequate and you had a goodnight's rest."

Some of them nodded and others mumbled their thanks.

"Good. I remind you that you are all still under

oath."

He looks down at our tables and says, "Counsel, are you ready to continue with this case?"

The district attorney stands up and says, "Ready for the people your honor."

Adrian gets up and says, "The defense is ready, your honor."

The judge looks down at the prosecution and asks,

"Does the prosecution wish to bring any new witnesses to the stand?"

"Yes, thank you, your honor. The People call Edward Simms."

The bailiff brings Mr. Simms to the witness stand. The clerk goes through the normal procedure of swearing in the witness and then instructs him to be seated.

The assistant district attorney gets up, stands in front of the jury box for a moment, then turns and faces the witness.

"Mr. Simms, you're employed as a computer technician with the Cambridge Police Department's Forensic division, is that not so?"

"Yes, that is correct."

"I believe that you have been searching through the files on the computer of the defendant to see if there was anything that would help in this case?"

"Yes, we have."

"Please explain what it is and tell me how you came by this information?"

"For the past two months, we have been pouring over the many files on this PC. Most of them are business-related and many are classified as confidential. There are a lot of technician data drawings, schematics, and stuff like that, where we required expert people to evaluate a lot of this information."

"Did you find any incriminating information in these files you mentioned?"

"No, we found nothing. We were about to pack it in when I thought I'd have one last look into the defendant's personal files which are small, only two or three files. One file was labeled Birth Certificates. In this file, there was a folder for Jason's Birth Certificate and another for Jason's Birth Certificate #2. I thought this was strange. Why would his son have two birth certificates? I opened it and found detailed drawings and plans on how to construct a detonation device, using a mobile phone as the trigger."

"Mr. Simms, do we have these images to display on the overhead monitors?"

"Yes, we have connected the defendant's laptop to the monitors, and my colleague John will take us to the files and folders in question."

The overhead monitors flash and come to life, the first image was the screensaver on my laptop.

"Please bear with us while my colleague pulls up the correct files," says Simms —— "ahh, there we are! There are four pages, this is the first page I wanted to show you. It's the date when it was downloaded."

"John, zoom-in to the top of that page that says: *How to build a cell-phone detonator.* On the left there, —— yes that's it, you can see the date is *September 23*, just over four weeks before the defendant came to Cambridge."

He shows another picture of a cell phone with its back removed, wires protruding out of it, and connected to some other device.

114

The jury and spectators are spellbound. The prosecution is doing an excellent job of putting me away for life. It is very disheartening to see they have found this sort of incriminating evidence on my PC. How it got there, I could not fathom.

"Thank you, Mr. Simms, I think we can switch the monitors off now. Mr. Simms, do you believe that such a device as we saw on the monitor, could have been used to ignite a fire that caused the Croning's home to be destroyed?"

Adrian jumps up. "Objection your honor, the witness is a computer technician. Not an expert on explosive and incinerating devices."

The judge looks at the prosecution with a disdained look and says. "Sustained."

"I'm sorry your honor, I have no further questions for the witness at this time."

The judge looks at Adrian and asks, "does the defense have any questions for this witness?"

Adrian gets up and says,

"Yes, thank you, your honor."

Adrian walks over to the witness box and says,

"Mr. Simms, did Mr. Hughes give you the access password to gain entry into his personal computer?"

"No, he didn't, we had to hack into it to gain access."

"I see, so this sort of thing is a regular day to day thing for you guys, I suppose?"

"Well yes, we have the skills to do that sort of thing, yes."

"I suppose you also have the skills to plant something on someone's PC without their knowledge?"

Up jumps the assistant district attorney.

"Objection your honor, the defense is implying

that the police department has planted the workings of this detonating device on the defendant's PC."

"Your honor that's an interesting theory but I was merely establishing ———"

Before he could finish, the judge was banging his gavel on the round sounding disc.

"Mr. Mink, I will have none of that in my court, do you hear me. The jury will ignore that last statement."

"I'm sorry your honor, I have no further questions for this witness."

"The witness may step down," says the judge.

"The prosecution may call their next witness."

"The People call Chief Fire Officer, Henry Bellmore."

The clerk goes through the swearing-in process, name, rank, occupation, and he sits down.

"Officer Bellmore, you were present at the fire at 44 Willow Grove Lane Cambridge on October 16 were you not?"

"Yes, I was in attendance there, it was quite a blaze."

"Officer Bellmore, you have vast experience in these matters, where do you believe this fire started?"

"It no doubt started in the garage and then spread to the rest of the premises."

"Did you find any evidence of how the fire was started in the garage?"

"No, unfortunately, the fire in the garage was so intense due to the combustion of the fuel in the three vehicles parked there, all evidence, if there was any, would have been completely destroyed."

"I see. Earlier on you saw on the monitor, pictures, and drawings, etc., of the so-called cell phone detonator. Have you seen one of those devices before, or have you had any personal experience with such devices?"

"No, fortunately in my career I've not had to deal with devices of that nature."

"But you are familiar with the nature of the device not so?"

"Yes, after we had the bomb scare at the Boston Marathon, a number of us in the department did a course at the FBI relating to such devices. The device we saw earlier is typical of the devices used in Afghanistan and other parts of the Middle East to detonate roadside and other types of bombs."

"Officer Bellmore in your professional opinion, could such a device have been used to start the fire at the premises of 44 Willow Grove Lane, Cambridge on October 16?"

"Yes, quite possibly."

"Thank you, Officer Bellmore, I have no further questions."

"Defense, do you have any questions for the witness?" asks the judge looking down at us.

"Yes, thank you, your honor," says Adrian as he gets up and walks over to the witness stand.

"Officer Bellmore, the device in question is basically a remote trigger device that can be activated by a cell phone, not so?"

"Yes, that's correct."

"Would it also be correct to say that the device could be used to trigger numerous other things like switch on lights, turn on the hot water tank, or the stove, I could think of a dozen things off of the top of my head, other than bombs and starting fires as advocated by the prosecution?"

"Well yes, I suppose so."

"Thank you, no further questions."

The judge looked at the prosecution as if to say, 'do you want to cross,' but he received no indication that they did and said, "The witness may step down."

The judge looks at his watch and down at the prosecution table and says.

"The prosecution may call their next witness."

This time the district attorney himself gets up and says, "The People call Mrs. Sylvia Croning to the stand."

There's suddenly a lot of murmuring and loud whispering going on in the spectator's area. The judge bangs his gavel on the sounding block.

"Quiet, quiet —— I'll have no discussion in my court. If you want to discuss anything take it outside and don't come back in until after recess. Is that clear? I've told you before I'll clear this court of spectators, I won't tell you again." As suddenly as it started, there is quiet again.

The bailiff escorts Sylvia to the stand, at first, I didn't recognize her. Her dark hair is cut short with silver highlights and has that pixie layered look, she has truly little makeup on and what she has applied makes her look twenty years older. She has on a double-breasted charcoal jacket and matching pencil suit skirt and low black heels. Very elegant. I believe the DA is pleased with what he sees approaching the witness stand because he bends over and whispers something to the assistant district attorney, who looks up, and they both smile. The clerk goes through the swearing-in routine and instructs her to sit down.

Looking at her now I have this feeling of utter contempt and disgust, that someone I trusted and regarded as family, could do this to me. What in heaven's name could possibly be her motive for

118

making these ridiculous allegations against me?

The district attorney walks up to the witness stand, "Good morning Mrs. Croning, I trust you are feeling better and managing to get your life back to some form of normality."

"Yes, thank you."

"I trust this will not be too stressful for you, if you need a break please indicate and we can do so."

"Thank you, I'm sure I will be fine."

"All right then. Mrs. Croning, we have your full statement, but what we don't have are the events leading up to the night of the murder of your husband, your rape, and beating. Could you take us through that period, let's say from the time the defendant arrived at your home on the night of October 15."

"Yes certainly, it was close to 11 p.m. when the cab pulled up at our entrance, my brother-in-law Grant got out of the cab and came up the stairs to greet me. We went inside and I offered him tea or coffee to drink, but he declined."

"Sorry to interrupt Mrs. Croning, but where was your husband at this time?"

"He was in bed asleep."

"I see, you had been waiting up for your brother-in-law?"

"Yes, I had received a call from him earlier in the evening that his flight had been delayed. So, I decided to go to bed, read, and wait until he arrived. When I heard the cab come up the driveway, I got out of bed, slipped on my bathrobe, and went down to meet Grant. I showed him to his room in the studio and mentioned to him that my husband and I were taking our boat out for a ride the next morning. We would be stopping for lunch at a restaurant close to a marina in the bay and I said it would be nice if he could join us. We said good night and I went up to bed."

"What happened the next morning?"

"Well, we got up at our normal time over the weekend, which was around 8:15 a.m. There was no movement from the studio where Grant was sleeping, so we made coffee and Bob read the papers and I watched some television. By 9:30 a.m. Bob was getting a bit agitated that Grant wasn't up yet. So, I went and knocked on the door and went in. He was still in his pajamas sitting at the table working on his laptop. I greeted him and asked him if he was having breakfast with us and then coming out for a run in the boat."

"What was his response?"

"He said he was sorry, but he would like to pass, maybe next time, as he still had some work to do on the paper, he was presenting the next day at the Convention Center."

"What happened then?"

"Well, as you can imagine Bob was fuming, he said fuck him he can get his own breakfast and lunch, we'll get breakfast at the club, and we left."

"Did you only see him again when you got back much later in the afternoon?"

"No, I did see him shortly before we left. While Bob was throwing a few things in the Land Cruiser, I stuck my head in the studio and said goodbye. I told him there was food in the fridge, he was to help himself and we'd see him later that afternoon."

"You see the main reason Bob wanted to take the boat out to the harbor was that he had arranged for the boat to be serviced on Monday, intending to leave it at the marina, and then get a cab back home. On Monday Bob would get a cab from home and go back to the boat at the marina and take it to where it was going to be serviced. This would save him a few hours having to queue at the Charles Dam River Lock."

"So, you went and had breakfast, got in your boat, went out into the bay, and then had lunch?"

"Yes, that's correct, we cruised around a bit and then moored the boat."

"Where did you have lunch Mrs. Croning?"

"At the Bayside Bar & Grill restaurant."

"How long were you at the restaurant?"

"It must have been at least an hour and a half; Bob paid the bill and we got a cab home around 4 - 4:30 p.m."

"When you arrived home, where was the defendant, was he still in his PJs?"

This got a few giggles from the spectators and frown from the judge.

"No, he was already dressed and sitting in the den watching a football game."

"Was this, then, the first time the defendant and your husband had seen each other since he arrived?"

"Yes, it was."

"I can well imagine that the reception was a bit cool, to say the least?"

"The reception between the two of them has always been cool to downright cold. My brother-in-law didn't have a lot of time for my late husband."

"Why was that Mrs. Croning?"

"Grant said Bob was just a glorified gambler, and all he did was gamble with other people's money and hadn't done a decent days' work in his whole life."

"So, I gather there was no love lost between the two of them?"

"Yes, that's correct."

"What happened then?"

"The men got some beers and continued watching the football game, there was no need for small talk I assumed, as it was quiet in the den. I started to prepare the evening meal. I had purchased some salmon fillets that I was going to bake. I had a potato and a Greek salad."

"Oh yes, I can clearly remember you telling me in my office, in no uncertain manner, that you knew exactly what your husband had to eat the night before his death, Mrs. Croning," the district attorney said looking at her with a smile on his face.

This brought some color to her pale cheeks.

"So, Mrs. Croning, I take it then that was basically all that happened up until the three of you had dinner together that night?" "Yes, that is correct." "As a matter of interest Mrs. Croning, did you manage to get your boat serviced?" "No, unfortunately not. Several days after the fire I remembered the boat was still moored at the marina and when I went to get it, it was no longer there." "Did you report its disappearance to the police?"

"Yes, I reported it missing to the police."

With that, the district attorney turns away from Sylvia and says to the judge,

"Your honor, I have no further questions at this time for this witness."

"Does the defense wish to cross-examine?"

"Yes, thank you, your honor, I have just one question at this time."

Adrian gets up and walks to the witness stand.

"Mrs. Croning, you mentioned that your husband was fuming and angry that my client had not gotten up and joined you for breakfast. Was it his nature to get annoyed by such things? What I'm trying to establish is, did he have a bad temper?"

"No, I don't think he had a bad temper, it's just that sometimes things upset him."

"I see, did you upset him sometimes, and did he ever lose his temper and assault you? Mrs. Croning before you answer, might I remind you are under oath."

Before she could respond, the district attorney was on his feet.

"Objection your honor, the defense counsel is badgering the witness."

The judge looks over at Adrian and says in a stern voice.

"Mr. Mink, —— any **reminder** that needs to be done in this court, will be done by me and not by you, is that clear," he says, emphasizing 'reminder.'

"Yes, your honor."

The judge looks across at Sylvia in the stand and says. "Please answer the question."

"No, he has never laid a hand on me."

"Thank you, I have no further questions for this witness at this time, but I would like to reserve the right to call this witness at a later time."

The judge says, "The witness is excused."

The judge looks at his watch. "Ladies and gentlemen, it is now 12:35 p.m., we will recess for lunch and be back here at 1:45 p.m."

"What was that all about?" I ask Adrian back at the table.

"Just laying the ground for what I hope is to come," he says.

"What is that?"

"We got a lucky break and managed to track down an old friend of your sister-in-law up in New

York. She remembers very vividly an incident when the three of them were at a restaurant and your brother-in-law had been drinking heavily. When the time came to settle the bill, he told your sister-in-law to pay it with her credit card and she refused. He became aggravated, he took her pocketbook that was hanging from the back of her chair and started to open it, she snatched it back from him. Then he really got mad and called her a fucking bitch, slapped her so hard she fell off the chair. She said she would courier an affidavit to us this morning and I'm hoping it will get here today or tomorrow at the latest."

"That I believe is the short version. Once we get the affidavit, we will see the full statement. Okay, I'm off to get a bite, and call the office. Can I get you the same as yesterday?"

"Yes please, that will be great thanks."

I sit in the holding cell waiting for my burger and reflect on Sylvia's testimony. Wow, she's good! It was perfect, she never hesitated once, and it came out so real I nearly believed her myself. Again, my burger comes, and I hardly have time to eat it and drink the Coke before I'm being escorted back into the courtroom.

I sit down at the table and a few minutes later Adrian comes rushing in out of breath and sits down.

"Phew! I didn't think I was going to get back in time, the office had the affidavit and I went to get it. We can submit it for evidence tomorrow. I don't want to give it to the next-door assholes to work on tonight. Here's a copy, take it with you and you can read it later, let me know tomorrow what you think?"

The bailiff calls everyone to order and we all stand while the judge takes his seat. The judge looks down at the prosecution and asks, "Is the prosecution ready to call their next witness?"

"Yes, your honor, the People call Dr. Gordon Ward."

The clerk gets Dr. Ward's details and swears him in. He was young, maybe in his late twenties just out of medical school. The assistant district attorney takes over again.

"Doctor Ward, you were on duty at the hospital's emergency department the morning of October 16 around 11:15 a.m. when the ambulance brought Mrs. Croning to the emergency section?"

"Yes, that is correct."

"Please describe what her condition was when you examined her?"

"She was semi-conscious, suffering from smoke inhalation, she had a swollen eye, a bloody nose and bruise on the left side of her face."

"Was that all?"

"Initially yes, that was until we got her stabilized in a room. Then we did a more thorough examination."

"What were your findings?"

"Well, it was evident from the type of facial injuries that she had been beaten. We were informed by the medics that she was found tied to the bed so we suspected that there may have been sexual activity. We immediately ordered a Rape Kit and a team to be on standby. We had to wait until the patient was conscious to obtain her permission to do a complete examination."

"So, you never examined her further."

"I, personally no, in cases like this we always hand over the examination to a highly specialized team, so as not to damage or contaminate any evidence that may be present."

125

"So, when the patient became conscious and they received her consent, the team conducted the tests, is that correct?"

"Yes, they then performed the necessary tests."

"What were their findings, doctor?"

"They found evidence of recent sexual activity and found traces of semen on the inside of her vaginal walls."

"Were these samples sent for analysis?"

"Yes, its standard practice that all the specimens we collect at such an examination go to either the police or the crime laboratory for analysis."

"Thank you, doctor."

"Your honor I have no further questions for this witness."

"Does the defense have any questions for this witness?" asked the judge.

Adrian stands up and looks at his notes, "Yes thank you, your honor."

He walks over to the witness stand and looks up at the doctor.

"Dr. Ward in your professional opinion, was the smoke inhalation the victim suffered, very severe, I mean, was it ever life-threatening?"

"Objection" protested the prosecution, "what relevance has this to the case, your honor?"

Adrian said, "Your honor, the prosecution has brought smoke inhalation up in their statements. I believe the jury has a right to know how severe it was."

"Overruled, the witness may answer the question."

"In my honest opinion, I don't believe it was very severe, certainly not life-threatening."

"One further question doctor, could a person fake semi-consciousness?"

"Objection your honor. The defense is implying that Mrs. Croning was faking her condition."

"Mr. Mink, I'm not sure I like where you are going with this line of questioning," The judge said, "so I'm not going to sustain that question."

"Your honor, I certainly did not imply that Mrs. Croning was faking her condition, but the prosecution brings up an interesting point. I have no further questions for this witness."

Adrian sits down. If looks could kill, the judge would have done it right there and then.

"Does the prosecution have any further witnesses?" the judge asked.

"The People call Doctor Alexander Mitchel."

The bailiff escorts the witness to the stand, the clerk swears him in and gets all his details for the records.

Dr. Mitchel was thin in stature, short maybe 5' 6" with thick grey hair combed back. His pale complexion, gaunt looks, and the thin-rimmed glasses give just the image of a person in a white coat standing at a lab table, looking through a microscope.

The assistant district attorney gets up and takes up his normal position in front of the jury box.

"Dr. Mitchel," he starts, and then turns and looks up at the jury. "As you are one of the specialists at the Criminal Laboratory, could you explain briefly the function of the Criminal Laboratory?"

"Well, in short, the crime lab is a scientific laboratory used primarily for the examination and evaluation of different kinds of criminal evidence.

There are different divisions within the department. The unit that I specialize in is the Biology unit. We analyze evidence like semen, saliva, skin, hair, nails, blood, bones, any body parts, and fingerprints that can be used to conduct DNA of the victim and the perpetrator."

"Thank you, doctor, for that brief and concise description. Your laboratory received samples of body fluids taken from the victim, as well as mouth swabs that were taken from the defendant, for evaluation and analysis, is that correct?"

"Yes, that is correct."

"Doctor, what were your findings?"

"We found a significant quantity of semen in the victim's vaginal fluids."

"Doctor, was this semen analyzed?"

"Yes, it was analyzed, and the DNA of this semen matched the DNA of the swab taken from the defendant."

"Thank you, doctor."

The assistant district attorney walked back to his table and says.

"Your honor, I have no further questions for this witness."

The judge sort of lifts his head and looks at our table and asks.

"Does the defense have any questions?"

Adrian gets up,

"Yes, thank you, your honor."

He turns and looks across at the witness.

"Dr. Mitchel," he says, and glances down at a piece of paper on the table in front of him, "In this case, the Crime Lab never mentioned receiving any evidence such as the skin of the victim, fingerprints, hair, fiber or any such matter that one usually finds in a rape crime scene. Why is that?"

"Well, apparently there weren't any," said the doctor.

"I see, did you not find that a little strange?"

"Yes, we did find it rather strange, because normally there are at least one or two other pieces of evidence left by the perpetrator in this type of crime."

"Thank you, doctor."

"Your honor, I have no further questions," and Adrian sits down.

"Does the prosecution wish to cross?" asked the judge.

The two district attorneys briefly confer, "Not at this time, thank you, your honor."

The judge looks across at the prosecution table, with a somewhat look of contempt, almost shrugs his shoulders, and excuses the witness.

The judge waits for the witness to leave the court and asks the prosecution,

"Do the People have any further witnesses?"

"Yes, your honor, the People call Mrs. Diane Hughes."

Diane is brought into the witness stand by the bailiff. She does not look at all well. She looks sick, and I'm not surprised, she must be under enormous stress. Her hair was pulled back in a bun and tied at the nape of her neck. She's wearing a two-piece grey mist color pants-suit with a single button jacket and a cream high-neck blouse, pearl-drop earrings. I can't ever remember seeing her in that suit before, but that's not to say she never had it before the court case.

The clerk says,

"Please raise your right hand," which she does slowly. "Do you swear that the testimony that you are about to give in the case before this court, shall be the truth, the whole truth and nothing but the truth, so help you, God."

"Yes, I do," she said in a quiet, creaky voice.

The clerk said, "Sorry Mrs. Hughes, would you please speak up a little."

She cleared her throat and repeated,

"Yes, I do." This time much louder. I could see she was uncomfortable and didn't want to be there.

As the district attorney gets up from the table, I say a silent prayer and I'm not religious.

'Please God let her speak the truth not for me, but for her sake and that of Jason, because the Lord knows the truth always comes out in the end and it will come back one day and condemn you of perjury.'

It looks like the district attorney has assigned the female witnesses to himself, for reasons only he knows.

"Mrs. Hughes, I'm so sorry to have to call you to stand witness here today to testify against your husband, the accused murderer of your brother-in-law, assaulter, and rapist of your sister. I did explain to you, did I not, the Federal Rule of Evidence 501 permits you from not testifying against your husband if you so wish, and that you alone hold the privilege to waive that choice."

"Yes, you did, and I agreed to testify. That was my choice."

"Thank you, Mrs. Hughes. When did you fly in from Philadelphia?"

"The day before yesterday."

"I see and has the state made adequate accommodation available for you?"

"Thank you, but I have declined the state's accommodation, as I am staying with my sister in

130

her temporary furnished apartment."

"Good, as long as you are comfortable."

"Mrs. Hughes, can we establish when was the last time you saw your husband before he left for Boston on the evening of October 14?"

"I'm not a hundred percent sure, he always liked to be early to catch a flight, it was around 5:30 - 6 p.m. I guess."

"When did you speak to him again?"

"It was the next morning, he called me from my sister's house to tell me he had arrived okay."

"Did he say anything else?"

"He said that Sylvia and Bob had gone out for breakfast and then they were going to take the boat for service or something and they would be back after lunch."

"Did you ask him why he didn't go with them?"

"Yes, I asked him and he said he declined as he had to put the finishing touches to his paper and anyway, he said there was no way he was going to spend four or five hours listening to Bob being so self-important and going on about his fantastic new boat."

I'm listening to this and I can't believe what I'm hearing. Is this my wife that I have been married to for ten years and have known for even longer? Is this the same person now standing in the witness stand being so deceitful? I'm shocked. I didn't know what I was expecting, but certainly not that she would be such a blatant liar.

"Now, on the morning of October 16 at 9:35 a.m. did you receive a call from Detective Burns informing you that there had been an incident at your sister's home in Cambridge?"

"Yes, I did."

"Did he give you any details at that stage?"

131

"No, not really, he said there was a fire and my sister had been taken to hospital and she was in a stable condition. I then asked the officer about my husband, was he alright? He replied they had not seen him. Then I told him that Grant had stayed there over the weekend, as he was presenting a paper at the Boston Convention Center on Monday. He told me my husband must have left the house early before the fire started. He said they had tried to call his number that they found on my sister's phone, together with my number, but there was no answer from him, that's when they got hold of me."

"Mrs. Hughes, when was the last time you spoke to your husband?"

"I spoke to him late on the afternoon of the 16th. By that time, I had already spoken to my sister in the hospital and I had taken a sedative, so I wasn't very responsive to him. Fortunately, my close friend Emma Curtis was with me at home and she spoke to my husband and arranged for an attorney to see him."

"So am I correct in saying that here in this court, is the first time you have seen your husband since he left home just over two months ago."

"Yes, that is correct."

"Thank you, Mrs. Hughes."

"Your honor I have no further questions."

"Defense do you have any questions?" the judge asked without even lifting his eyes from the paper he was reading.

"Thank you, your honor, I'll be brief."

Adrian gets up and has a piece of paper in his hand and walks to the witness stand.

"Mrs. Hughes, I cannot even imagine the heartache you must have gone through in deciding to support your sister and not your loving husband who has supported you and your child for, mmm let me see now, ——" and he looks at the paper, "you have been married for just over ten years" and he looks up at Diane and says, "Is that right, Mrs. Hughes?"

She nods.

"Sorry I didn't hear that."

"Yes, ten years."

"Mrs. Hughes, in the ten years that you have been married, has your husband ever been unfaithful or two-timing, has he been unloving in any way or not provided for you and your son?"

"No," she mumbles.

"I'm sorry Mrs. Hughes, you'll need to speak up for the jury to hear you."

"No," she said loudly.

"Thank you, do you and your sister have a very close bond?"

"Yes, we have been very close since we were just toddlers."

"Even though you aren't really sisters in the true sense of the word?"

"I'm not sure I know what you mean, she's my sister."

"Yes, she is an adopted sister, not a blood sister, that's what I mean Mrs. Hughes. I find it very admirable of you to support her in this way. Considering the circumstances, I assume you would do almost anything to support your adopted sister, is that not so?"

"Well, yes I would and so would she do the same for me under the same circumstances."

"I see and would treason and perjury fall into that statute?"

The district attorney is on his feet in a flash.

"Objection your honor the Defense is ——."

He never gets to finish his sentence because Adrian had already turned around and was walking back to his seat saying, "No further questions your honor."

He comes back and sits down. The district attorney gives him a contemptuous look and then looks up at the judge and says,

"Your honor the people rest their case."

"Ladies and gentlemen as the hour is getting late, I suggest that we recess for the day."

The judge banged his gavel on the sounding block and said, "Court is adjourned, we will restart tomorrow at 10 am."

After everyone stands, the judge leaves the bench and goes into his chambers, I say to Adrian, "Well that concludes business for day two. Diane didn't look at all too happy up there. I thought at one time she may burst into tears, but she held it together. Christ,—— the two of them have really concocted quite a conceivable story."

"Yes, and tomorrow will be your day to give your 'story' testimony," says Adrian.

"Look it's just 4 p.m. I'll ask the guard if he will take you to the interview room and we can quickly go over our strategy for tomorrow."

With that, he gets up and disappears through the side door of the courtroom. A few minutes later he comes back with the guard in tow, "Okay, he'll give us thirty minutes."

We sit opposite each other in the small interview room on plastic stacker chairs.

"Okay, this is what I propose we do tomorrow. First, I will introduce the affidavit of your sister-in-law's friend, Jennifer Small from New York. You had a chance to read her statement, what did you think of it?"

"That's typical of what that dickhead would do when he'd had a couple too many. Yes, I think it's good."

"The prosecution is going to bitch like hell when I bring it up, but I'll deal with that. I don't want to disclose it to the jury until later when I have your sister-in-law up on the stand again."

"You will be my first witness and I want you to read your statement to the jury just the way we typed it. I'll give the clerk a copy of it so he has it on record. I know the stenographer will be taking notes, but I want a written copy to be available for the jury just in case they want it at the time of deliberation."

"After you have testified, I'm going to recall your sister-in-law and see what she has to say about your testimony. That's when I will bring up Jennifer Small's affidavit. Okay, that's it, I'm not sure if I'll re-call your wife, we'll see how things develop."

"I'm also going to call on Fireman Johnson, he's the one that pulled Sylvia out of the fire. I want to see what he has to say. I have a notion about your sister-in-law."

"Yes, I have several, —— but what's yours?"

"I know you're pissed but we need to be focused here. Let's say she staged this whole thing, or she had someone to help her. Either way, there is no way that she was going to just lie there on the bed naked and hope the firefighters get to her before the fire consumes the whole house with her in it."

"Yes, so what are you implying?"

"She must have worked out a means of escape from being tied up, that's why I want to question

Clive Johnson the Fireman. Okay, you think about it, I'm heading home before the rush, I'll see you in the morning. "

CHAPTER 11

It's a restless night for me. I'm trying to weigh up in my mind what the odds are for and against me. Notwithstanding the good job Adrian is doing, it still looks depressing. Sleep eventually comes but I am tormented with dreams of pigs running around with human heads and Bob lying in bed with a bloody pig's head. I wake up in a cold sweat and lie awake until the lights come on.

The early morning just drags on, I suppose because I was awake so damn early. I'm dressed and ready and it seems like hours before the guard and bailiff come and get me. This morning as I enter the courtroom and look around there are definitely more people in the spectator gallery. The 'Odd Couple' as I call them are sitting in the same place and Diane and Sylvia are sitting to the left of them. Diane is wearing a navy floral short-sleeved dress, she looks elegant. I think my heart does a little flutter and despite everything, I still have feelings for her. Her hair still in a bun, secured with a bow in the nape of her neck.

Adrian is already seated when I arrive, we greet each other, and I sit down next to him.

"So, are you ready for the final stretch?" he asks.

"As ready as I can be, I didn't get much sleep as I was mulling over all the stuff."

"Well, don't worry, just be yourself and do what we said yesterday. By reading it you don't have to remember anything. That's why I got you to write it in the beginning, because I know what it's like when it gets this far into the case. Now you know the asshole district attorney is going to have a full go at you when he crosses, so keep your cool, don't let him rattle you."

"All rise," calls the bailiff, "Judge Kenneth Gould now presiding."

The judge comes in, takes his seat, and instructs everyone to be seated.

"Good morning ladies and gentlemen, we are now entering our third day of trial, the defense will put forward their case."

The judge glances down at Adrian and asks, "Is the defense ready with its case?"

"Yes, your honor, the defense is ready. However, before we proceed, we would like to submit a new piece of evidence. I understand it's late, but like the prosecution, we have also been looking for new evidence and this arrived late yesterday evening."

Before Adrian could finish, the assistant district attorney was up on his feet protesting.

"Your honor, this is very late in the proceedings to be presenting new evidence that we haven't had a chance to see," protests the assistant district attorney.

"Well, in all fairness, the prosecution had an opportunity to bring late evidence to this case, so why don't you let me be the judge on what I will, or I will not allow. Mr. Mink let me have a look at what you have there," says the judge.

Adrian walks over to the clerk's desk and hands him the affidavit from Jennifer Small. The clerk examines it and hands it up to the judge.

The judge reads it, looks up, then reads it again, and asks, "Mr. Mink, how do you propose using this affidavit?"

"Your honor, as we heard, Mrs. Croning testified that her husband was not at all abusive or bad-tempered. I wish to show the court we have

138

found at least one witness who refutes that statement."

"Umm ——," he gives the document back to the clerk, "I'm going to allow it."

"Thank you, your honor, I have a copy for the prosecution."

He walks up and places the affidavit on the clerk's table. The clerk examines it to see if the two documents are the same and then hands the copy to the prosecution.

Adrian, back at the table says,

"Your honor, the defense wishes to put the defendant Grant Hughes on the witness stand."

The bailiff escorts me to the witness stand, where I must take the oath. It wasn't necessary to state my details as they were already on record.

"Mr. Hughes, you have been locked away here in a Cambridge jail now for how many weeks?" asks Adrian.

"Nine weeks."

"You have never been in jail before as I mentioned in my opening statement. No doubt, this must be quite a traumatic experience for you, especially seeing you are being framed for a crime you never committed. Your sister-in-law has accused you in no uncertain manner of murder, rape, assault, and theft, and the state is accusing you of arson. How do you view these accusations, Mr. Hughes?"

"They are all lies."

"Well, then Mr. Hughes, why don't you tell the court what actually happened on those days leading up to October 16 when you were arrested."

"Your honor, Mr. Hughes has written down in detail his movements and the events from the time he left home in Malvern on Saturday afternoon

October 14, at 5:15 p.m., leading up to the time he was arrested on Monday, October 16. He will read this written report word for word because this is exactly what happened. I have copies here. He placed several copies on the clerk's desk. You may want to follow what Mr. Hughes is reading in his written report." Nobody moved or indicated they wanted a copy.

"Mr. Hughes please proceed with your testimony."

It took me twenty minutes to read slowly through the report, emphasizing certain points as I went along, and being a proficient speaker helped. There were murmurs and whispers from the spectators at the part where Sylvia had fucked me, and the judge had to bang his gavel a few times to get silence. All the time Adrian was seated at the table, he was adding to his notes. When I finish reading, he gets up and walks opposite the jury box and addresses me.

"Mr. Hughes, now that explains does it not, how your semen was found in your sister-in-law's vaginal fluids by the crime lab and why there was no other form of evidence found in the bedroom or on her body. That's because you were never in the bedroom when she said you were there."

"Yes, I remember her stuffing tissues between her legs and darting upstairs," I say.

"Aah! That would explain it, she probably saved some of your semen in a container and inserted it into her vagina on the morning of the 16th, very clever."

Up jumps the district attorney, "Objection your honor, this is pure speculation."

"Mr. Mink, please confine your probabilities to yourself. The jury will ignore the counselors'

140

statement." "Yes, thank you, your honor"

"Now this next part is where the story gets even more confusing because your sister-in-law said you never went on the boat with her, and yet you could quote all the details of the boat and what alterations they had done to it. This was no standard craft anymore, so there was no way you could have gotten this information from anyone other than from her or her husband. How do you explain the fact that you knew all those details?"

"The reason I can explain, knowing all the details as you put it, is because I was on the boat. We went up the river through the lock, she even explained to me how big the locks were. We cruised around the bay and ended at the restaurant, where we had lunch and she tricked me by paying the bill."

"That's right Mr. Hughes, we checked with the restaurant and they confirmed your sister-in-law did pay the bill as you said, but she used her husband's credit card. I wonder why she did that."

"I have no idea,"

"I think I know why, because in her statement she said her husband paid the bill, mmmm interesting."

"Mr. Hughes when you got back to your sister-in-law's house, you helped your sister-in-law prepare dinner. You cut the cheese with a large kitchen knife, the same knife they found under the bed, is this correct?"

"Yes, it certainly looks like the same knife."

"Was it just after this that she asked you to reload her gun that was in the drawer of the sideboard?"

"Yes, that's correct."

"That would account for your fingerprints being

all over the gun and on all the remaining bullets in the magazine, is that not so?"

"Correct".

"You never helped clean up after dinner did you, you went straight to bed?"

"Yes, that is correct, but only after sitting in the living room for an hour or so finishing off the wine, while Sylvia told me about her life in California and how she met Bob."

"So that knife you cut the cheese with, could easily have found its way upstairs into the main bedroom after you left the kitchen?"

"Yes, it's quite possible,"

"Now the next morning Mr. Hughes, you say your sister-in-law came and woke you up, let's say more conventionally," and he emphasizes the more conventional way with his hands sort of raised, "at around 6:30 a.m."

This gets a few snickers from the spectators; the judge looks up and there's immediate silence.

"Yes, that's correct."

"You then showered, went into the kitchen for a cup of coffee. While you were drinking it, Mrs. Croning came in with a plastic bag and said she had a few things for your wife and son, is that correct?"

"Yes, she asked if there was room in my bag for it and I told her I was sure she could squeeze it in somewhere."

"So that could account for how the money got into your bag without you knowing about it, is that not so?"

"Yes, that would explain how it got there."

"When you finished your coffee, you picked up your bags from the bedroom, came back into the kitchen, and waited for the cab. The cab arrives, you say your goodbyes to your sister-in-law, but just before you step outside, she hands you a knotted, white plastic bag and asks you to throw it in the trash out front when you go by. She told you it's the wine bottle and some other trash that may as well go out today with the main trash. Do I have that correct?"

"Yes, that's right."

"So again, that would account for how the gun got into the trash can outside, is that not so Mr. Hughes?"

"Yes, that would explain how it got there."

"Now the last piece of evidence the prosecution brought forward was the information on how to make a remote trigger device using a mobile cell phone that they alleged was found on your PC. Mr. Hughes, have you any idea how that piece of information came to be tucked away in a file under your son's birth certificate?"

"No, I have no idea, I have never seen that document before."

"Mr. Hughes, is your PC password protected?"

"Yes, it is."

"Who besides yourself knows the password?"

"Just my wife and my business partner."

"So, let me get this straight, the police department confiscated your PC on the day of your arrest October 16, and they had it all the time, up until the second day of this court hearing. The prosecution then came forward with startling new information, having found this piece of evidence on your PC. So, let's see now, working back from 22nd November, to the 16th October that is —— mmmm 35 days, I think. In that time, they managed to hack into your PC without your password, search through all your company and personal files, of which I'm sure there were a great number and do to your PC whatever they wanted."

The assistant district attorney was on his feet "Objection your honor, the defense is implying that the police planted the document in question on the defendant's PC."

"Mr. Mink, what is your point, do you have a question for the witness?" asked the judge.

"Your honor, I was just about to ask my client a question, may I continue?"

"Yes, Mr. Mink please continue and try not to make any insinuations towards the police department, because I've spoken to you about this before Mr. Mink, you are walking on a very thin ice."

"Yes, —— thank you, your honor."

"So, then Mr. Hughes, if that incriminating document got onto your PC before being confiscated by the police, it could have been planted there any time, by your wife, or by your partner, not so?"

"Yes, I suppose, but it's highly unlikely that my partner would do that."

"Yes, but what about your wife?"

"I hate to think so, but considering all that has taken place, I must say yes."

"Mr. Hughes, you testified that you are a very deep and sound sleeper, is that correct?"

"Yes, that's right, I sleep very soundly, and you could carry me away in my bed and I would unlikely wake up."

"Please relate one of the many incidents while you were at college that you were carried away in your bed while asleep."

"One of the incidents was when a group of fellow students came into my room in the early hours of the morning and carried me in my bed out to the women's residence. They left me at the main entrance, where I remained fast asleep until I was woken by a group of women poking me in my ribs."

"That must have been very embarrassing for you Mr. Hughes?"

"Yes, it was, but that was only one of the many incidents. It got so bad that my grades started to drop, and my parents brought me home to attend the local college in West Chester."

"Mr. Hughes, is there anyone that can testify to you being such a deep sleeper?"

"Well, yes there is, my mother for one, but I would not like to put her on the stand to testify. Then there is my wife of course, but again I doubt under the present circumstances she will admit that I have a deep sleep problem. Colleagues from college days would certainly remember me. I'm sure they would be able to confirm what I have told you is true."

"Yes, Mr. Hughes, I can understand you not wanting to put your mother under the stress of testifying. As far as your wife is concerned, we know full well she will deny the fact that you have a sleep problem. Fortunately for you Mr. Hughes, your sleep habit created such a sensation at the college you were even mentioned in the yearbook with a picture of you in the bed outside the women's residence. We were able to get in touch with half a dozen people who remember you. So, if necessary, we can call on any one of them to come and testify or send us a signed affidavit."

"Now Mr. Hughes, you mentioned that your wife had the password for your PC, correct?"

"Yes, she had the password because there is some of our private information stored on my PC and there were times when I was not around, and

145

she needed access to this information."

"So, given the close bond of your wife and her sister, would you say that your wife would impart secrets to her? What I'm trying to say is, if she were asked to give your password to her sister, do you think she would do that?"

"Had you asked me that, say six weeks ago, I would have said no, but now I definitely think yes, she would,"

"Let's go back then to the nights October 14 and 15 you slept at your sister-in-law's house. On those two nights where was your PC?"

"It was in the bedroom where I was sleeping, lying on the table."

"So Mr. Hughes let's assume your sister-in-law has your password and given the fact that you sleep like Goldilocks, on any one of those two nights, your sister-in-law could have come into your bedroom, opened your PC, inserted that 'trigger device' document into your son's Birth Certificate file and you would be none the wiser?"

"Yes, that's quite correct, she knows my son's name, birth date, etc., and it would be easy for her to find the file and to put it there."

"Thank you, Mr. Hughes."

"Your honor I have no further questions for my client at this stage."

The judge looks down at the district attorney's table and asks,

"Does the prosecution wish to question the accused?"

"Yes, thank you, your honor." The district attorney gets up and walks over to the clerk's table and picks up a copy of my detailed written statement. He shuffles through the pages, as he slowly makes his way to stand opposite the jury.

He turns to me with a smirk on his face and says,

"Mr. Hughes —— this is quite a story; you could be up for a Pulitzer award."

This brought a few sniggers and giggles from the spectators, which had the judge banging on his gavel.

"Unfortunately it's not a story," I say, turning around to face the gallery, "the storytellers are sitting over there," trying not to show my contempt for them, while pointing to where Sylvia and Diane are seated in the spectator stand.

"Your honor, please restrain the defendant from making comments unless he is requested to do so."

"Mr. Hughes, you are to restrain yourself, only answer questions and reply when asked to do so, is that clear?" says the judge.

I nod.

"Excuse me, Mr. Hughes I never heard you," he says, putting his hand to his ear.

"Yes, your honor, it's clear."

"Thank you, Mr. Benmin please continue."

"Yes, Mr. Hughes, your account of how your semen ended up where it did is an interesting story, I'm sure, but let's leave that for the moment. I want to ask you about your sister-in-law's boat you said you were on. You said you were on the boat because you can remember all the modification details done to it. Is that correct?"

"Yes, that's what I said."

"As you know Mr. Hughes the boat is missing, poof gone, nowhere to be found, so how can we verify these modifications to which you are referring? So likewise, Mr. Hughes, your proof that you were on the boat are also poof gone, out the porthole so to speak."

147

"Mr. Hughes, you said that the knife found under the bed in Mrs. Croning's bedroom was the same knife you used to cut the cheese. Is that correct?"

"Yes, I said that could be the knife I used to cut the cheese."

"Correction Mr. Hughes, you said, and I quote, 'Yes the same knife,' "that's what you said, we can have the court reporter read it back if you so wish."

"That won't be necessary, that's correct."

"Mr. Hughes, can you remember how many similar knives there were in the drawer when you selected that particular one to cut the cheese with?"

"No, I can't remember,"

"Can you perhaps remember what the type of cheese you took out of the fridge that you cut several slices from?"

"No, I can't,"

"Mr. Hughes I find it very strange that you can't remember some very basic aspects of the event, but you can clearly identify the very knife that is now in a plastic bag, sitting on the table over there on the clerk's table. Mr. Hughes, I would suggest that the only reason you know that is the knife, is because you accidentally left it behind. Your story of cutting the cheese if I may say so, is very cheesy to me."

"I have no further questions for the accused your honor." With that, the district attorney went back to his table.

"Does the defense wish to redirect?" asked the judge.

"No thank you, your honor," said Adrian.

"In that case," the judge said looking at his watch, "it's now 12:15 p.m. I suggest we recess for lunch and be back here sharp at 1:15."

The bailiff calls everyone to stand while the judge leaves the court.

While standing there at the table, Adrian looks at me and says, "I think that went okay, you came across very sincere, I think the jury are scratching their heads a little. I'll call your sister-in-law again after lunch, let's see what she has to say about having an abusive husband. Look I'm going to get a bite, can I get you the usual?"

"Yes, please but skip the Coke and get a coffee instead, thanks."

The coffee and hamburger were cold when they eventually got to me, but this did not matter as I only had a few minutes to eat the burger and wash it down with the cold coffee before I was being escorted back to court.

The bailiff calls everyone to stand while the judge enters the court. He comes in, sits down, and instructs everyone to be seated.

Once everyone is seated and quiet, the judge asks,

"Does the defense wish to call another witness?"

"Yes, thank you, your honor, I wish to call Fireman Clive Johnson."

The clerk does his normal swearing-in and gets all Johnson's details.

Adrian gets up and walks over to the witness stand and addresses the witness.

"Fireman Johnson, you were at the scene of the fire at the premises of 44 Willow Grove Lane, Cambridge, Massachusetts, on October 16 is that correct?"

"Yes, I was there, I was the person that brought the victim out of the fire."

"Yes, thank you, Mr. Johnson, we are always

most thankful for the dedicated and self-sacrificing services that the fire department performs. Could you please briefly explain what transpired that day?"

"Our fire truck was the first to arrive on the scene, the fire was already burning through the upper floors. My fire chief told my partner and myself to put on our extraction suits. We suited up and went into the premises, through the front door which we had to break down. The kitchen and dining room area were already burning profusely, flames were leaping up the stairs and smoke was thick all around us. Fortunately, we had breathing masks and goggles. We ascended to the second floor and I thought I could hear someone coughing. I ran into the main bedroom and saw the victim lying naked tied to the bed. I cut her feet free and loosened her hands, before picking her up and carrying her down to the medics outside. My partner brought out the body of the deceased. By this time, the fire was raging, and we just hoped there were no other folk inside."

"Thank you, Fireman Johnson. Question: how did you cut the victim's feet free? Did you find the knife on the floor to do that with?"

"No, I didn't see any knife, there was too much smoke. I used the blade of my ax to cut the strips of material that were tied to her feet and then there was enough slack to slip the noose off around her wrists."

"That was quick thinking fireman to get her out of there fast. Did you perhaps notice how tight those restraints were?"

The prosecution jumps up, "Objection your honor. What has this got to do with this case?"

"Mr. Mink, where are you going with this?"

"Your honor, the prosecution brought up the restraints not me, I'm trying to demonstrate for the jury just how this was done and how effective this was or wasn't."

"I will allow it. Carry on Mr. Mink but please get to the point."

"Thank you, your honor. With the court's permission, I would like to demonstrate how the victim was restrained with the strips."

"Yes, Mr. Mink if you must, but make it brief."

Adrian walks back to the clerk's table and rummages through the brown paper bag holding the sheeting strips until he finds the longest piece. It's about 4 Ft. in length. He brings it back to the witness stand.

"Fireman Johnson, this is the longest piece that was used to tie the victim's hands, you may not recognize it as it is a little scorched by the fire, but it is this piece because, in the photographs taken of the scene after the fire, the picture shows this tied to a slat of the headboard. It was doubled over like this and the two ends were tied to the slat. This loop I have made here is what I assume you slipped off the victim's wrists. Let me demonstrate to you if I may."

Adrian goes up to the witness and says, "Place your hands together like you are praying,—— there you go, —— and I will slip this loop over them and pull it tight around your wrist. How does that feel? —— is that sort of how you remember the victim's hands were restrained?"

"Yes, that's exactly the way they were tied."

"It's sort of like a dog's choke collar, when it's tight it restrains and when there is slack one can slip the noose?"

"Yes, that's correct," he says.

"Of course, Fireman Johnson you wouldn't know if there was enough slack in this piece before you untied the victim, for the victim to slip the noose so to speak, would you?"

"No, I wouldn't."

"Thank you, Mr. Johnson, I have no further questions, can I have the strip back please," and he walks back to the clerk's table, stuffs it back in the brown paper bag and walks back to our table, and sits down.

"Does the prosecution wish to cross?" asks the judge.

"No thank you, your honor."

"Does the defense wish to call another witness?"

"Yes, thank you, your honor, I wish to recall Mrs. Sylvia Croning to the witness stand."

The bailiff escorts Sylvia to the stand, who today is dressed in a cream blouse, black tight-fitting jeans, with a plaid detail grey coat with white trim on the sleeves and pockets. She looks a lot sassier than the first day she took the stand.

"Mrs. Croning, may I remind you that you are still under oath," says the judge looking down at her over the rim of his glasses. She nodded and the judge said,

"Please proceed Mr. Mink."

Adrian gets up from the table, gathers up a few pages he had been going through, and walks over to the witness stand.

"Mrs. Croning, we have now heard both sides of this case, both intriguing. I'm sure the jury at this stage must be in a bit of quandary as to whose story they believe. The reason I say this is that there are some of the facts that just don't seem to add up in my mind."

"For instance, let's take it from the time you were at the restaurant. You say your late husband Bob paid for the meal and you left there at around 4 - 4:30 p.m. Is that correct?"

"Yes."

"Now we checked with the restaurant and we have a copy of the credit card slip. Yes, quite right, it's your late husband's credit card, but the signature does not match other signatures of his. Furthermore, when we questioned the waitress, whose number was on the slip, she said she remembered the transaction because you left her a large tip. When she thanked you, the waitress told us you had said, and I quote, 'Don't mention it, he's loaded.' Do you remember paying the bill Mrs. Croning?"

"I don't remember, maybe I paid for it with my credit card, or maybe I used his card, so what if I did?" she says, getting a bit agitated.

"What if you did, you say? But in your evidence yesterday you said your husband paid the bill. So, what is it, did you pay the bill or did your husband pay the bill?" "As I said, I often use his card, I can't remember if he paid or I paid using his card."

"You see, in your brother-in-law's statement, he said that you paid for the meal that the two of you had together. Now, how would he know you paid the bill if he was not there?"

When after a few minutes Sylvia hasn't answered, Adrian prompts her.

"Mrs. Croning that is a question."

"I don't know," she curtly replies.

"Okay, then you left the restaurant at around 4 - 4:30 p.m. by cab, when did you get home?"

"I don't remember the exact time; it must have

been well after 5 p.m. as the traffic is normally bad at that time of the day."

"Give or take five or ten minutes, then it would be 5:15 - 5:30 p.m., would that be a good estimate?"

"Yes, that would be about the time."

Adrian shuffles his papers and looks at them and then looks up at Sylvia saying,

"So, when the two of you arrived home, you find your brother-in-law in the living room watching football and drinking a beer, is that correct?"

"Yes, that's what I said."

"Mrs. Croning what type of beer does your husband drink, I'm sorry your late husband, what brand did he like?"

"He mostly drank Bud Lite."

"I see and I assume that would be a bottle and not a can?"

"Yes, that's right."

"Again, I assume that the defendant was also drinking a Bud Lite when you got home?"

"Yes, he was."

The DA gets up from his seat and says, "Your honor, where is this line of questioning going, are we going to have to listen to the defense question the witness in such detail?   Next thing he will be asking what type of salad dressing was used?"

Of course, this brings a few sniggers and giggles from the spectators.

The judge bangs his gavel and says, "Thank you Mr. Benmin, I don't need any snide comments from you."

Mr. Mink, I trust you are going somewhere soon with this line of questioning?"

Adrian turns to the bench and says, "Yes your honor. If it pleases the court to bear with me for a few more minutes, I will get to the point."

"Very well then Mr. Mink, you may proceed, please make it brief,"

"Thank you, your honor."

"Mrs. Croning did you perhaps see if the defendant, your brother-in-law, had drunk more than one beer, were there any empty bottles standing around that you noticed? You see —— " and Adrian looks at the paper in his hand and reads, "you said——'we all had a fair amount to drink,' " What I'm trying to establish is how much the defendant had to drink before you came home, which could have made him so hostile and agitated during dinner. Did you see any empties lying around?"

"I am not sure; I think there may have been one or two empty bottles on the side table."

"Let's say he had two beers and then you came home and the guys got some more beers and continued to watch football, until you called them to dinner, say 6:30 – 7 p.m., would that be about right?"

"Yes, that would be correct."

"By this time, the guys would have consumed maybe another two beers each before they came to the table, would that be about right?"

"Yes, I think that would be a good guess."

"At the table, did the guys continue to drink beer or did they drink wine?"

"We all drank wine at the table."

"Well, I can see how my client got hostile and agitated after drinking five or six beers and then switching to wine, we all know those two don't mix too well."

"Mrs. Croning, can you perhaps remember by the end of the night how many bottles of wine the three of you consumed?"

"Yes, we consumed two bottles."

"I think your assessment of a 'fair amount to drink' was a little on the lenient side."

"So after the three of you had all this to drink, my client started to get upset about the money his wife had invested with your late husband, 'he got incensed' were your words and he then stormed off to bed. Is that correct?"

"Yes, that's correct."

"Then you cleaned up the kitchen, packed the dishwasher, and went to bed. Sometime in the early hours of the morning, you wake up with the light going on and you see my client standing at the foot of your bed with a gun in his left hand and a knife in his right hand. Is that correct Mrs. Croning?"

"Yes, that's correct."

"Mrs. Croning, how well do you know your brother-in-law?"

"Fairly well I think."

"I'm going to ask you a question and I want you to look at me when you answer, not at your sister in the gallery. Do you know whether your brother-in-law is ambidextrous?"

"No, I —— don't know."

"Now Mrs. Croning I want you to be very sure when you answer, in what hand did my client hold the gun, left or right hand —— look at me Mrs. Croning."

"—— Mrs. Croning I'm waiting."

"I can't remember for sure."

"Isn't that strange, a minute ago you said the gun was in his left hand and the knife was in his right hand"

"Now if I read your statement here ……." And

Adrian takes one of the sheets of paper he has, holds in both hands, and reads the passage.

"You say and I quote, 'He had a gun in his right hand and a kitchen knife in his left hand.' Now you were quite clear in your original statement, but now you are not sure, is that correct Mrs. Croning?"

"It's been several weeks, and I can't be expected to remember all the details," she says.

"Maybe you will remember this. Was your brother-in-law wearing gloves?"

"No, I don't think so."

"Alright Mrs. Croning, let's see how much more you can remember or should I say, have forgotten. You say in your statement, as I read it here, 'he came around to Bob's side of the bed, took a pillow, pushed it over Bob's head, put the gun against the pillow, and shot him three or four times, I think.'"

"Now at this stage, when my client went around to that side of the bed, was your late husband lying with his head on his pillow?"

"Yes, he was lying down."

"So let me get this clear, first your late husband sits up in bed and protests, then he lies down again, my client walks up to him, takes a pillow and covers his head, have I got that right?"

"Yes, I suppose so."

"Mrs. Croning, — let's just say for argument's sake, my client had the gun in his right hand and the kitchen knife in his left hand. Which hand did he hold the pillow with and from where did he take it?"

"I don't remember."

"Mrs. Croning, you were lying next to your late husband and you can't remember if my client took your pillow from your side of the bed or pulled the pillow out from under your late husband's head. Do you remember if he dropped the knife to perform this task?"

"No, as I said I don't remember."

"Well, my client must have put the knife somewhere because he could not have taken a pillow and pushed it over your late husband's head with a knife in his one hand and the gun in the other hand, could he? Maybe he put the knife between his teeth, you know like Tarzan did in the movie?"

Of course, again this brought a few sniggers and giggles from the spectators and again the judge had to bang his gavel to get silence.

"No, he didn't put it in his mouth," she says.

"Aha yes, I'm sure you would have remembered that."

"Let's get to the part where you state that my client tied you up and raped you. I'm hoping your memory will be a little better in this instance, seeing that you were the victim."

"Mrs. Croning, can you remember what you were wearing at the time?"

"Yes, I was wearing a short nighty pajama top and panties."

"Mrs. Croning, when you had finished counting the money, my client told you to remove the top sheet from the bed and hold it for my client to cut into strips, is that correct?"

"Yes, he cut several strips from the sheet."

"Yes, we have seen the strips he allegedly cut."

"Could you please demonstrate for the jury just how you held the sheet so my client could cut it into several strips?"

"That's a bit difficult, I don't have a sheet."

"Oh —— that's not a problem," says Adrian and walks back to the table and from a large brown paper bag, takes out a folded sheet, and holds it up to the judge. "With your permission, your honor, may I?"

The judge looks at Adrian with a disdained look and says, "Yes Mr. Mink if you must, —— carry on."

"Thank you, your honor."

With that Adrian walks back to the witness stand and unfolds the sheet, holding it up to Sylvia. She stands up and reluctantly takes the sheet from him and stands to hold it draping down in front of her legs.

"Okay, Mrs. Croning I'm sure you can remember how you held the sheet so my client could cut all those strips. Just demonstrate please, how you held it."

Sylvia's face was flushed, she looked like she was about to burst into tears. She looks down at the sheet in her hands and then looks up at the judge, shaking her head.

"I'm sorry your honor I can't remember, this is very stressful for me," said Sylvia.

"Fine Mrs. Croning," said the judge, "would you like a break —— or some water?"

"Thank you, your honor, some water would be nice."

"Bailiff please get Mrs. Croning some water."

While the bailiff is getting the water, Adrian relieves Sylvia of the sheet, folds it up, and brings it back to the table.

"That was quite a performance," I whisper.

"Just getting started," he whispers back.

Sylvia drinks her water and has recovered some of her equanimity.

The judge looks across at her and asks, "Mrs. Croning, are you feeling better, can we continue?"

"Yes, thank you, your honor."

"Mr. Mink you may continue."

Adrian thanks the judge and walks back to the witness stand, with the sheet for Sylvia to hold.

"Mrs. Croning, you have the sheet and my client has the gun in his right hand pointing at you I suppose. He is cutting the strips with the knife in his left hand, something like this ——."

Adrian makes his right hand like a gun with his forefinger sticking straight out and thumb up, arm extended, and with his left-hand points his index finger as if it's the knife, making up and down strokes.

"Or you may have been holding the sheet sideways, then, of course, he would be cutting across like this," and again he indicates with his left hand a cutting action going across the sheet. "So, which one do you think is the one most likely Mrs. Croning?"

The DA was upon his feet.

"Your honor, we have already heard the witness state that she does not remember how the sheet was cut. The defense is laboring the point unnecessarily."

"Mr. Mink, what is your point?" asked the judge.

"Your honor I'm only trying to demonstrate to the jury just how difficult such a feat would be for one holding a gun in one hand, and being in such close quarters to the victim, being able to cut several long strips from a sheet with the other hand. I certainly can't visualize how such a feat was possible."

"I think you have made your point Mr. Mink, please move on," said the judge.

"Thank you, your honor." Adrian takes the sheet from Silvia and brings it back to the table, turns, and walks back to the witness stand.

"Mrs. Croning, did my client threaten you with the gun constantly? What I mean is, did he have the gun pointed at you while he was tying you to the bed?"

"Yes, he must have —— but maybe he put it down to tie me to the bed, I don't remember."

"What about the knife, I suppose my client dropped that under the bed, did you see him do that?"

"No, I didn't see where the knife went."

"So now you are all trussed up on the bed, hands and feet tied and he beats you about the face. Why did he beat you, did you provoke him, or say something that would have made him do that to you?"

"No – I said nothing to him, he just beat me with his fist."

"So then after he's beaten you, he removes your sleepwear and rapes you. Is that how you remember it?"

"Yes, that's how I remember it."

"But if you are all tied up, how does my client remove your sleepwear?"

"Well, he didn't remove them completely, he just pulled my panties down around my ankles."

"Does he then rape you?"

"Yes, I think that was when it happened."

"Mrs. Croning, we heard earlier on from the fireman how he found you all trussed up. It must have been very difficult for my client to have penetrated you with your legs tight together, your ankles tied to the bottom of the bed, while being stretched out with your wrists tied to the top end of the bed. Are you sure he raped you while you were all tied up?"

161

"I don't remember, maybe it was before he tied me up."

"Now you say you aren't sure if he raped you before he tied you up or after he tied you up. Mrs. Croning —— I believe anyone having been raped would surely remember being raped with their hands and feet all bound up. So, when did the rape take place, before you were tied up, or after you were tied up?"

"It must have been before."

"I see, are you now quite sure it was before he tied you up?"

The DA is on his feet again.

"Your honor, the defense is belaboring the point unnecessarily."

"Mr. Mink, I think Mrs. Croning has given you her answer, move on."

"Yes, your honor, thank you."

"Alright Mrs. Croning, so you are now lying back on the bed in your pajamas, he pulls your panties down to your ankles with just the gun in his hand now, because you said he dropped the knife, but he had the gun in his hand all the time. Is that how you remember it?"

"Yes, I think that's how it happened."

"Then he rapes you and beats you with his fist I think you said, while still holding the gun pointed at you."

"Yes, that's what I said."

"Then he removed your panties from around your ankles, stuffed them in your mouth, tied you to the bed, and then left with the money in the bag. Do I now have the sequence of events correct?"

"Yes, I think that's how it all happened."

"So, when did you or someone remove the top of your sleepwear?"

162

"No, only my panties were removed, not my top."

"So, if you say my client never removed the top of your sleepwear, how is it Mrs. Croning that when the fireman found you, you were all trussed up completely naked, can you please explain that for the jury."

"No, I can't remember how they came to be removed."

"Yes, maybe your dead husband miraculously got up and removed them for you."

The DA is on his feet again.

"Your honor, does the witness have to bear testimony to these ridiculous innuendoes."

The judge looks towards Adrian and says, "Mr. Mink, I think I have allowed you enough leeway, so please finish up with this witness without any further remarks or overtones. Is that clear?"

"Yes, thank you, your honor, I only have a few more questions."

"Mrs. Croning, I asked you before if your late husband was ever abusive to you, and you replied he had never laid a hand on you, or words to that effect. Am I right?"

"Yes, that's correct."

"Mrs. Croning, do you remember your friend in New York, Jennifer Small."

Warily, not knowing where this question was leading, she answered "Yes I remember her, we were roommates for a while."

"Well, I have an affidavit from her which came in this afternoon. Your honor, with your permission, may I show this to the witness?"

"Bailiff please hand the affidavit document to the witness," says the judge.

The bailiff promptly gets up, taking the affidavit

from the clerk, walks over to the witness box, and hands it to Sylvia.

"Mrs. Croning," said Adrian "would you please read the contents of this affidavit so the jury can hear you."

Sylvia looks at the paper, reads it to herself, and looks over at the table for the prosecution, who looks straight back at her without any expression on their faces.

"Mrs. Croning,—— we are waiting," says the judge.

She starts to read it and the judge has to ask her to speak up. She finishes reading and puts the paper down on her lap.

"Mrs. Croning, do you remember the incident where he hit you so hard, you fell off your chair and you landed on the floor, and the waiter came and helped you up?"

Several minutes passed and Sylvia sat staring at the paper in her lap as if she were in another world.

"Mrs. Croning, I'm waiting," says Adrian,—— still nothing.

"Your honor, will you please instruct the witness to answer the question."

The judge looks over the rim of his glasses and says, "Mrs. Croning —— you will please answer the question."

"Sorry your honor, what was the question?"

"Mr. Mink please repeat your question to Mrs. Croning."

"Thank you for your honor."

"Mrs. Croning, my question was, and I repeat. Do you remember the incident in the restaurant where your late husband lost his temper, hit you, knocked you off your chair and you landed on the floor?"

"Yes, I remember it."

"Thank you, so your memory is not that bad after all."

"Mrs. Croning, now that we have sorted that out, I must then take it that when I asked you sometime before if your late husband had a bad temper, was abusive to you and you answered, 'No, he never had a bad temper and never laid a hand on me,' that was a lie, was it not?"

Another long wait, ——— "Mrs. Croning, ——," and before Adrian can speak or ask her again, the DA jumps up.

"Your honor, I must protest, the defense is treating the witness like she is on trial here."

"With all due respect to your honor, what I'm trying to establish here is that the prosecution's witness may not be as truthful and trustworthy a witness as they have portrayed her to be. If she is willing to perjure herself, I believe the jury has the right to know this," he says.

The judge looks down at Sylvia again and says, "Mrs. Croning, please answer the question."

"Yes," she says.

"Yes, what Mrs. Croning?"

"Yes, I was lying," she said indignantly.

"Thank you, Mrs. Croning, for clearing that up. I wonder how many other lies you have been telling the jury during this trial?"

"Objection," shouts the DA, "Your honor, the defense is badgering the witness."

The judge looks across at where Adrian is standing and says in a somewhat drained voice, "Mr. Mink, I think you have made your point, move on."

"Thank you for your honor."

"Mrs. Croning, how much was your late husband's life insurance worth?"

Again, the DA objects "Your honor, I must strongly object to this line of questioning, it has absolutely no relevance to this case."

The judge looks down at Adrian and asks, "Mr. Mink, where are you going with this line of questioning?"

"Your honor, I believe this has relevance in the trial for the following reasons. We have heard the testimony from my client, and we heard the DA label it as fiction, a pack of lies, a story worthy of a Pulitzer award. We also heard the testimony of the victim, Mrs. Croning in this case, who also happens to be the only witness. We have also just established that this witness may not have been as truthful as she was originally made out to be. In the end, the jury is going to have to look at all the facts and not the lies. It's a fact that Mrs. Croning may benefit from this crime via an insurance policy taken out on her late husband's life, and I believe the jury is entitled to know about it."

The DA was on his feet again, "Your honor, this is absolute nonsense and needs to be struck from the records. The defense is making —— "

"Mr. Benmin please sit down before I strike you off the records," said the judge in an irate tone.

"Ladies and gentlemen of the jury, we will take a short break."

The judge looks down at the prosecution's table and then over at Adrian standing by the witness box. "Counselors — in my chambers — now." Emphasizing now.

"Bailiff please," says the judge.

The bailiff follows formalities, we all rise, the judge leaves the bench, and the prosecution and

Adrian follow him into his chambers.

Ten minutes later the two DA's and Adrian come out and sit down at their respective tables.

"What's going on?" I whisper.

"I'll tell you later, let's see what the judge has to say."

The bailiff calls us all to order and the judge comes back in, telling us to sit.

"Ladies and gentlemen of the jury, given that we are into the late afternoon, I'm going to call a recess for today and we will be back in court here tomorrow at 10 a.m. sharp."

"Mrs. Croning please ensure that you make yourself available again tomorrow to complete where we left off today." "Bailiff please."

The bailiff does his thing. The judge leaves the bench and Sylvia steps down from the witness box as the court starts to clear of spectators. Sylvia looks around for the DAs as she reaches their table, obviously wishing to speak to them, but they, expecting this, have retreated out of the side door.

Adrian finishes packing his briefcase, and says, "Look they will be coming for you soon, so sit down and let me fill you in quickly as to what transpired in his 'Lordship's Chambers.'"

"The judge was furious, he climbed into the DA like you can't imagine. He told them that they, their mayor, and his fucking incompetent police department had screwed up this case by trying to push it through before Christmas. This was supposed to be an open and shut case, a few days in court and it would be all over.

The judge said, "And now you two clowns, where do you think this case is going? I'll tell you where it's not going, and that is it certainly will not be a guilty verdict. How the hell did you two not foresee that Croning had life insurance on her husband? Did it not even enter your thick skulls that she may have bumped her husband off for the insurance? No of course not, you were so fucking sure you had an open and shut case, you never looked elsewhere. You two have your fucking heads so far up the mayor's ass, you can't see the light of day. Now I sit with the mess, I have to let Mr. Mink here pursue his line of questioning, because if I don't, the press will be all over me and the jury will be wondering why I cut his legs from under him. Guess who will be calling for a mistrial," and he looks over at me. "So, gentlemen, we are going back out there and I'm going to call it a day and I'll sleep on it. I'll decide what course of action I will take in the morning, now get the fuck out of my chambers."

"Whoa!" I said, "That's good news. No wonder the DA shot out of here so quickly."

"Okay Grant here comes your escort, tomorrow will be interesting, sleep well, and I'll see you then. Here's a copy of yesterday's paper, they sure painted a debauched picture of you. It'll be interesting to see what the press has to say in the morning about today's proceedings. I'm also ducking out the side exit, I don't want to make any comments to the press."

CHAPTER 12

Adrian was right, the press had a field day with reporting on the trail, printing all the gory details. It was all on the front page with a picture of Bob's blown away head next to that of the pig. How the fuck did they manage to get those pictures? Someone had leaked them to the press I bet. There were pictures of the two DAs standing on the court steps, taken while being interviewed by someone, both having grins as wide as a mile on their mugs. They were lapping up all the limelight. There was a picture of me, this time just head and shoulders.

Shit, this was not good, as it was sure to get into the press further down the coast and my family was soon going to be involved in the repercussions of this bad press. I'm not sure what my parents had been told and I'm sure Diane hadn't spoken to them. So sooner or later they are going to read about it in the press down there if they haven't already. What has Diane done with Jason? Did she leave him in Florida with her aunt while she is up here, I certainly hope so?

All this negative press about me is unquestionably not good for our company. Norman must be pulling his hair out wondering what the hell I've got myself involved in. I bet the shareholders are asking questions he can't answer. The fact that I can't even talk and explain things to him, is just so fucking frustrating I can scream.

Friday morning couldn't come fast enough for me. I was already in court sitting at the table when Adrian comes in and puts his briefcase on the table.

"Good morning Grant, how was your night?

Not too good I imagine after reading the paper, but today is going to be our day."

"Yes, I hardly slept. I couldn't get the front-page images out of my mind. How the hell did the press get hold of those two pictures?"

"They more than likely have a connection within the police department, or with the fancy cameras they have today, they may have shot them from inside the courthouse when they were displayed on the screen. It's done and there's nothing we could have done about it anyway."

The bailiff announces the judge, he enters, and we all stand while he takes his seat at the bench.

He sits down, adjusts his glasses, and looks up and around at his audience and over at the jury and says,

"Good morning ladies and gentlemen, you may be seated. Bailiff, you may bring in the witness please."

We wait until Sylvia is brought back into the witness stand. She doesn't look at all happy at being there, the self-assured attitude she portrayed earlier on in the trial has vanished. Today she was wearing a grey formal business suit, jacket, and matching pants with a white blouse.

"Good morning Mrs. Croning," said the judge. "May I remind you that you are still under oath?"

"Ladies and gentlemen of the jury, yesterday, shortly before we recessed for the day, the prosecution objected to the line of questioning that the defense had assumed. I have since then considered the prosecution's objection and I have decided to allow the defense to continue.
Defense, you may continue with your questioning."

Adrian gets up and says,

"Thank you, your honor," and walks over to the

witness stand and faces Sylvia.

"Good morning Mrs. Croning, I trust you had a good night's rest." Not allowing her the chance to reply, he continues.

"Do you remember my last question Mrs. Croning, but maybe it's better that I repeat it?"

"How much was your late husband's life insurance worth?"

There was a long delay and finally, she said.

"I think it was five million."

"Mrs. Croning didn't you just three weeks ago receive a check from the insurance company that insured your late husband's life, for the exact amount of five million dollars?"

"Yes."

"So, what was your reason for saying, 'You think it was five million'

No answer was coming forth, so Adrian said,

"Let me help you out here. Maybe you got a little confused with all the insurance policies that you have. Mrs. Croning is that perhaps the problem?"

"I'm not sure what you mean," she says.

"Oh! I'm sure you do Mrs. Croning, let's see now," and Adrian unfolds a piece of paper he has in his hand and reads aloud.

"According to my sources, your house was insured for six million, and the contents one hundred and fifty thousand. The Mercedes SLK, sixty thousand. The Lexus LS 500 ——

"Your honor," protests the DA, "this is not the line of ——"

Before he could finish his sentence, the judge had banged his gavel so hard on his sounding board, it fell off the bench, and the court clerk had to pick it up and place it back again on the bench.

"Mr. Benmin, I have already ruled on this and I do not wish to hear from you again regarding this matter, now sit down," he almost shouted. His face was red, and his hands were shaking.

"Mr. Mink, continue."

"Thank you for your honor." Adrian looks down again at his paper in his hand.

"The Lexus LS 500 was insured at seventy-five thousand and the Toyota Land Cruiser, fifty-thousand. Let's not forget the controversial boat, at two hundred thousand. Then to top it off there's the Key-man business insurance of three million from your late husband's business. If my source is correct, you are also the beneficiary there as well. So, if my math is correct, that all adds up to the tidy little sum of fourteen million, five hundred and thirty-five thousand dollars. It's no wonder Mrs. Croning that you are a little confused as to the amount. Fourteen million, five hundred and some change is quite a nice incentive for murder."

The DA was up on his feet again and before he could open his mouth, Adrian cut in, "I have no further questions for this witness your honor."

"Does the prosecution wish to redirect?"

The DA gets up and says, "No thank you, your honor."

The judge looked contemptuously across at Sylvia and said, "Mrs. Croning you may now step down."

"Does the defense wish to call its next witness?"

"Yes, thank you, your honor, I wish to recall Detective Alan Burns to the stand."

Alan Burns is duly called, and the bailiff brings him to the witness stand, where the judge reminds him that he is still under oath.

Adrian walks over to the witness stand and addresses Detective Burns.

"Detective, the team of investigators who found the plastic bag with the gun and wine bottle, did they perhaps find any other empty wine bottles in the trash?"

"No that was the only one that we found outside the property in the trash can."

"What about the trash can in the kitchen, were there any bottles in there?"

"The kitchen was pretty badly damaged by the fire with water, so it was difficult to say what was in the kitchen."

"Detective that may be the case, but we also took some pictures of the fire scene soon after we were permitted to look around. I have a photograph of the kitchen and I can see a bent and buckled metal trash can lying on its side," and Adrian is looking at a picture he has in his hand. "Did you find any bottles in it?"

"No, we didn't."

"No, you didn't look in it, or no you didn't find any bottles in it?"

"No, we found no other bottles in the trash can or the kitchen."

"Detective, in your professional opinion, do you think that the six or seven empty beer bottles and two or three wine bottles that Mrs. Croning referred to in her cross-examination, could have melted in the fire? That's a heap of bottles that just disappeared, you know, poof out the window."

"No, I have no opinion as to what could have happened to those bottles."

"Detective, did you or your team come up with an explanation as to how the bullets in the magazine clip got my client's fingerprints all over them?" "Yes, they explained that the defendant retrieved the gun from the drawer, seeing the magazine only holds a few rounds, he fills the magazine before going upstairs and shooting Mr. Croning" "Now let me see the detective, if I have this right. My client picks up the gun from the drawer and sees that it only has say one, two, or three rounds in the magazine and proceeds to reload it with the exact number of rounds to fill the magazine. Is that what you're saying?" "Yes, that's correct." "So, someone must have known how many rounds to leave in the drawer to exactly fill the magazine. Because you stated that no other rounds or shell casings were found near the sideboard. That's quite a coincidence, don't you think detective"? "Not really, the husband could have left the gun in the drawer with the exact number of rounds, meaning to reload the magazine at a later stage."

"I see a detective, so now you're suggesting that my client picks up each of the rounds in the drawer that the husband left there, wipes off the fingerprints of the husband, and then proceeds to load the magazine. Do I understand you correctly?"

"Well, maybe the husband just tipped the shells out of the box and counted the number he needed and put the rest back in the box."

"Okay detective let's leave it at that because I think you and your team are both flummoxed as to how the ammunition only has my client's fingerprints on them. One last thing. Dr. Mitchel from the crime lab also found it strange that no other samples of hair, nails, skin, or material had come back from the crime scene, even though the defendant was not wearing gloves, according to your witness. Care to make any further comments, detective?"

"No, I don't think so."

"I didn't think so either," Adrian says, as he walks away from the witness stand.

"Your honor, I have no further questions for this witness."

"Does the prosecution wish to redirect?"

The prosecution declines.

"Does the defense wish to call its next witness?"

Your honor, the defense rests its case.

Adrian walks back to the table and sits down.

The judge looks at his watch and looks up and says, "Ladies and gentlemen, I think we will have an early recess for lunch and after lunch, we will hear closing statements from the prosecution and the defense. Please be back here at 12:45 p.m."

We all stand, as the judge leaves the bench.

"Wow! That will give the jury and everyone else a lot to think about, nicely done Adrian," I say.

"Well, one thing we know, the judge is pissed off with the DA and I was surprised he let me continue my line of questioning this morning."

"It'll be interesting to see what the press makes of all this now."

"I'm going to get a bite to eat, same again for you Grant?"

"Yes, please, and make it a large whiskey instead of the coffee."

"Wish I could, but wait until this party is over, then I'll buy you a case of the best."

Once everyone was again seated for the afternoon session, the judge addressed the jury.

"Ladies and gentlemen of the jury, you have heard the witnesses for the prosecution, and you have heard the cross-examination of these witnesses, by the defense in this trial. The prosecution and defense will now give you their closing statements, which are basically a summary of the past four days."

The judge looks down over the rim of his glasses at the DA table and asks.

"Is the prosecution ready to make their closing statement?"

"Yes, thank you, your honor, the prosecution is ready."

"Please proceed then."

"Thank you, your honor," and the DA strolls over to the middle of the floor facing the jury.

"Ladies and gentlemen of the jury, over the past three and a half days you have heard the testimony of various witnesses in this trial. You have also seen evidence, pictures, and demonstrations. Let me remind you that many of these witnesses were experts in their respective fields. However, the defense has tried by all manner of means to discredit these witnesses and the evidence brought before you. That is his job, that's what he gets paid to do. So, don't be fooled. He is very clever, manipulative and would have you believing things that may not be factual.
Remember what we are dealing with here is factual evidence."

"So, let me summarize the facts for you.
We have the weapon with the defendant's fingerprints all over it.

We have the knife with the defendant's fingerprints all over it.

We have the DNA proof that the defendant's semen was found in the private parts of Mrs. Croning.

We discovered $65 000 dollars in cash in the defendant's overnight bag.

We have a witness that was at the scene of the crime and was a victim of the crime.

We found plans and drawings of the mobile phone trigger device on his computer.

Now you ask — did the defendant have a motive for committing the crime?"

Of course, yes — he did. His wife had invested $50,000 with Mr. Croning and he wanted that money back, with interest."

The DA turns, looks at me, and points saying, "Then this man here takes a pillow and covers Mr. Croning's head and blasts him, bang, bang, bang, three times point-blank through the pillow, into his head, dead, dead, dead. All because he would not open the safe and give him the money."

He turns back to face the jury.

"He then forces the dead man's wife to open the safe and give him the money. Not satisfied with what he has already done, he beats and rapes her. Then ties her to the bed and later to cover his crime, he sets fire to the house hoping to destroy all evidence."

"Ladies and gentlemen," again he turns and points at me. "This fine looking and respectable man, do you think he could have planned all of this?"

"Oh yes, —— you can be sure he did. This was a premeditated crime, believe me. He had planned this all along. Remember we found the plans and drawings of the mobile phone trigger device on his computer. It had been downloaded weeks before he came to Boston."

"Ladies and gentlemen of the jury, considering all the overwhelming and compelling evidence in this case, there is no other considered verdict in this trial, than that of guilty on all accounts."

The DA struts back to his table, looking at us as if to say, 'beat that you losers.'

The judge looks down at our table and asks, "Does the defense wish to make a closing statement? If yes, then please proceed."

"Yes, thank you, your honor," and Adrian walks over to face the jury.

"Ladies and gentlemen of the jury, today you have the most difficult task of judging a man of either being guilty or innocent of a serious crime, for which if he is found guilty, could face the death penalty. Not a comfortable decision for anyone to be making."

"Therefore, it is of the utmost importance that you carefully weigh all those facts that the prosecution has laid before you and examine them carefully before you make your judgment. The prosecution will have you believe that the evidence is factual, but we know their key witness has lied several times under oath and this witness should therefore not be considered a reliable witness. The prosecution's whole case hinges on this witness and without her, there is no case against my client."

"I have pointed out so many anomalies in this case, that the prosecution and the police department have not been able to clarify."

"Remember the gun, there is still no clear explanation of how my client's fingerprints were found on the bullets in the magazine, other than when he loaded it for his sister-in-law as he stated."

"Yes, they found his fingerprints on the knife, but as he admitted, he cut cheese with a knife the night before."

"His sperm was found in the vaginal fluids of

Mrs. Croning, and we know from Mr. Hughes's statement that the sperm got there in the manner in which he described in his statement."

"They found sixty-five thousand dollars cash in my client's bag. He told you how that happened when his sister-in-law asked if she could put some things in his bag for his wife and son. There again a feasible explanation."

"Then we have the drawings for the trigger device, found on my clients PC. How it got there, he does not know and given the fact that his PC was out of his sight for more than a month, it is also possible that it was planted there by someone. Furthermore, they assumed the fire was started by such a device. Remember there was no proof that this was the case."

"Last but not least, we have the one and only witness to the crime, who also happens to be the victim. We have heard on several instances where Mrs. Croning has lied, she can't remember whether the gun was in my client's left or right hand. She can't remember whose pillow was taken when she alleged that my client shot her husband. She can't remember what my client did with the knife when he held the pillow over her husband's head. She can't remember how she held the sheet she alleged my client cut, while she was holding it. She can't remember being raped before being tied up or after, we still have no explanation of how her pajama top was removed."

"There are just so many anomalies that her story just doesn't hold water. Let's take the beer and wine bottles. She said they had about six or seven bottles of beer and two bottles of wine to drink. The police found only one empty wine bottle. So where did the rest of the empty bottles go? Poof out the window, as the prosecution would say."

"Then, what a surprise to learn that the key witness and so-called victim is about to gain a large fortune of over fourteen million dollars in insurance."

"It is not my duty to prove that my client is being framed. That is the job of the police department. My responsibility is to prove that the evidence that has been presented does not prove beyond a reasonable doubt that my client committed any of the crimes for which he is being charged."

"Ladies and gentlemen of the jury, I must, therefore, appeal to you, that if there is any doubt in your minds as to whether my client is guilty or innocent, you should find him not guilty."

Adrian walks back to the table and sits down. I whisper out of the side of my mouth.

"Nicely done."

The judge looks down at the DA and asks, "Does the prosecution wish to rebuttal?"

"Yes, thank you, your honor," and the DA walks over to face the jury again.

"Ladies and gentlemen of the jury, you have heard the defense criticize our key witness and repudiate her statement. Can you imagine having gone through the traumatic experience she went through?"

"Seeing her husband shot next to her, then being beaten, raped, and left to burn? Now she is being treated for PTSD, and for those of you who don't know what that is, let me explain. It stands for post-traumatic stress disorder and is a mental condition that results in a series of emotional and physical reactions in individuals who have witnessed the most horrific and traumatic event."

"My goodness, no wonder she could not remember all the facts, I doubt if anyone in those same circumstances would be able to."

"Ladies and gentlemen of the jury, you have heard and seen the compelling evidence in this trial. You now must find the defendant guilty of the crimes as charged."

The DA walks back to the table and sits down.

The judge takes off his glasses and looks up at the jury.

"Ladies and gentlemen of the jury, the charges against the accused, including that of first-degree murder and rape are the most serious charges in our criminal justice system. You have heard from both sides of the case and now it is your duty to try and separate facts from fiction. You should not be influenced by the personalities of any of the parties. There should be no dislikes, opinions, prejudices, or sympathy. That means you must decide the case solely on the evidence brought before you. Whichever way you decide, guilty or not guilty, the verdict must be unanimous. I urge you to deliberate honestly and considerately. Remember you took the oath to do so."

"You will now go into deliberation and I instruct you to choose a foreperson. When you have reached a unanimous verdict, the foreperson will write this on a slip of paper and hand it to the court clerk when you re-enter the court. Thank you, ladies and gentlemen."

The judge then instructed the bailiff to take the jury out to the jury room.

He then informed us that the court was in recess and would reconvene as soon as a verdict was forthcoming from the jury.

Adrian looks at me and says,

"Well, that's it, now we wait. That was a nice touch the DA threw in there at the last moment about your sister-in-law suffering from PTSD, quite touching I must say, had me almost in tears."

I was taken back to the holding cell and sat there with my thoughts to myself, wondering what my chances were. Adrian, I believe, had done a great job and I couldn't have asked for better representation.

Two hours later we are back in the court.

The jury is brought back into the court and the foreperson, in this case, a black woman, gets up and hands the clerk a piece of folded paper. There is a sudden hush all over the courthouse, I swear one could hear a pin drop. The clerk unfolds the paper, reads the verdict, and passes it to the judge.

The judge looks at the paper, removes his glasses, and looks at the foreperson.

"Madam, I see that you have not reached a unanimous decision, and I see," he says, looking again at the paper in his hand, "the deadlock is pretty strong on both sides, almost equal."

"Yes, your honor," she replies.

"Ladies and gentlemen of the jury, I could request that you all go back and deliberate again, but do you think you will be able to come up with a unanimous decision either way if I do?"

There's a lot of shaking of heads in the jury stand and the foreperson says,

"Your honor, with all due respect to you and the court, I think we would be wasting the court's time." There's a lot of nodding in the jury box.

The judge nods his head and says, "In that case, I must declare this a hung jury. Ladies and gentlemen of the jury, I thank you for your time and service to the community. Madam foreperson, you may now sit down."

The judge looks down at the prosecution table and asks,

"At this time does the prosecution wish to pursue another trial?"

The two DAs are whispering to one another.

The judge said,

"Gentlemen I'm waiting for your answer."

"Your honor, the people would like a few days to confer on this matter before making a decision."

Immediately Adrian is on his feet,

"Your honor this is unacceptable, my client has the right to know now where he stands in this case."

The judge shakes his head and says,

"I'm sorry the defense has a point. The prosecution has had ample time over the past days to discuss the possibility of a mistrial. Please make up your mind, I'll give you five minutes."

There was a lot of heated argument going on in hushed voices coming from the DA's table and it was obvious there was not a consensus as to what to do.

Eventually, the judge says,

"Gentlemen your decision please."

The DA gets up and says,

"Your honor yes, the people wish to reschedule another trial."

"In that case, the defendant will be held in custody until a new trial date has been assigned," says the judge. He bangs his mallet on the sounding board, announcing, "This court is now adjourned."

We all get up and the judge leaves the courtroom.

"Disappointed," asks Adrian.

"Yes, somewhat but glad it wasn't guilty," I say. "When you put the DA under pressure there to make a decision, I thought for a few minutes I may have a chance to walk."

"Yes, that was my plan, it didn't work but it was worth the try. Anyway, I wasn't going to let you stew for weeks not knowing if there was going to be a trial or not."

"So, what happens now?" I ask.

"Well, unfortunately we are still in the hands of the district attorney's office and you can bet they will be in no hurry to reschedule this retrial date. They will want to sit back, lick their wounds, and hope the whole thing will just go away and someone else will have to pick it up. This is not good for Mr. DA's political career. The mayor is going to be pissed big time not having got a conviction. I know this doesn't help you."

"Yes, it sucks," I say.

"I'll see if our office can pull some strings with guys we know in the Supreme Court. Hopefully, they will put some pressure on those assholes to at least set a date to meet with a judge and set a new trial date. Then I'll get another chance to request bail, and this time they can't refuse. That's the immediate plan. They are going to take you back to jail now at Robert W Healey."

"Okay, that would be great if we could get bail. Do you think I'll be allowed to make a phone call when I'm back in jail?"

"I don't see why not now your trial is over, you won't be in solitary anymore either and there is no longer any reason why you should not be allowed, visitors. You can make calls, but you will be restricted by how many you can make, and you'll

184

have to phone collect. Who do you want to call?"

"I want to speak to my folks; they have not heard from me since I left home."

"Yes, I'm sure your dad wants to hear your side of the story having heard what your wife has had to say."

"Yes, he will be anxious to hear from me. I doubt if my folks would have had any contact with my wife as they don't get on together."

"I'll try and get to see you as soon as I have some news. Look you're going to need some money in there, did you have any on you when they arrested you?"

"Yes, I had about two hundred and thirty in my wallet."

"Okay, I'll see if I can get it released. In the meantime, here are a few dollars." He took out two tens, a twenty, five singles and put them in my hand.

"Just hang in there, we are more than two-thirds of the way there," said Adrian as he shakes my hand, picks up his briefcase, and makes his way out of the side exit of the courthouse.

CHAPTER 13

I was put in a cell with another person called Jeffery Spencer, still a kid in his early twenties I would guess. He was in for grand auto theft for the second time and was waiting for his trial date to come up in January. He'd been in the slammer for two months, so he had the routine well figured out by this time. It was nice to have someone who could show me the ropes and that helped me not to screw up too much.

The second day I asked him, "Hey Jeff, what's the procedure if one needs to make a call?"

"You pretty much have to bribe the guard to let you use the phone," he says.

"How much?"

"Two to three dollars, but when you ask the guard permission to use the phone, he's going to ask you what you got? You say two. He may say okay, he may say phones engaged all-day. In that case, you can say, would three help? He would say I'll check. He would come back shortly and say phones free for three, make it snappy. Or, if you're not in a hurry, you can say okay, I'll try again tomorrow. Then maybe a little later he may come back and say, phones open two for two, make it snappy."

"What's two for two mean?"

"Two bucks two minutes, that's all you get, that's why you gotta make it snappy."

I have waited six weeks to speak to my folks, but I thought I would try the two-dollar trick first and see what happens.

Jeff was right, a few hours later the guard comes back and says the phone is free, so I slip him the two bucks and he takes me to the phone box.

Speaking to my dad is not easy. Somehow, I feel like I'm twelve years old again having to explain to my father about the note I brought home from the school principal. Why I should feel guilty, I don't know, maybe because my dad has always said there is something funny going on with those two Robert girls. My folks never hit it off with Diane. I tell him I will soon need to borrow a large sum of money to secure bail, and can he please help. He says tell your attorney to call me with whatever he needs.

Three days later back in my cell I'm informed there's someone to see me. I'm taken to the common visitors' room, where there are no barriers anymore, this is a nice change. There are a table and chairs and sitting at the table is a person I have never seen before. She has a dark complexion and thick black hair tied with an elastic-band left hanging below her shoulders. I'm thinking maybe Asian or Indian descent. Her makeup is sparse except for the bright red lipstick that enhances her rather large mouth. I can see under the table as I walk in, she is wearing a light green pantsuit. Green on a woman is not my favorite color.

"Hi," I say, "sorry, I don't think we've met."

Before I can even pull out the chair, she pushes her card across the table towards me. There is no gesture from her to shake hands. I sit down, pick up her card, and read, Ms. B. Langley, Attorney-at-Law.

"Oh," I say. "Where's Adrian Mink?"

"Mr. Hughes I'm not here to represent you, I'm here representing your wife."

"My wife," I say —— "what has she done?"

"Mr. Hughes, your wife has done nothing. It's

you that has done everything, and she is suing you for divorce, full custody of your son Jason and half of your assets," she says with a little smug smile.

"Oh, gee whiz! Only half my assets, why not all?" I say sarcastically.

"Mr. Hughes the court would never allow that."

"Oh —— I don't know why not? The court has me up for murder, rape, assault, theft, and arson. They want to send me to prison for life, the gas chamber, or whatever they do these days. So, my life is fucked, so why not take it all, what can I do with half my assets in jail or dead. So, there you go, you may as well change it to read all my assets."

"Mr. Hughes, this is not a joke, your wife is suing you because of what you have done to the family, and you have humiliated and embarrassed her. She is under a huge mental strain now. She is seeing a doctor because of the anxiety attacks she is having because of all the physical and mental strain you have put her under. I have a report here from her doctor," and she opens a file and before she can pass it to me, I say, "Let me guess, she's suffering from severe PTSD."

"Yes, —," she says surprised, "how do you know?"

"Oh, did my wife not inform you?"

"No, tell me what?" she says getting all defensive.

"That I'm telepathic," I say, smiling my best smile, "and I'll also tell you the doctor's name. Dr. Ann Madison from Los Angeles, not so?"

"Yes, Mr. Hughes, that's correct. Post-traumatic stress disorder is not a nice condition to be suffering from," and she pushes the document back into the file.

My sarcasm went over her head and she continued.

"Mr. Hughes, we don't want to stress your wife any more than necessary, so I would like you to sign these documents," as she pulls out a wad of papers from the folder and starts to lay them out in front of me. "We can clear all this up in a few weeks I'm sure and it will be the best for your son and also for you in the long run."

I pull one page over and read it and then the others, until I've read them all.

"Mmm," I say, "I see from the dates these documents were drawn up —— let me see now, that would be three,—— no four weeks ago, is that right?"

"Yes, Mr. Hughes that is correct. I have been trying to get to see you, but the district attorney's office would not give anyone access to you until two days ago."

"So, if my memory serves me correctly, my wife must have started divorce proceedings shortly after I was arrested, is that correct?"

"When were you arrested, Mr. Hughes?"

"October 16."

She takes one of the documents, looks at the date, and says.

"Yes, that would be correct, twenty-eight days yes, on the twenty-fourth."

"I can now imagine how distraught my wife must be having to wait all this time to serve these papers on me, no wonder she is close to having a nervous breakdown."

"Yes, Mr. Hughes, it is very sad."

"If I don't sign, I suppose this could result in a long-drawn-out court battle with lots of tears and bad feelings between us all, which could well push her over the edge, so to speak, with her being in this fragile state of mind."

"Yes, I'm afraid so Mr. Hughes" and she hands me her pen.

I take the pen and ask her.

"Ms. Langley, are you familiar with the habits of the Algerian monkeys?"

She looks up at me, not quite sure where this is going.

"No, not really, why do you ask?"

"Well, they have the nasty custom of taking peanuts and shoving them up their backside. Now I would like you to take back your pen and perform the same custom with it. You can also tell my wife and her sister that they both can go and fuck themselves, and the next time I'll see them will be in court, one way or the other. Good day, Ms. Langley —— nice meeting you."

I get up, bang on the door, the guard comes and takes me back to my cell. Phew, that was close, I had to take control of myself with Ms. Langley. I felt like I wanted to reach out and put my hands around her neck and squeeze it until that smug little smile of hers disappeared down her throat.

I think I'm slowly getting the picture. These two half-sisters have concocted this whole thing to get rid of their respective husbands, collect a heap of cash, buy a boat, and take my son sailing off into the fucking sunset.

Well, Diane my dear, if you think I'm just going to roll over, I've got news for you. If you think I'm going to sign everything I own and worked for, over to you, then you have misjudged me all these years we have been together. It just shows you that although you may think you know someone, you don't really. This has been proven so many times. One hears of cases where a partner, friend, wife, or a family member has let someone you know down. You tell yourself that kind of thing will never happen to me because I know my friends, my family, my wife, and when it does happen, you wonder how you missed it and why you didn't see it coming.

Life can be cruel for no reason, it's just like that sometimes. When you are down, there always seems to be a line of people out there waiting to kick you.

The next day while having breakfast, the guard came and said I had two visitors waiting to see me.

"Two?" I said.

"Yes, two in suits."

I am not surprised to see Norman, my business partner, and Eric Greenway, our business attorney sitting at the table when I get inside the visitors' room.

"Hi Norman," I say as I reach out to shake his hand. "So nice to see a familiar face, I was wondering when you were going to manage to get to see me."

"Hi Grant, how are you doing man?" You know Eric. Eric stretches out his hand shaking mine, and I sit down facing them.

"Well, not too good, five and half weeks in jail for something I didn't do, and because of a hung jury, I'm sitting here pending a new trial date," I say.

"Yes, we've sort of been following the case as best we can from the press and you have been taking a hammering from them on all sides, up here and down our way. Grant, I don't know what you've got yourself mixed up in, all I know is that it has had a huge negative effect on the firm. We are basically on the brink of losing everything."

"That's what I was afraid of when I saw the first press report."

"Well, I don't know how to tell you this in any way that's not going to make you feel bad, so I'm just going to tell you as it comes out. You are no longer CEO and co-owner of the company; the shareholders have unanimously voted you off. We haven't appointed anyone to replace you and we likely won't for a while."

"Fuck me, you can't do that, it's my firm, I founded the company."

"Grant, remember when we went for the IPO with the sole purpose of raising cash to finance the Micro Bridging Project, we gave up our rights as owners? You and I each hold thirty percent of the shares. The forty percent balance is held by the shareholders. So, their forty and my thirty gave us the majority to vote you off."

"Christ Norm, why would you do that?"

"Grant I had no alternative, the company was going under, the share price dropped by half and is going down every day and unless we can pull off this Micro Bridging Project within the next four weeks, we can kiss our asses goodbye. You know I mortgaged my house to the hilt to put money into the company. My in-laws bought stock in the company, and friends of mine bought stock. I've got young kids in school. I don't want to end up on the street. How do you think I feel having to tell you this?"

"Which brings me to the next point, why the fuck did you put personal stuff on your company laptop? All the stuff you've been working on is locked up in that PC and we have no way of getting to it. Without it, we can't finish the fucking project. We have been trying for weeks to get your laptop released and at last, we have an order from the Supreme Court for it to be released. Now, all we need is your signature permitting us to get it from the police department."

"Eric, do you have that document?"

Eric opens his briefcase and takes out a document and slides it across the table to me with a pen and says. "Write your full name here, sign at the bottom, and date it," he says.

"That asshole of a DA only permitted us yesterday to visit you, so we flew up last night. Now we must get down to the precinct, pick up your laptop, and hope they aren't going to give us a hard time."

"Look, Grant, I'm sorry I have to do this, there is no other way. I hope to God this whole thing you've got yourself mixed up in with your family will eventually come out with you smelling like a rose. Because there is something very smelly somewhere. I think I know you better than the person the press is portraying you to be."

"Look we have to go; we've only got weeks to get Micro Bridge to the market. Your shares are still there so if we get this thing right, you will come out okay."

"Who knows what's going to happen to me in the future Norm. All I can tell you is that this is all a load of bullshit. Yesterday I realized Diane and her step-sister are screwing their respective husbands and are about to sail off somewhere into the sunset with my son."

"Yesterday, her attorney was sitting exactly where you are sitting today with papers suing me for divorce and half of my assets. The papers were drawn up a week after I was arrested. She didn't even want to know if I was found guilty or not.

Christ, you live with someone and you think you know them."

"Jees Grant buddy, what can I say, certainly nothing that's going to make things right, just hang in there, I have faith that in the long run, good will prevails,"

He and Eric push back their chairs and get up, we shake hands and they leave. I sit there for a few minutes weighing up all that has happened in the past few days. Then the guard comes and escorts me back to my cell.

Two weeks after the trial, Adrian comes to see me, advising that he has managed to get a date to sit with the judge and prosecution to decide on a new trial date. As we expected, the DA has handed the case down to his deputy and one other junior advocate in the office. A new judge will be presiding over the retrial. Adrian will be meeting with them the first week in December to decide on a new trial date which will be set sometime in the new year. He said he will then again push for bail with the new judge. He is confident we will be successful. So at least I can look forward to being out on bail before Christmas.

CHAPTER 14

The weeks in jail go by without incident and I soon get into the daily routine of jail life. True to his word Adrian meets with the new presiding judge and negotiates a bail of one million dollars. He also arranges a bail with a bond agent for them to take up the bond for a ten percent fee. He has spoken to my dad, who arranged a one hundred-thousand-dollar EFT from his bank to Adrian's company's bank.

Other conditions are I must surrender my passport, wear an electronic ankle bracelet, and report once a week to my probation officer in Paoli. I'm restricted to travel only within the state of Pennsylvania, except for when I would need to travel to Massachusetts for my trial.

Three days later all the paperwork is complete and a flight ticket to Philly is arranged by Adrian and his office. With my cell phone returned to me, a few personal possessions, and my overnight case, I'm escorted out of Robert W. Healey Public Safety Facility by a plain-clothed police officer who's accompanying me to the airport to ensure I get on a plane for Philadelphia. At the airport, I feel as if everyone is staring at me, but I'm sure they aren't, it's all in my head. My dad is at Philly airport to meet me and we drive back to their home in Wayne which is about 35 minutes from the airport. On the way back I use my dad's mobile to call the probation officer in Paoli to inform them I have arrived in Pennsylvania, as Adrian instructed me.

It was Saturday midday, and I was wondering if the office was open over the weekends, but then I suppose probation officers need to be on call 24/7.

I was put on hold for what seemed an age, at last, a female voice says,

"Yeah, what'cha want?" I explained who I am, giving her my case number, saying I'm supposed to report to her in a week.

"Yeah, Friday, 10 a.m., and make sure you're not late." Bang, she puts the phone down. I thought to myself, this is going to be another interesting experience I can do without.

We parked in the garage adjoining the house. I get out and go inside and greet my mom who just holds me in her arms for a few minutes and says,

"Good to have you, home son. You can sleep in your old room. Give me all your clothes to throw in the washer, then at least you'll have something clean to wear."

My mobile was dead, so I put it on charge and used the landline to call Norman at home. The phone rings a few times and is picked up by one of his kids. I assumed it was Alex.

"Hi, this is Grant Hughes, can I speak to your dad please?" There was an "Oh yes" silent pause, and a hand went over the mouthpiece of the handset, —— "Mr. Hughes, let me find my dad for you." I can well imagine what was being whispered while Alex went to find his dad. A few minutes later Norman comes on the line.

"Grant, where are you calling from, the jail?"

"No Norm, I'm not in jail, I'm at my old man's place in Wayne, got out on bail today and flew in this afternoon. Sorry to call you at home like this, but I knew you would want to hear I'm out until the new trial date sometime in the new year. Look, how's the project doing, did you manage to finish it, and can I be of any assistance?"

"Hell Grant, that's great news, yes we have

finished it, but we have a few glitches in the software that we are trying to iron out. You could really be of help on that side. It's part of your design program that's giving us a bit of a headache. If you could investigate that, it would be a great help. Our shareholders are very anxious, and I must say they have been very patient, but I think their patience is starting to wane, so any help to speed this along would be beneficial."

"Well, why don't you come over this evening. Pick up my laptop from the office on your way here, I assume that's where it is, and we can go over the program. I can then work on it from home. I do not need to come into the office and upset the staff. Let's just keep it low profile and we can communicate over the internet."

"Sounds like an excellent plan, see you at about 5:30. Do your folks still live in that big old Dutch Colonial house in Baker Street?"

"Yes, the very same one I grew up in, see you later," I put the phone down and tell my folks about the arrangement Norman and I just made.

At 5:30 sharp Norman pulls into the driveway and dad goes out to meet him. They both come in laughing about something one of them has said.

"Hi Norm, do you remember my mom? Mom, I'm sure you remember Norman, he was my best man at our wedding."

"Yes, of course, I remember Norman, how are you, it's been such a long time?"

"Yes, I'm ashamed to say it has Mrs. Hughes, far too long."

"Oh, don't you come with that 'Mrs. Hughes' here, Pat will do fine. Come and sit down in the den. What can I get you all to drink, coffee, tea, lemonade or are you guys going to have something a little stronger?"

"Something a little stronger please," says dad, "If you don't mind."

"Okay mom, I'll get it. Dad, Norman, beer?" I ask.

Both say yes to a beer and mom says she will have a glass of wine.

When everyone has their drinks and were relaxed, I say,

"Now that I have all the most important people in my life here, and before Norman and I get down to discussing business, I would like to take this opportunity to tell you exactly what happened to me in Boston, from the horse's mouth and not what you may have read in the press, if that's okay?"

Everyone nods their heads.

So, I start my tale of woe from the time I arrived at Sissy's front door ending up with me being accused of murder, rape assault, robbery, and arson.

As I'm telling the story, I could see my dad is getting more and more agitated and upset, and by the time I'm finished he looks at me and says,

"Grant, I told you ten years ago that woman was not good for you, but you wouldn't listen and as for her sister, well she always was a slutty thing in my eyes."

"Now Jack that's not fair, you don't know what you're talking about," says my mother.

"I know what I know, and I see what I see," says my dad.

"Hell Grant, that's quite something," says Norman. "So where are Diane and Jason now?"

"I have no idea. As I told you she has filed for a divorce. So sooner or later she is going to have to come back from wherever they are and go to court to fight this thing through. But as things stand now, I don't have much of a chance of getting any custody of Jason as long as this crime is hanging over my head."

"What are your chances at a new trial?" asks Norman.

"Well, according to my attorney Adrian Mink, we have a particularly good chance of winning it. We now know all the evidence they have against me. We can now pull it completely apart, show the cops up as being incompetent, and having an unreliable main witness who has perjured herself several times. So yes, we are pretty confident that we will win this one." I say.

"That's good to hear Grant. As I need to be getting back, can I show you what symptoms we are getting on the program? The problem being they aren't there all the time; they seem to be intermittent. Maybe you can work on it and see what you think is bugging the program."

"Okay let's go and sit at the dining room table and you can show me quickly what the problem is."

We excuse ourselves from the folks and sit in the dining room with my laptop, while Norman explains what seems to be causing the hiccup in the program software.

Twenty minutes later I have a good idea of what the problem can be so I will investigate it first thing in the morning. Norman says good night to my folks and leaves.

The next morning mom shakes me awake early as I'm eager to start to look at the programming software problem. I work on it solidly the whole day, checking and rechecking circuitry for any flaws. By late afternoon I think I have nailed the problem down to what must be a chip malfunction. The chip was designed to offload a specific task from the accelerator to the CPU on the motherboard and this doesn't seem to be performing that task all the time. I e-mail Norman my theory, telling him what I suspect and that he needs to get hold of Eagle Electronics, the motherboard sourcing company. They need to do a dry run test on the motherboard for us and specifically on that one component, I identified.

On Monday morning I asked my dad to drive me over to my house. I need to start getting used to the fact that I'm now on my own. I can't expect my folks to put me up forever. I must get my life together and the sooner I start the better. On the way over my dad says,

"Son, what are you going to do about Jason, we haven't seen him in months and now it looks like we may never see him?"

"Dad, with all due respect, I'm out on bail. I've really no resources at my disposal to search for him and his mother. They could be anywhere in the world now for all I know. I'm as anxious as you and mom to find the little guy, but my hands are tied. We will just have to wait and hope he is fine. She will have to bring him back when she eventually has a court date for the divorce hearing."

But more and more I'm thinking, those two girls have skipped the country with Jason. They know that their time is running out. There were just too many anomalies in the statements Sissy gave. The lies she told must have left a lot of unanswered questions with the police department. I would think the police are quite anxious to know a lot more about all the money she inherited, because of Bob being murdered.

I have no idea what I was going to find when I

got home. Will my car still be in the garage, will there be furniture in the house and what will the garden look like? These are the things running around in my head as we drive home.

Well, the first thing one sees when driving up to a house that hasn't been lived in for months, is the state of the garden. Thank goodness all the utilities and mortgage payments are on a debit order and are paid automatically every month, otherwise, I probably would see foreclosure signs outside my house.

We park in the driveway and go through the front door. The house is cold and smells musty from being locked up. Thank goodness we haven't had a freeze yet or the pipes could have frozen. From a cursory glance, everything seemed to be still there, and I see both my car and Diane's are in the garage.

I turn on the thermostat to get some warm air into the place, then I open the refrigerator, and immediately I know I have a problem. Whatever was in there has gone bad and is smelly. I closed the door and told myself that's a job for tomorrow.

I go upstairs to Jason's room and open his closet, noticing some of his clothes are missing. His baseball mitt and ball are gone from where he normally keeps them. Good, I'm thinking, at least he has something to play with. Everything else seems okay. I sit on his bed and pick up a bronze medal on a lanyard he received for coming in third in a running obstacle race. I was so proud of him, I remember he was wet through and covered in mud, but not once did he complain. He said, 'it was a lot of fun dad.' Gee —— I miss my little buddy!

In our bedroom I open Diane's closet, finding some empty hangers, clothing seems to be missing from shelves, as well as underwear in the drawers. Always difficult to know what she is wearing anyway, and what she has put away for winter. It sure looks like she was traveling light. I check the rest of the house and all seems to be normal.

Dad says I can come back to the house and have dinner there. I declined saying I need to start cleaning up the place and get to the post office to see what they have done with our mail.

I contacted our garden service and explained there had been a problem and could they come and clean up the place the next day and I will give them a check for what we owe them and for this clean-up.

The Post Office gives me a box full of mail, mostly junk and a few outstanding bills, nothing of real importance. I then stop off at the local supermarket and get some basic supplies and a dozen beers.

I picked up a pizza from our local place and that night I sat in my favorite chair, watching TV for the first time in months. It feels really good sitting there eating pizza with a cold beer in my own home.

CNN news has just started when my mobile phone rings. I pick it up, but I don't recognize the number.

"Hello,"

"Hello, is that Mr. Grant Hughes?" says a female voice.

"Yes, this is he," "How can I help you?"

"My name is Clare Gibbs. I'm a private investigator working for Insurance Investigations Inc. I have been following your case and I have some information that may be helpful in your new trial. I was wondering if I could set up an appointment to come and see you."

"Can't we discuss whatever you have, over the phone?" I ask.

"No —— not really Mr. Hughes. I would rather speak to you one on one if you don't mind. I have a picture that I would like to show you. I could fly down any day that is suitable for you."

"Where would you be flying in from? "I ask.

"I'm stationed in Boston, but my job takes me all over the US."

"Well, if you have been following my case, then you know that I'm out on bail and unemployed. So, I have plenty of spare time. Pick a day and come down."

"Thank you, I'll get a flight tomorrow and I'll see you in the early afternoon if that's okay?"

"Where would you like to meet?" I say.

"Can we meet at your house, it's more private if you don't mind?"

"Okay that's fine, let me give you my address," I say.

"No, that's okay, I already have it. I will rent a car from the airport. I'll text you when I pick up the car, that way you'll get my ETA. See you tomorrow.

With that, she hangs up. Must be quite an efficient organization, she already has all my details, I say to myself. Should be interesting to hear what she has to say.

The next day the garden service arrives, and the place soon looks neat and tidy again with the grass mowed, and all the leaves picked up. Emptying the refrigerator reminded me of the last time I threw something in the trash, it got me put in jail. I suppose those memories will be with me for the rest of my life.

At 1:37 p.m. Clare Gibbs texts me saying she

will be leaving the car rental service now, so I estimate she will take approximately 35 to 40 minutes, depending on the traffic to get here. My estimate is not far out as 45 minutes later she pulls into the driveway. I watch her through the front window, get out of the car, look around, then she goes to the back and gets her computer bag. She is slender in build, say 5'7" with brown hair cut shoulder length. I would say mid to late thirties, it's always difficult to judge a woman's age. She was wearing grey pants with a matching grey London blazer that covered her hips. Her sleeves were slightly rolled up revealing the long sleeves of a black polo shirt with a few buttons down the front. She looks vaguely familiar as she walks towards the house along the sidewalk in black wedge heeled pumps.

I open the door before she gets to the top step and I greet her. "Hi – Mrs., Ms. Gibbs?" I say.

"Just Clare will do fine," she says as she stretches out her hand to shake mine in a firm grasp.

"Come in," I say. "Can I take your jacket, or are you comfortable with it on?"

"Thanks, I'll leave it on, I can always take it off later if I get too warm," she says.

"So where would you like to sit, at the dining room table or in the den?"

"I think the dining room would be just fine thanks," she says.

"Okay follow me," I say, as we walk through into the dining room, "take a seat anywhere. Can I get you something to drink? Coffee, tea, OJ, sorry I don't have any fizzy drinks, I do have water, but sorry no ice. My ice maker has not got back to normal yet, my fridge had to be defrosted?"

"Water without the ice will be fine thanks," and she puts her laptop shoulder bag on the table.

When I get back with the water, she is looking at the photo display on the sideboard. She has a picture frame in her hand and turns to me and asks, "Is this Jason in his baseball uniform?"

"Yes," I say. "How do you know Jason, my son?"

She puts the picture back on the dresser, pulls out a chair, and sits down.

"Mr. Hughes, as I said, we have been following your case right from the start, that's why I know about your son."

"Wait a minute, — I know now where I've seen you. You were the lady with the elderly portly gent that was sitting in the second row on the left in court every day. My wife sat near you a few times. Am I right?"

"Quite right Mr. Hughes, I must tell my partner you referred to him as a portly elderly gent, he'll get a kick out of that. He is mostly referred to as the 'fat old fart' by most people we know," she said with a smile.

"So, you left him behind, coming here on your own to face a murderer, rapist, women beater, and an arsonist in a house all alone, are you out of your mind?"

"Well, thanks for your concern Mr. Hughes, but firstly we suspect you are not guilty, and secondly I'm an ex-police officer and I'm carrying." She flips her blazer flap back to reveal her sidearm.

"What do you mean you suspect I'm innocent? Who the fuck are you? You come in here and you tell me you suspect I'm not guilty, how the hell do you know that? How long have you known and not said anything?"

"Calm down Mr. Hughes. Let me explain. My partner's name is Joe Phillips and we both work for the same investigation company. He's showing me the ropes before he retires. It's a long story, maybe I'll tell you about it if we have time later. Let's see how things develop here with what we have first. The only reason he isn't with me here today is that he is not well. He is suffering from severe COPD and he should be in hospital, but he is a stubborn old fool and won't listen to anybody."

"Long before I joined this investigation firm, Joe had been assigned the insurance case of the Croning senior's boat called the Mystical, that mysteriously went missing off the Gulf of Maine. Did you know about that accident?"

"Yes, I did, but only recently from my sister-in-law over the weekend, when it was alleged, I shot her husband. She told me about it in one of our conversations."

"Although you may not know this, it's standard practice for insurance companies to do reference checks on people taking out large insurance policies, and your brother-in-law's late father's name came up on the system. As his boat disappeared or sank under suspicious circumstances, and because they had the same second name this immediately raised a red flag. The insurance company Croning used to insure his boat contacted our company, Insurance Investigation Inc., and Joe was assigned the investigation job."

"Now when the Croning's had the interior of the boat remodeled and the insurance evaluators went out to see the finished work on the boat, Joe went along with them. He confirmed exactly what you described as being the new inside layout."

"Fucking hell, so you knew that I had been on that boat and that I was speaking the truth, but you guys didn't come forward and say anything. Why didn't you guys speak up?"

"Sorry Mr. Hughes, I knew you would be upset, that's why I had to come down to see you personally."

"Upset," I said, "doesn't even come near to how I feel at the moment."

I get up from the table and walk over to the window with my back to her.

"Have you any idea what I have been going through these past months in jail. Have you any idea what this has done to my family, my company, that I don't even own anymore. No, of course you don't, how can you fucking know how I'm feeling?" I say.

I stood looking out of the window at the freshly cut grass trying to regain my composure. Several minutes later I return to the table, sit down, and drink some water.

"Well, I suppose you have a very commendable explanation as to why you didn't come forward," I say sarcastically.

"Look, Mr. Hughes, you are correct, I have no idea how you are feeling and what you went through. I'm sorry for your losses and suffering. We acted the way we did at the time because we had our reasons. We can carry on with what I came down for, or I can just leave now, go back to Boston and things will eventually take their course. It's entirely up to you."

"Well, you are here now, so I may as well hear your side of the story, what have I got to lose?"

"Alright then, let me try and explain as best I can. It would have been pointless for either Joe or me to have tried to convince the police department that you were innocent, because we both have a somewhat strained history with the department."

"What do you mean by 'strained'?" I ask.

"I'll explain and I hope you will understand," she says.

CHAPTER15

"Joe Phillips and my late dad were on the force. They were both detectives with the Cambridge Police Department. My dad and his partner were on a stakeout one night in an old warehouse down at the dockside where a drug deal was supposedly going down. The information they initially got was sketchy. They had been hiding inside the warehouse for several hours before this expected deal took place."

"They soon realized when the thugs arrived that this was no small-time drug bust. They could see there were four or five heavily armed thugs on the scene; this was a well-organized deal going down. They called for heavy backup, however the deputy superintendent on standby brushed it off and said he was not calling out the SWAT team. He would dispatch other detectives and a patrol car in the area to assist my dad and his partner and they should take care of it. The other detectives were Joe and his partner."

"The patrol car in the area was first on the scene, coming under automatic fire from a sniper who had been placed somewhere on a roof, overlooking the warehouse. Both officers took hits in the arms and legs but managed to get back around the corner of the warehouse. Their radio had been hit so they couldn't call it in. Joe and his partner came in from the other direction and experienced the same heavy gunfire, Joe was hit in the shoulder and leg. His partner who was driving fortunately wasn't hit and they accelerated past the warehouse zigzagging to avoid shots coming from the roof. When they were out of firing range, they immediately called again for more backup."

"Inside the warehouse, my dad and his partner heard all the shooting, thinking that the cavalry had arrived, they came out of their hiding and started shooting. They were outgunned with their handguns, the hoods had automatic weapons, resulting in dad and his partner getting killed."

"By the time, the cavalry did arrive, the party was all over, the hoods had gone with their drugs, leaving two dead officers and three wounded."

"It became a big political drama, everybody blaming everyone else. The press had a field day. My dad, now dead, took the full brunt of the blame for not obeying his commanding officer's orders and not engaging until the SWAT team arrived. Joe, who was always too outspoken, hearing over the radio my dad's call at the time, asking for heavy back-up, and the superintendent telling my dad to handle it, he said what they were saying was a load of political bullshit, and he would not back down. He was subsequently dismissed from duty as unsuitable, insubordinate, and uncooperative, or some bullshit clause they dug up in the HR file to get him out. So, with his history, there was no way the Cambridge DA was going to listen to his story. There would have been all sorts of accusations like, 'How much is he paying you, Joe, to make this statement?'"

"Mr. Hughes, do you see the predicament we were in?"

"Okay, I see. The Cambridge DA would never have taken Joe's word for it; they would have needed to see the boat for themselves before they would even consider that evidence. You also mentioned you had a strained relationship with the police department. Would this be the same police department in Cambridge?"

"Yes, the very same one that Joe worked at."

"Okay I get it, you and this Joe Phillips guy worked together in the police force in the Cambridge Precinct."

"No, not quite. I only knew Joe because he worked with my late dad back then," she says.

"So how did you and Joe get mixed up in the insurance investigation business together?" I ask,

"It was about six months ago when my front door intercom buzzed, and a husky voice asked if I'm Clare Gibbs. I replied, 'yes but whatever you're selling I don't want any, goodbye.' The voice said, 'Wait Clare wait, it's me, Joe." I told him I didn't know any Joe, and he should get lost. Then he explained 'Clare it's Joe Philips, remember I worked with your dad.' Then I knew who was speaking, and replied 'Christ Joe, what are you doing here? How did you find me? I'll open for you to come on up. I'm on the third floor, number 22.'

"After what seems an age there's a knock on the door and there he is, standing leaning over holding onto the door frame, panting, completely out of breath he must be 190 lb. if not more and Joe is short maybe 5-8. I thought he was going to have a heart attack right there and then. He complained, still struggling to breathe, 'Jees Clare, there should be a law against landlords not installing elevators in buildings like this!' "I helped him inside, inviting him to sit in the living room on the couch, but he reckoned I'd need a crane to get him out again. He preferred to sit in the kitchen, and after drinking some water, and a few minutes later, he took out the rescue inhaler, taking two puffs and told me he has COPD." "I asked him how he found me. He said he still had friends in the department, bumping into one the other day who mentioned my little ordeal with the mayor's son, and he pulled some strings and got my address. He told me he wasn't well and needed to retire, his boss asked if he knew of anyone who he could recommend as a replacement. Joe said he couldn't think of anyone reliable until he heard about me from his friend. He told me about his job and suggested we go and see his boss, which we did. After a few more interviews, I liked what I saw and heard, and here I am. As I said before, Joe's health is not good, he needs to pack it in, and I will eventually take over from him." "How long had you been in the force?" I ask, "About eleven and a half years." "Wow, that's quite a few years, what rank did you reach?" "Detective Sergeant." "So, this incident that took place must have been quite serious, to make you quit after eleven years." "Well, it's a rather long story, you sure you want to hear it?"

"I'm not going anywhere. You've come all this way from Boston, so the least I can do is hear you out, so go ahead."

"OK, but first can I take you up on that offer of something to drink?"

"Yes sure, what can I get you?"

"A beer would be nice if you have one."

"Sure, they are fresh from the market, I picked them up yesterday."

"Glass, — or is the bottle okay?"

"Bottle is just fine, thanks."

I get two beers out of the fridge, open them, hand her one, and sit down opposite her.

"Okay,— let's hear your story."

"One of my colleagues tried to rape me in the women's locker rooms."

"Whoa!— no, not another rape thing" I say.

"Yes, it was a Friday evening, my partner

Donald Stanley and I had just come back into the precinct from a stakeout at a bar down in West Cambridge, it must have been close to midnight."

"Excuse my interruption so this is the same precinct as the one that I was detained at?"

"Oh yes, this is the same one you got arrested at, Robert W. Healy,"

"Okay interesting, so you started there a few years after Joe Phillips left?"

"Yes, that's correct."

"Sorry, carry on,"

"Anyway, we go up to the general offices on the second floor, the place is like a morgue. Don says he's going to his desk to file a quick report. I go to the women's locker rooms to clean up. I go into the washroom, have a pee, and walk back to the lockers. My locker is situated towards the back. I opened it, removed my gun from my purse, and put them both on the top shelf where I had left my holster and belt. Remember we were dressed for nightlife, sort of casual, I was wearing a short skirt and a tank top and high heel pumps. I kick off my shoes and bend down to get my flat shoes at the bottom of the locker. The next thing my head and shoulders are jammed into the second shelf of the locker, my arms are trapped against my side."

"The next thing my skirt is up, and my panties are being pulled down. I'm shouting and screaming, trying to straighten up and whoever is holding me keeps banging me back into the locker. My nose hits the shelf and there's blood streaming out of it. He tells me to shut the fuck up and enjoy the ride. By this time, he has my panties down and around my ankles. I can feel his dick against my ass. I push back again as hard as I can. He swears at me and slams me back into the locker. Hits me in my

213

kidneys with his fists and shouts 'Shut up you little cock teaser bitch.'"

"Next thing I hear a thump and a grunt, and he's off me. I straighten up and Don is standing over this guy rubbing his knuckles. I pull up my panties and look at my assailant and recognize him as Patrol Officer Archer Lance, the mayor's son. I didn't want to believe it at first but, yes it was him, the drunk and useless scumbag Archer Lance."

"I was so mad. I was insanely mad. I snatched my gun from the top shelf of the locker and walked up to where this scumbag was lying on the floor rubbing his jaw. I lean over him with blood from my nose dripping all over his face. I put the gun to his head, cock it, and said, 'say goodbye you fucking scumbag.'"

"Wow!" I said interrupting her. "That must have taken some restraint, not to have pulled the trigger right there and then."

"Yes, you are right. If it weren't for my partner, I would be in jail now. He kept saying 'Clare, Clare, don't do it, don't do it, he's not worth it.'"

"I just stood there, — for I don't know how long with both hands on my gun and the barrel pressed hard against his temple. Eventually, I backed off. I was shaking and I was so furious. He was scared maybe for the first time in his whole fucking life."

"Don kept saying to me 'it's okay Clare, it's okay, it didn't happen, you're okay, take your things and get out of here, go, go.'"

"I took my stuff out of my locker, banged it closed, and started to walk away. By this time, the scumbag Lance had got some of his drunken macho courage back. Realizing he's not going to die, he shouts. 'Hey Don, why don't we both do her, she'd like that.' Don turns and kicks him a few times in the crotch and he doubles up on the floor moaning. Don tells him he's a fucking disgrace to the force and that's how I left them."

"You must have been so mad. Did you go home then?"

"Yes, but I went into the bathroom first and washed my hands and face. I had blood all over my blouse and skirt. There was nothing I could do about it. I looked like a total mess and had to stuff some toilet paper up my nose to stop the bleeding. I walked back out into the locker room; they were still there with Lance on the floor. I shook my head in disgust and went home."

"As soon as I got home, I jumped into the shower and put it on as hot as I could stand it, I felt so violated. I just wanted to wash away the feeling of his hands on my body, his dick on my ass, and the smell of his alcoholic breath. It was his every presence I needed to wash away. I wanted to forget it ever happened, but I knew that tomorrow I would have to file a report and it would all come back again and again, every time I had to repeat it to some committee or board."

"When I got out of the shower, I slipped into my sweats and made myself a hot drink. I was sitting on the side of the bed when my mobile phone rang. It was Don, my partner. He wanted to know how I was making out. I told him I was okay and thanks for literally saving my ass."

"He tells me he just had a call from mayor Vernon Lance. He says the mayor was most upset about what happened. He says I should tell you that he is so sorry for the actions of his son."

"How did the mayor get to know about it so quickly I ask?"

"Don had dropped the scumbag back at the

mayor's home, as he was in no state to drive."

"Don then tells me the mayor is going to recommend a transfer of Archer to another precinct. He says there is no need for us to make out a report that morning. We should just keep it between the four of us and the mayor will see that there's a nice promotion in the system waiting for me in the future. But what got to me then was when Don said, 'Clare, let's face it, nothing really happened to you, other than you got a bloody nose.'"

"Hell, I bet you were pissed," I interrupted again.

"Pissed, —— was an understatement, Mr. Hughes, I was fuming —— fucking, hopping mad, I wanted to jump down that phone and kill him."

"I shouted at him over the phone, 'Don are you for fucking real? — If you hadn't interceded, he would have raped me. You want me to just drop this like it's just some piece of shit I picked up on my shoe in the street?'"

"What did he have to say?" I ask.

"He said, 'Claire, you know as well as I do, the superintendent is not going to go up against Mayor Lance. So, whatever you say doesn't matter. Archer is going to walk into another job in some other department or precinct.' "

"I said to him, 'but Don you were there, you were my witness, you ditched the asshole. How many other women in the department has he groped and how many have filed complaints about his lecherous behavior? He's got to fall this time.' "

"He says, 'Sorry Clare I can't be that witness. I have a young family, two kids in school, you know I'll lose my job sooner than later. I can't afford to be without a job, sorry Clare they have me by the

216

balls.' "

"I tell him 'fuck you, Don,' I switch the phone off and throw it on the bed in absolute disgust. I know it wasn't him. He was just caught up in the fucking political ass-creeping bullshit that we all had to put up with, within the department."

"I wasn't about to go to sleep, so I get out my laptop and start to write a formal grievance complaint of sexual harassment and attempted rape against Archer Lance. When I finished, I must have read it ten times, making changes before I was happy. I printed it, signed it, and put in an envelope and addressed it to the Superintendent Cambridge Police Department."

"By the time I close my laptop it's close to 4 am, so I lie on the bed in my sweats and eventually I fall asleep. I think having got it down on paper, sort of got it off my chest and because I was so exhausted, I just died."

"Yes, I remember having finished writing my ordeal down on paper and it was a sort of relief and I got some sleep after that. Did you go into the precinct that day?"

"Yes, I eventually woke up about 9 a.m. had a much-needed coffee and breakfast, got dressed, and drove into the office at around 10 am. Put my things down at my desk and walked up the stairs to the superintendent's office. I put the envelope on his secretary's desk. I told her it's a grievance complaint and to please make sure the superintendent gets it today. I then went back down to my desk. It must have been an hour later I got a call from her that I'm to come up to the sup's. office."

"When I got there, my immediate boss Lieutenant John Littleton was there seated at the conference table, with the Superintendent Mike Ross seated at the head of the table."

"I assume this was the same Mike Ross who together with Detective Alan Burns, interrogated me?" I ask.

"Oh yes, —— the very same asshole,"

"They told me to sit at the other end of the table facing the sup. He had my letter of complaint in front of him, as well as a file I assumed was my personal file. He opened the file, glanced at it, and looked up at me and asked me how long I have been in the force?"

"I told him eleven and almost six months."

'Six as a Patrol officer, three as detective and two-plus as detective Sergeant,' he says, 'and I see you also have a degree in Criminal Justice.'

He then said, 'Sergeant Gibbs, the allegations that you have made against one of your colleagues is quite dramatic and unsettling, would you not say?'

I said, 'it wasn't an allegation Sir, it actually happened.'

"I could already see where this was going and the hair on the back of my neck was starting to bristle. I thought fuck them, boss or no boss, they are going to hear what I have to say."

'Sir, with all due respect, an allegation is a statement made without necessarily giving any proof of any wrongdoing. I can assure you that what I have reported in my letter of complaint is factual and yes, dramatic.'

"The sup. was somewhat put out by my brusqueness, but soon recovered his composure and asked if I have any witnesses to this alleged incident?"

"I told him 'Yes, as you have read in my

218

complaint, my partner Detective Donald Stanley was there.'"

They must have had Don waiting on call somewhere close. He buzzed his secretary, asked her to call Detective Stanley, and tell him to come up to his office. We waited a few minutes and Stanley knocked and came in. The sup. asked him straight out if he had been anywhere near the women's lockers at around 12:05 a.m. this morning. He said no, he had not been anywhere near the women's lockers at that time of the morning, he said he'd been writing up his report at his desk at that time. I felt bad for him, knowing full well he was caught up in all the political bullshit that goes on, but I'm still pissed at Don. I could see he is very embarrassed and uncomfortable.

The sup. looked at me and said, 'Well Sergeant Gibbs, it seems you don't have a witness and your statement is purely an allegation, and quite a serious one if I must say so,' and he had this smirk on his fucking face. I felt like climbing over the table and taking his tie and throttling him. 'Of course, you would know with your degree in Criminal Justice,' he went on to say, 'this could be classified as slander. You could be sued in a civil court for something like this.'

"That will be just fine superintendent, because then I will get the opportunity to show the court the two pictures I took as I left the locker room on my mobile phone's camera, of the witness Donald Stanley and the scumbag that tried to rape me, lying on the floor. The picture even shows the date and time. It will be interesting to see how they explain that away." I say.

"Oh, and for my safety, I have emailed a copy to myself and a very good friend, saying what to do with the pictures if anything should ever happen to me," I say.

"Christ, I would have loved to have been a fly on the wall in there."

"Yes, there was a deathly silence in the room. Eventually the sup. dismissed Donald with a warning not to speak to anyone about this. They told me to step outside the room and wait in the secretary's office. After about twenty minutes I got called back into the office again and the sup. informed me I'm to immediately go home on full pay. I'm not even allowed to go back into the general office. I shouldn't speak to anyone about this and they will contact me in a few days."

"Three days went by and late on the third day I got a call from the sup's secretary informing me to come into the office at 6:30 p.m. I should come straight up to his office on the third floor and not to go to any of the other departments."

"I got there, and the third floor is empty, not even the secretary is there. My boss Lieutenant John Littleton invited me in and directed me to a chair. The sup. was at the conference table, along with the state attorney, Matthew Gordon, to make sure everything is above board. They had a proposal they wanted to put forward to me, but first I had to listen to the sup. spouting off about what a great person my dad was and his exemplary record in the force, how I had shot up through the ranks to Detective Sergeant in such a short space of time and all that bullshit, and as this unfortunate incident could destroy the professions of so many, it would be better —— bla-bla-bla."

"Anyway, what they proposed was a retirement package for twenty years at my present salary, in exchange for all the pictures. I told them no deal, because a few years down the line if they suddenly decide to change their policy and rules, just like they're always doing, and I'd be left with nothing."

"I told them I want retirement on my present salary for life. They wouldn't get any pictures, as they are my insurance policy. They could take it or leave it. If they cared to leave it, I would take this to my union, and we'd go to court. I got up and left the room."

"Wow! Clare, you've got some balls, sorry just a figure of speech. Did they agree to your terms?"

"You see Mr. Hughes——"

I stop her and ask her to call me Grant.

"Okay, Grant. You see, I had nothing to lose really, my career in the Police Force was finished as I had reached the pinnacle of my career. My ambition of making a superintendent was a pipe dream. I was not politically connected and certainly didn't have the family background to get me into higher circles to mix with the politically correct crowd."

"Two days later I got a call requesting that I go to the district attorneys' offices in Lower Cambridge to see Mr. Matthew Gordon. When I got there, he had all the necessary papers ready for me to sign. I was told not to go back to the department, I was to hand in my gun, badge, keys to my desk and locker and he would see that my personal things would be cleared out and brought to my home."

"I suppose Joe knows all about this?"

"Yes, I told him about it, and he was thrilled to hear I had put one over on the department for a change. He wanted to know if I really took the pictures."

"So, what did you tell him?"

"I told him he asked too many questions."

CHAPTER 16

"Now Mr. Hughes, —— sorry Grant, maybe now you can understand why it would have been completely a waste of time telling the DA that we thought you were innocent. With my department record, they would have just laughed at me and told me to F-off. Without the boat as proof, you haven't got a leg to stand on. It is our objective to find the boat, not necessarily to prove you are innocent but to get the insurance company's money back, that's our job. Does that answer your question somewhat?"

"Okay Clare I get the picture; I can understand now why you didn't come forward with this information earlier. So where does this leave me and what are you guys doing to try and find the missing boat?"

"Sorry to say this Grant, but you must also understand where my company is coming from. Their main objective is to recover insurance fraud. Your verdict doesn't even feature in their investigation. We have no obligation towards you. The only reason I'm here is because there is a connection between our investigation and your case. We are not only representing the one insurance company that insured the boat. We have the three other insurance companies for whom we are doing an investigation and they are all linked to your case."

"Sorry Clare, you lost me there, what three other insurances are you referring to?"

"Well, there's the death of Robert Croning, that's one policy. Then the cars that burnt in the fire, they are a separate policy. The Croning's house destroyed in the fire is a separate policy and his company Croning Investments, Key-man Insurance is a separate policy. As you know from your trial, it's a sizable sum of cash that these insurance companies have forked out, so they are damn well interested to find out if fraud has been committed. That's why we were present every day at your trial to see what leads we could pick up."

"Of course, Clare I see where you are coming from, this is not about me, it's all about the fucking money the insurance companies have paid out. As you say, I don't even feature in this, so why have I been listening to you for the past hour? Your story was very touching but thanks, I'm still out on bail, have another trial date next year and who knows if I'll get a verdict of not guilty," I said with some frustration in my voice.

"Look, Grant, get down off your self-pity high horse. I told you on the phone before I came down, that I thought we may be able to help each other. OK, now I want you to look at this picture, it's a bit grainy. Tell me if you recognize the person in the picture on the right, standing at the counter."

Clare opens her laptop shoulder bag, takes out a full-page photo, and slides it across the table to me.

I look at it for a few seconds and look up at her and say, "This is Bob Croning, must have been taken some time ago before my time. I never saw him with a beard and long dark hair."

"Are you sure it's him?"

"Absolutely, I'd know that face anywhere, where did you get that picture of him?"

"Well, now, the situation starts to get even more interesting," she says. "Let me explain. Remember I told you earlier that Joe had seen the Croning's boat with the insurance assessors?"

"Yes, I remember you said he went and saw it after they had done the modifications."

"What I didn't tell you was that at the time he secretly installed a miniature tracking device in one of the light switch outlets. The reason I didn't tell you this before was because I wasn't sure how far to trust you. I'm sure you know it's illegal to install any such device on anyone's equipment without their prior knowledge and permission," she says.

"So why haven't you been able to find the boat if it had a tracking device fitted?" I ask.

"You may remember your illustrious sister-in-law only reported the boat missing to the police about a week after it went missing. Then another week went by before she reported it to the insurance company giving them the police case number and all the details. Then it took them another week to give us the case to investigate."

"We immediately got the tracking company to activate the device on the boat. They tried and there was no feedback from the device. What we assumed happened was the boat had either sunk, or it was stored somewhere, and the batteries had been disconnected. We were hoping it was the latter."

"Damn that was unfortunate," I said.

"Well, yes but hear this. Four days ago, we got a lucky break. We got a call from the tracking company who reported they had received a brief signal from the boat. They had pinpointed it to an address in New Jersey."

"In New Jersey," I said, "that's brilliant."

"Wait, it gets even more amazing," she says. "I flew down there the day before yesterday and saw the manager, Rory Smith at Bluefin Marina Sales and Service, situated in Cape May. Once I explained who I was, showed him my credentials, reports, and dockets from the police of the missing boat, he was very cooperative and helpful."

"Rory said they bought the boat approximately six weeks ago from a guy that sailed it,—— he thought, from New York. The guy told him he was getting a divorce and had to sell the boat as part of the settlement. The manager said he gave the guy $145K for it, which he thought was a fair price for a boat with those features."

"Did you see the boat?"

"No, he had just sold it the day before."

"You're joking, he sold it before you got down there. Didn't you call before you went down to make sure it was there and that it was the right boat?"

"Yes, sure I called the guy," — "Hi! Sir, sorry to worry you, the illegal tracking device that I installed in one of your boats has just sent me a signal. Could you please go and substantiate it for me?" "I think fucking NOT," she says, getting all tense.

"Yes, sorry, – stupid of me, I guess not."

"Look it's getting late Grant, it's already dark and I have to find a place to crash. If you are free tomorrow, we can pick this up again. I have to make some calls back to the office and update Joe."

"Yes, I'm sorry the afternoon has just flown by. This time of the year it gets dark very early. Look without being presumptuous, you are more than welcome to crash here. We have a guest room that is all made up. It won't be inconvenient, and the company would be nice. We could then carry on where we left off. What do you say?"

"Well, —— that's very nice, you sure it's not

going to be a problem?"

"Look around, — it's only me and I have no problem, so if you want to get your bag from the car, I'll show you where you can bed down."

Clare gets her overnight bag from the car and I take her upstairs and show her the guest room and bathroom. I leave her to make her calls.

Thirty-five minutes later she comes down. This time she isn't wearing her blazer and I cannot help but notice her shapely figure. She has also removed her holster and gun, so I gather she feels comfortable with me. Anyway, there is no way I'm going to mess with any ex-police officer. Clare looks like the sort of person who can handle herself very well, with or without a firearm.

"For dinner, we have a few choices. We can go out, there are some nice places within fifteen minutes, we can have leftover pizza, or I can make a mean double cheeseburger with a salad."

"I don't know — but a mean burger sounds good to me," she laughs.

I take the patties and cheese slices for the hamburgers out of the fridge as well as the fixings for a salad, open a bag of fresh rolls, and start the grill on the deck. Thirty minutes later we both have a glass of wine and a double cheeseburger in front of us at the dining room table. We sit eating and discussing my case in a fair bit of detail.

Clare says, "As you can see from my case and what happened to Joe, those assholes in Cambridge Precinct aren't going to cut you any slack. Even when they are so wrong and it's staring them in their fucking faces, they will disagree and twist it this way and that way, so they always come out smelling of roses."

We clear the plates, pack them in the

dishwasher and go to sit in the den.

"Okay," I say, sitting down in the comfortable sofa chair. "I'm anxious to hear what else you found out in New Jersey."

"Well, as you can imagine I was as disappointed as you are, learning that I had just missed seeing the boat. I ask Rory the manager for the name of the guy who sold it to him. He gets out the file, pages through the papers, and hands me a copy of the bill of sale. The name Mark G. Edwards appears on it with a New York address and driver license. I take down all his details and call them through to Joe later that day, who said he would check on them. While I was talking to the manager, I noticed that the premises have CCTV, so asked him if the CCTV system was working which it was, and whether he had the day's recording when Mark Edwards came in."

"He called one of his staff members and asked them to have a look at the bill of sale date recording. It takes a while but then he showed me a few clips of the guy. I asked him if he can make me a copy of the DVD, but he told me the law doesn't permit that. He allowed me to take a picture of the screen with my cell phone camera, which I did and the picture I showed you is the one you said is Bob Croning. Well, that is the same guy who calls himself Mark Edwards."

"That's — uncanny, how can that be Bob. He is dead and buried," I say.

"Yes,—— that's the big mystery. When I told Joe, he said he knew there was something fishy about your case. So, if that is Bob Croning in the picture and you are sure of that, then who the hell is the dead guy buried in his grave?"

"We have to be absolutely sure that the guy in

the picture I showed you is Robert Croning and not Mark Edwards."

Clare gets up from the couch and goes up to the guest room, returning with the photo.

"Here," she says handing me the photo, "take another careful look at it, make sure you see what you think you're seeing."

I take the picture, get up, and hold it under the light. The more I looked at it, the more I'm convinced it was Bob. The features are his and no mistaking those dark black eyes.

"It's definitely his picture," I say. "My wife has a photo album of family pictures, let me go and see if she has one with Bob in it and you can tell me what you think."

I go upstairs, search through the filing cabinet and find some of Diane's old photo albums. I quickly page through them and find one where Bob is in the picture. Fortunately, it's a clear shot of him and Sylvia at some function. I pull it out of the insert, pleased with my find, go back downstairs, and show it to Clare.

"Here have a look at this, see what you think?"

"She looks at the two pictures together and says, 'Yes, I must agree there is a definite likeness there.'"

"Now what?"

"Nothing now. Joe is going to contact the office first thing in the morning. The office has contacts in the FBI. He will ask them to get the FBI to check on this guy Mark Edward's credentials. Depending on what they come up with, we may have to go down to Cape May for you to see the clips and make a positive ID of Robert Croning."

"Okay that sounds like a plan, but how come your office has contacts in the FBI?"

"Grant our company is big, it's international, and we have offices in most major cities in all the first world countries. Because of our international connections and investigations, we deal a lot with foreign agents and law enforcement, hence our office here in the US is regularly involved with the FBI."

"Wow! I hadn't realized that it was such a big organization."

"Oh, believe it! If you think insurance of fixed assets like buildings, cars, planes, ships, and property is big, what about the financial world, banks, financial institutions, stocks and bonds, patents, it's huge. People have made a profession out of being insurance fraudsters. Insurance fraud is a multibillion-dollar enterprise."

"A multibillion-dollar fraud enterprise, you make it sound like a business."

"That's right, most people don't know that, but yes, it is a business. Very few people know companies like ours even exist," she says.

"It's late, I think I'm going to call it a day," says Clare, "I'll see you in the morning. What time do you normally get up?"

"Well, about seven unfortunately for you, I will be using my alarm clock that you no doubt heard about in my trial. You will more than likely have a rude awakening because you will hear it."

"Aha! That's good, because if you were hoping I was going to come and give you your sister-in-law's routine of waking you, you better think again," she says, with a grin on her face and disappears up the stairs.

The next morning we finish breakfast and I pack away the dishes and clean the kitchen. Clare has gone back up to the guest room to brush her teeth.

Her mobile is on the sideboard and is buzzing. I pick it up and answer it.

"Hello, this is Clare's phone."

The croaky voice on the other end said, "Hi you must be Grant, this is Joe, is Clare around?"

"Yes sure, she's upstairs brushing her teeth or something of that nature,"

"Okay," he says, "tell her to call me as soon as she's finished with the nature stuff," and he hangs up.

Ten minutes later Clare comes down and I give her the message.

"Sorry," she says, "I should have taken my phone with me upstairs. I'll go and make this call and see what news Joe has." She picks up her phone and goes back upstairs.

After what seems an age, she eventually comes down.

"Wow! A lot has transpired since last night. First things first. Joe has taken a turn for the worse and is being admitted into hospital later this morning. His wife will take him there. We have both been nagging him for weeks to go and get treatment, but he is a stubborn old fool, and now his breathing is so bad he has to be admitted."

"Now it seems the FBI has taken an interest in your case after they got all the details from Joe. Because this is no longer in the Massachusetts region, it automatically becomes an FBI case, so they are sending two guys from Philly within the next hour or so to pick us up and we are going to Cape May."

"Whoa, what about my ankle bracelet alarm?"

"You and your freaking alarms, I nearly crapped myself this morning, I thought the house was on fire when your stupid alarm went off. As to that bracelet thing, don't worry, you are now officially FBI property. The Cambridge DA no longer has any jurisdiction in this case. The FBI is taking it over. This is going to piss-off the DA and the Cambridge precinct big time, man I wish I could be a fly on the wall when they get the message," Clare says with a smile on her face.

"Did they perhaps find out who this Mark Edwards is?"

"Yes, apparently he has been missing for some years. He just went off the radar so to speak, it doesn't look like he has any relatives or family. So, another mystery. Look I suppose we better get ourselves organized, these FBI agents will be here soon, and they don't like to be kept waiting,"

The two FBI agents arrive about forty minutes later. We are ready and waiting, sitting in the dining room. I see their car pull in behind Clare's rental. We go outside. They get out and come over and introduce themselves as Agent Miles Jackson and Jerry Cooper. I couldn't help but think of all the movies I've seen where cops say, 'Okay, here come the suits,' and you see these guys arrive dressed in smart suits and highly polished shoes. Well, these FBI agents didn't look at all like that. They were very casual, wearing grey pants, a jacket, and no necktie.

The trip down to Cape May took just over two hours and the agents questioned me virtually the whole way. By the time we arrived, I think they had a particularly good picture in their minds of the whole case and how it unfolded.

The Manager at Bluefin Marina Sales and Service is expecting us. Clare called warning him she would be visiting again, but this time with the

FBI.

He already has the DVD player hooked up to a monitor when we arrived. He has his tech guy go back on the DVD to the day before when the boat was still moored on the dock. The security camera is mounted high on a post and some distance from the dock, but you can see a person tying up the boat and when we zoom in, I'm sure it's Bob. I also recognize the boat and I can just make out the name Taimen written on the side. We then switch to the scene in the store where two guys are standing at the counter. Here we get a clearer look at him, we freeze the picture to give me a better look. There's absolutely no doubt in my mind that this picture is Bob, despite the beard and the darker long hair.

"Well," said Miles, "If your identification of that person is who you say it is Mr. Hughes, then you have certainly been framed. I must say from the family photo you showed us there is a definite resemblance. But the proof of the pudding will be in the eating, so to speak, when we have that body exhumed and we see who is in that grave."

Miles tells the manager "Oh — we will be needing a copy or preferably the original of that video footage please."

"We will also need the name and address of the person who just bought the boat because the boat is listed as stolen. Buying stolen goods is a crime, although unbeknown to Bluefin Marina, it still amounts to the same thing. The police will be confiscating the boat at some time from the new owner after this whole mess is cleared up. The Manager says these things happen and that's why we take out insurance." Clare looks at me, shakes her head, and chuckles.

"I don't know about you guys," said Miles, "but I can really do with something to eat."

"You are always hungry," said Agent Cooper, "you've got a python in that stomach of yours. Look at you, you never put on an ounce and you eat like a horse."

"Aww cut with the lecture, find us somewhere to eat."

We find a Burger King along the road and pull in. The three guys have burgers, Miles has a double with fries and crispy onion rings, which he polishes off before we finish our singles. Clare has a Caesar salad.

On the way back the two agents question me as to where I think they may find Sylvia and Diane. I tell them I have no idea, only that I suspect Sylvia has bought a catamaran boat she'd told me about, and that they may have sailed off into the blue yonder somewhere. But now of course with Bob being still alive, this theory goes 'poof out the porthole' as the DA would say.

"Well, no, — that may not be too far from the truth," says Agent Cooper. "Maybe this was their plan all along. Your brother-in-law and his wife both being water lovers, maybe they planned this all along. Collecting the insurance money, she wires the money to a local bank account that he has set up. He takes some cash and buys a nice —— what size 'cat' did you say, Mr. Hughes?"

"My sister-in-law said she would love a 35/40 Ft. 'cat,' fully equipped for long sea trips."

"Okay, he buys this 40 Ft. 'cat,' fully rigged," he says. "Then your brother-in-law with his vast experience of foreign finance buries the rest of the money in some offshore bank, where we have no jurisdiction. Then he meets the girls and they all sail away. What do you think about that scenario?" says Agent Cooper?"

"I like it except, if he has the boat and the cash stowed away in some offshore account, why would he need two women and a young kid hanging around his neck cramping his style?"

"Yes," said Agent Jackson, "I can't see any advantage for him having three extra people trailing along with him. —— Okay he will need a crew, but he could always hire a crew with that sort of bread tucked away."

"Well, you can well believe that my sister-in-law would not have let him go off with a bag of loot and her dreamboat. She would have made sure she had some watertight hold on him, making sure her husband didn't screw her —— like she screwed me!" I say.

"Point taken Mr. Hughes, we can speculate forever, but we won't be able to do anything until we get that body exhumed," said Agent Cooper.

We are dropped off back at my house later that day and they tell me they would be in touch as soon as they have the body exhumed and identified. They tell me I am to assume I am still out on bail and nothing has changed until they say so.

Back inside the house, I say to Clare.

"I don't think I thanked you for coming down to see me. I'm glad you persuaded me to listen to your story otherwise we may not be in this position now. I feel quite elated knowing that this whole thing is going to end sooner than I expected. Are you flying home tonight, or can I persuade you to have dinner with me and it won't be a hamburger? We can go somewhere nice I promise."

"You know Grant, as much as I want to, I

should get back. I need to see how bad Joe is and brief him of today's accomplishments. He is going to be ecstatic. I'll take you up on that dinner sometime later, we are still going to cross paths several times before this case is over, believe me."

With that, she goes and gets her bag from upstairs, comes down and we shake hands and say goodbye. I walk her to her car, and she gets in and opens the window.

"I'm glad I got to spend some time with you, Grant."

"Yes, me too Clare, take care," and she backs out of the driveway.

Back inside the first thing I do is to call my dad and give him the basic details of the past two days. He tells me to get my PJ's and toothbrush, close the house, and come over. This news calls for a celebration with them and I wasn't staying alone tonight. So that's exactly what I do.

CHAPTER 17

In the morning I call Adrian and give him the news and he is delighted.

"We're going to sue their fucking asses off, just you wait," he says.

I tell him not to jump to any conclusions, as the FBI still must dig up the body, identify it, do all the forensic analysis and toxicology studies to see how this guy died. The FBI guys were telling me in the car they would want to know if this John Doe was drunk or drugged before he was shot.

"Remember, Adrian, my clever sister-in-law got the DA to release the body before the coroner could complete his investigation. So, they will have to do that now, to get all the evidence that may have been missed by the original coroner's office." I give him Clare's number, and he says he remembers her and the fat guy sitting in the same place every day in court. He says he will give her a call and thank her. I asked him if I'm still obligated to report to the probation officer down here now that the FBI has taken over the case? He says

"Yes, better stay within the law until this thing is final and you are cleared. Be forewarned, those probation officers can be right assholes, little power mongers, so keep your cool. You may be lucky and get a decent one who is more human. I'll check with the DA's office to see what they say about the FBI involvement and keep you posted as to how things progress."

"Okay," I say, and hang up.

I e-mail Norman and give him a quick update and ask him to call me when he's private. An hour later he calls me, and we have a long chat, he too is thrilled to hear my news. I asked him about the fix I suggested on the project.

Norman says, "Eagle Electronics has done a few dry runs, they were getting intermittent signals and they are still checking the components. In the meantime, they have built a new motherboard using another company's components. We got the new motherboard yesterday and we are busy building them back into the CPU. We hope to do some tests later this afternoon and crossing our fingers it works." He says he will keep me informed.

Two people who I'm apprehensive to call and I haven't spoken to, are our best friends Jim and Emma Curtis. I still need to thank Emma for being there for Diane and organizing the lawyer for me. I have Jim's mobile number and I think I will give him a call first and see how the reception is and take it from there.

I call and he answers, "Grant, —— fucking hell, I saw your name come up on my screen, where are you?"

"I'm at home, where are you at the moment, are you alone?"

"Yes, alone, I'm in the car on the speakerphone driving to a client. How come you're not still in jail?"

"I'm out on bail, it's a long story, I was hoping to see you guys sometime, but I was hesitant to call, I wasn't sure what sort of reception I could expect."

"Fuck Grant, we are buddies, what's this reception shit? Come over tonight if you can, we would love to see you. I'll call Emma. She hasn't heard from Diane for months. Come and have a bite with us around 6:30, if that's okay?"

"Jim that will be great, see you then."

Well, that was a relief, I don't know why I was uncertain about calling friends, but as I have been screwed and kicked in the teeth by people I trusted most, I suppose now I wasn't sure who was sitting on which side of the fence.

Jim and Emma lived on the west side of Paoli, not far from the Paoli Hospital in one of the nicer old suburbs. Jim had inherited his dad's old house when he passed several years ago, and they had remodeled the interior. They didn't have any kids, not because they didn't want any, but Emma had some problems and was not able to have kids. I know they spoke about adoption several times, but nothing ever seemed to come of it. They were always very fond of Jason and they spoiled him terribly.

I arrived there just after six, pulling into the long driveway and parked in front of their double garage. I have a bottle of red Castiglioni Chianti 2010 that I know Emma will enjoy and walk to the front door and ring the chime.

Emma opens the door and stands back and looks at me sort of up and down for a few seconds and says, "You don't even look like a convict, where's your striped PJs? Come in you stupid ass, how can you think we would treat you any differently,—— give me a hug."

Well, that was that. "Jim is in the shower, he only just got home a few minutes ago," says Emma. I put the wine on the kitchen counter, pull up a barstool, and sit and chat with her as she prepares whatever we are going to eat.

"Are you just going to sit there and stare at that bottle of wine you brought, or are you going to open it? You know where everything is," she says.

"Christ, you're just as bossy as ever, how the

hell does Jim put up with you?"

"Open the wine and stop asking stupid questions, glasses are on the table."

I open the bottle, get three glasses from the table, and pour a glass for each of us and give one to her and say, "To the future."

"Yes, I'll drink to that," she says, and we clink our glasses.

We speak about everything except me, Diane, and my sentencing. Jim comes down from upstairs and we shake hands, hug big bear hugs and chat as if we'd seen each other just weeks ago.

We finish the bottle of wine before dinner and Jim gets another bottle that's just as good and have it with our meal. After dinner, we sit in the living room and Jim pours me a hefty scotch on the rocks and he has bourbon straight up. He mixes what looks like a mean Manhattan for Emma. The gas fire is burning, the room is warm and with friends, it has a nice homey feel about it.

"Okay, Grant tell us what has happened in your life, but before you do, let me say this, — we haven't heard a thing from Diane since the day Emma spoke to you on the phone in your house months ago. Where she is, we have no idea. We only know what we have read in the various newspapers over the weeks."

So again, I tell my story, but this time of course I confirm a lot more details than I previously knew, which is very comforting now knowing I'll soon be a free man again.

Emma says, "You know Grant, for some months leading up to this whole thing, I had a feeling there was something wrong with Diane, somehow she wasn't her normal self, she sort of withdrew. We had lunch a few times and I asked her what was worrying her. She said it was her mom's Alzheimer's, it was getting worse and she was worried about it, I left it at that." "Wow! — are you saying that the two sisters and Bob had been planning this for some time? Christ Grant, I can't believe it."

"No, neither can I, but that's how it looks."

Jim, shaking his head in disgust, says, "Now little Jason is caught in the middle of all this."

"Yes, unfortunately, that's the sad part about this whole thing, he is now going to have a split family,"

After chatting with Jim and Emma, I said "Look, guys, it's late, it's been great catching up with you, but I must be on my way; I must meet with my probation officer tomorrow. Sorry for my initial reaction. I'm just so ultra-sensitive now, I suppose I'll get over it in time."

"No need to apologize, we fully understand. Look bro we are here for you any time, just shout, okay," says Jim.

I drive home through all the back roads as I don't want to be stopped by the cops close to midnight and asked to blow into a breathalyzer, because I'm sure I'm over the 0.08 limit. That's the last thing I need at this stage of my life, to be charged with DUI. Thank goodness I get home without incident and park in the garage, lock up the house, and go to bed, and have a good night's sleep.

The next morning, Friday, I have breakfast, get out the paper they gave me for the probation officer, check the address, which I enter into the GPS from my car. It was only twenty minutes away, so I thought I would leave at 9:30 giving myself time to find parking and get to their office in plenty of time.

The address is in Paoli, on the north side of the main rail line going to Philly, not the nicest of areas. As I drive over the railway bridge the GPS tells me to turn right in 160 yards into Luke Street. I drive a farther half a mile past an old rundown building and old boarded up shops that have graffiti all over them. This doesn't look like an area where the government would have an office. I drive on, the GPS instructs me to turn left at the next intersection and my destination will be on the right.

Yes, that's the address, 322 Baker Street. There's an old tennis court opposite the three-story building. The tennis court has seen better days. The fence was rusted and collapsing, the asphalt court is full of cracks with weeds growing out of them, a few black kids bounce a basketball around on the beaten-up court.

Now to find parking in this neighborhood. I must drive another two blocks before I find a spot. I'm not too happy about leaving my car here, not knowing if it will be here when I get back or if it will be broken into, but I have no option as there's no other parking in the area. I must walk briskly to get back to the probation offices to reach there in time for my 10:00 a.m. appointment.

The offices are on the second floor of the three-story, brick-face building. Three other people are waiting in the waiting room, sitting on white grubby plastic chairs. There is no receptionist, only a closed frosted glass sliding window that is shut. On the shelf next to the window is a clipboard with a pen tied to it with a piece of string. I pick it up and assume one is supposed to write one's name, case number, and time of arrival on the form.

This I do and sit down next to a young black

girl with dreadlocks, a ring in her nose, earphones plugged into her cellphone and her eyes are closed. There are two white guys, I guessed, in their late twenties/thirties. They have their heads down, stuck in their iPad playing games. Twenty minutes later the window slides open and a large hand comes out with long black painted fingernails and a half a dozen rings of various shapes and sizes on all the fingers. It clasps the clipboard and pulls it through the window. A woman calls from inside. "Vanesa Croon." The board gets placed back on the counter and the window slides closed.

Five minutes elapse and the window opens again and the same voice shouts this time.

"Vanesa, are you fucking deaf?"

There is no response from anyone sitting there, so I nudge the kid next to me and she opens her eyes and sort of half looks at me as if to say, 'what the fuck do you want.'

I say, "Are you, Vanesa?"

"What?" — she says, pulling the earplug out of her ear. I now can hear loud music coming from the earplug.

I ask, "are you, Vanesa?"

"Yeah, what of it?"

"They're calling you."

"Oh fuck," she says, jumps up and storms through the door to my right marked 'Interviewees'.

Forty minutes later she comes back out and I can see she's been crying as her mascara has run down her cheeks. She pulls her hoody up over her head and goes out of the main door.

Ten minutes later the same procedure, the window opens and the voice calls 'Taylor Jackson.' One of the guys gets up and walks through the door still with the iPad in his hand playing the game.

I ask the other guy, "Excuse me, if you don't mind me asking, what time was your appointment?"

"10 am," he says, without taking his eyes off his screen.

"So, we are all for 10 am?" I ask.

"Yeah, that's the way the bitch sets it up, don't worry you should be out of here by 12:15 pm. You're lucky, there are only three of us here today," he says.

It's 12:30 before my name is called by the person the guy called 'the bitch' and when I set eyes on her, I immediately know why. She must weigh two hundred pounds plus, blond, crew-cut hair, black eyebrows, and long false eyelashes. Three piercings in her left ear with outrageous earrings. Her upper arms are as big as my legs, with tattoos up and down both sides. She's sitting behind a cluttered desk with a bunch of filing cabinets behind her. The office reminds you of a 1970 movie scene.

"Paper."

I hand her my form, she looks at it, says, "Sit," indicating me to the bench against the wall. She opens a drawer in her desk and comes out with a small plastic bottle.

"Here, take this into the restroom, piss in it and bring it back here," she says.

"What for, I'm not here on any DUI or drug charges. Why do I need to be tested for whatever?" I say.

"Look Mr., in this office you do as I say, I don't give a fuck what you have been arrested for."

Remembering Adrian told me to keep my cool, and don't rock the boat, I get up, take the bottle into the restroom, perform the task, and bring it back to

244

her.

She picks up the bottle and wheels her desk chair to a counter on the other side of the office where there's a basin. She opens the bottle and places a strip of paper inside the bottle that is protruding from a handheld Alcohol Urine Tester. Waits for a few seconds, she removes it, ejects the strip into a waste container and empties the pee down the drain, rinses the bottle and places it upside-down on the counter with several others. Scoots back to her desk and says, "You've been drinking."

"Yes, last night so what?" I say. "There is nothing in my probation that says I can't have a drink."

"Look Mr. I'm only going to say this one more time, in this fucking office you do what I say and what I want you to do. So as long as I am your Probation Officer you will adhere to my rules and my regulations, is that clear now?"

I just look at her and say, "Okay, is that it, can I go?"

"Not until you pay me forty bucks."

"Forty dollars, for what?" I ask.

"Administration fees, this job doesn't get done for nothing. We don't take cards, only cash or checks."

I take two twenties out of my wallet and put them on her desk.

"Receipt please."

She opens a drawer and takes out a scruffy looking receipt book and writes out a receipt, tears it out, and pushes it across the desk to me.

"Thanks," I say, "now can I go?"

"The FBI called the other day to get travel clearance for you, what was that all about?" she asks.

"Classified information," I say and walk out.

CHAPTER 18

There's a cold wind blowing when I get outside, I wrap my coat around me and walk to my car, hoping to still find it there and still in one piece, which it is. I drive home thinking what a terrible probation officer that was and how the authorities can employ someone like that to perform such an important task.

I spend the weekend with my folks and go back home again on Monday to do some cleaning up around the house. Norman calls to tell me it would appear from all initial tests that the fix I suggested, has worked. They have ordered another ten motherboards with the new components and hope to build them into prototype machines by early January, and have them out in the field, being tested by customers soon thereafter. This was all good news and I hoped that as soon as I was cleared of this crime, I could get on with my life and back to work. I'm sure the shareholders will have no problem with that.

Later that day I got a call from Adrian informing me that I was to appear in court on Wednesday at 11:45 am.

"What is all this about Adrian?"

"They are going to acquit you."

"Wow! —— that's the best news I've heard in a long time, do you have any details?"

"No, the DA's office isn't saying a thing as usual. So, give me a call when you arrive in town and we can meet and go to court together, see you then."

A few minutes later I got another call. This time it's from Clare Gibbs.

"Hi, I heard from my source in the DA's office

they are going to acquit you on Wednesday!"

"Yes, I've just a few minutes ago spoken to my attorney and he told me I am due to appear in court at 11:45 p.m."

"Grant, I have a lot I need to discuss with you, is it at all possible for you to come up this evening?"

"Sure, let me see if I can get a flight, it shouldn't be a problem."

"Also, I have a big favor to ask,"

"Okay, what is it?"

"I have some sad news, — Joe my partner, he passed on Sunday afternoon and is being buried tomorrow. Could you accompany me to the funeral tomorrow? There will be people from the Cambridge precinct there and I could truly do with a little support?"

"Sure, no problem, let me see if I can still get a flight out this afternoon."

I tell her I'll call to let her know if I'm successful or not and hang up.

I quickly look for flights leaving Philly for Boston this afternoon and evening. I found one leaving at 4:30 p.m. There are only business seats available, but I think, 'what the hell', and book business class. I call dad to give him the good news and tell him that I'll keep in touch. I book an Uber car to pick me up in an hour, throw a few things in an overnight bag, and jump in the shower. I dress in a dark suit that I will need for the funeral and could also wear to court the next day. While I'm waiting for Uber, I call the Hilton DoubleTree in Chelsea and book a room for two nights. As Clare's phone is engaged, I text her that I have a flight, with my ETA.

It is 6:30 p.m. by the time I get to the hotel. I have already called Clare from the cab and we have arranged to have dinner at a restaurant she chose, somewhere near to where she lives in Somerville, and tell her I'll pick her up at her apartment at 7:15 p.m. I quickly go up to my room, change into something more casual, and call a cab.

The restaurant was full for a Monday evening but as Clare explained, it is one of the most popular in the area. The food was excellent, Mediterranean cuisine, and we had a bottle of Saldo Zinfandel red to go with it. Clare was in no mood to discuss my case seeing as how it touches on Joe and she is a little emotional now. So, we just chat about her and me in general and have a great evening.

I walk her back to her place which happens to be only three blocks from the restaurant. She put her arm in mine and we walked in silence. At the front door, she punches in the door code and it opens.

"Come on in, I'll make some coffee," she says.

We climbed the three flights of stairs to her apartment.

"You don't even have to go to the Y," I say, slightly out of breath.

"She laughs, that depends just on how many times a day one has to do this."

Her apartment building looked quite shabby on the outside but so did most of the old buildings in this neighborhood. Inside it had been remodeled, was modern and well furnished.

We remove our coats and she hangs them in the hall closet. I go and sit on the couch in the living room. The small but adequate kitchen is just off the living room and dining room. I can see her hovering over the coffee mugs.

"How do you take your coffee? With a little cream if I remember right?" she asks.

249

"Good memory," I say.

She comes back with two mugs of coffee and she sits down next to me, kicks off her pumps, and curls her legs up under her. I asked her what time the funeral is in the morning and she said at 11 am. The service will be held in the Catholic Church in Malden and he'll be buried in the Holy Cross Cemetery nearby.

"It's not going to be anything big, certainly not official. His wife Martha wanted a plain private funeral because that was Joe's wishes."

We finished our coffee. I checked my watch; it was close to midnight.

"I had better be getting back and let you get some sleep," I say.

She puts her hand in mine and looks at me and says, "I don't want to be alone tonight, please stay over."

We lay on our backs in bed, me in my briefs and Clare in her PJs —— it's an awkward moment for the two of us, just lying there with the lights out. Then Clare turns on her side facing away from me and pushes against my side.

"Grant, —— just hold me please, just hold me."

I turned into her, put my arm around her waist, and snuggled into her. We fall asleep, spooned together. Sometime in the early hours of the morning, we both must have turned in our sleep. I'm now lying on my back when Clare shakes me awake.

"Hey! —— wake up you sleepyhead, you really do sleep like you're dead, look at what time it is."

I sit up, rub my eyes, and say, "Wow —— you're up and dressed already, what is the time?"

"It's 8:30 am, you want some coffee?"

"Yeah, that would be nice."

I get up and head for the bathroom, wash my face, look in the mirror, I have a stubble of a beard, no razor, no toothbrush. I could be back in jail, I smiled to myself. I finish dressing and I'm sitting on the bed tying my shoes. Clare comes in with the coffee and puts it on the side table, leans over and kisses my forehead, and says, "Thanks Grant for last night, I needed the comfort."

We have a quick breakfast of cereal and fruit. I call a cab and we agree to meet outside the church at 10.50.

After getting back to the hotel, a quick shower, and dressing in my dark suit, I call another cab to take me to the church, getting there just before eleven. Clare has already gone in and is seated in the second row from the back on the side near the windows. I check my coat and sneak in and sit down beside her. She's dressed in a black straight dress, black tights, calf-length black suede boots with wrap-over fur tops. The dress has a low neck and she is wearing a three-strand pearl choker necklace. Her hair cascades onto her shoulders, glinting in the light coming from the window whenever she moves her head. I know it's a funeral, but I can't help but think how stunning she looks and that I shared her bed last night.

She whispers, "I thought you deserted me."

"Sorry," I whisper back, "got caught up in the traffic."

There was only one eulogy, given by one of Joe's old buddies that had been with him in the force. It was touching, and he mentioned the incident where John Gibbs and his partner lost their lives and Joe with two other guys got shot up. He went on to say what a great man Joe was, a good friend and the sort of person one could always rely

251

on, —— that was Joe Philips.

Clare needs a Kleenex and we sit and wait until everyone has left the church. There weren't many there, I would say maybe thirty people. We go to the cemetery and stand in the background. Clare points out people she knew. Joe's daughter is there standing next to her mother, she lost her husband in Vietnam and never remarried. There are a few officers from the Cambridge precinct present.

The ceremony is over and most of the people have left, we make our way over to where Martha and her daughter are standing, about to get into the car to leave. Clare introduces me as a friend, and we give Martha our condolences. Martha insists that we come back to the house for some cake and refreshments.

We are standing drinking coffee when Martha comes over and speaks to us about Joe.

"You know, Clare was like a second daughter to him," she says to me. "He got a kick out of working together with her. So, Mr. Hughes, you'd better look after her, or Joe will come and haunt you," she says with a smile.

"At the moment I think she is looking more after me than I am after her."

"Remember Clare I called you just before he passed," Martha said. "Joe could hardly speak. I had difficulty understanding what he wanted me to ask you. He kept saying 'the photos, ask Clare about the photos, ask her, yes or no?' I had no idea what he meant, but after asking you his question, then telling him your answer was 'no,' he smiled and passed with that lovely smile on his face. I don't know what it meant to him, but it must have been important. I'm so glad I managed to get hold of you," she says.

By the time we leave Joe's house, it is too late for lunch and too early for dinner, so I say,

"As we are not far from my hotel why don't we go over there. We can sit in the lounge or we can go up to my room, order a drink and you can tell me what you wanted to discuss with me."

"I've got a better idea. Why don't we go back to your hotel, you can check out and come to my place and spend the night there? I need to show you some things on my laptop and it's a lot quieter there than the hotel," she says.

"Are you sure?"

"Yes, why not, I think I know you by now. As you said, I'm looking after you, and I need to make sure the hotel management doesn't file charges against you for disturbing the peace with that stupid alarm you have."

"Oh, I see now —— that makes perfect sense," I say with a smile.

I get my bag, check out of the hotel, and walk out to Clare's car in the parking lot.

Sitting next to her in the car as we drive to her place, I ask, "Clare, I'm curious to know what it is Joe wanted to know just before he passed. You obviously gave him the right answer. What was it that put the last smile on his face?"

"Aha — he wanted to know, 'yes' or 'no,' whether I really did take those photos in the women's locker room," she says.

"Ms. Gibbs, I think I heard Martha say you told him 'no,' —— am I correct?"

"Mr. Hughes, you ask too many questions," and we look at each other and both burst out laughing.

Back at her place, each with a beer, sitting in

the living room, she says. "Let me tell you what the FBI has revealed to us so far. First, they were pleased with the fact we tracked the boat and identified Robert Croning. They gave us the full report of what they found when they dug up John Doe. Without boring you with all the forensic details and stuff, take a guess whose body it was?"

"I have no idea,"

"Mark Edwards."

"What!! —— The Mark Edwards whose identity Croning is now walking around with?"

"Yep, the one and only, —— apparently this Mark Edwards from Maine has been missing for years. He lost his wife to cancer and had no immediate family. He went off the rails and his friends said he just disappeared, never heard from him again, so they reported him missing. The FBI tracked him down in Boston, where he'd been living as a tramp, was a confirmed alcoholic visiting the AA on and off, mainly to get company and warmth in the winter months."

"It was pretty easy to identify him, his prints, mug shot, blood type and DNA were on file for DUI. The toxicologist found heavy traces of prescription sleeping drugs in his stomach."

"Christ I'm slowly getting the picture," I say.

"What do you mean," says Clare, "what picture?"

"Bob is also a confirmed alcoholic; he still went to AA meetings. I bet you he befriended this Mark Edwards at the meetings and then invited him to stay in the studio with them, until shortly before I arrived."

"What makes you think that?" asks Clare.

"Well, I never thought about it until now, but while I was at my sister-in-law's place, I noticed a few odd things, but I never paid too much attention to them at the time. For instance, Sylvia said to me I could hang my stuff in the closet. She said there were some of Bob's old clothes hanging there, so I should just push them to the side as there's plenty of room. I didn't pay much attention to what was in the closet, as I was tired, and it was late. The next day after the 'rude awakening,' whilst showering I noticed there were black hairs in the drain. There were old clothes in the closet when I dressed, but they weren't what I'd call Bob's style, although they were clean, they smelt of cigarette smoke. You know how clothes seem to retain the smell of cigarette smoke, even when they have been laundered. Neither Bob nor Sylvia smoked, so I thought that was odd. There were a pair of old and stained sneakers on the floor with holes in the toes, and I wondered why he would want to keep them."

"So now I'm thinking maybe it was this Mark Edwards staying there before I arrived, they drug the poor guy with sleeping pills and keep him in the basement or one of the rooms upstairs. All the time Bob is at home, not out playing golf. Christ Clare, what do you think about that for a scenario?"

"I think you may be onto something; we need to speak to the Feds about this," says Clare.

"Yes, I think we do,"

I get up and pace around the room hitting my fist into my hand.

"Just think, they could have then carried him upstairs when I left that morning and staged that whole thing. No wonder Sylvia was so anxious to get the body released before they could perform an autopsy. If they had, they would have discovered the overdose of sleeping drugs. Fuck me, I'm sure I'm on the right track."

"Come and sit down, relax before you have a heart attack," says Clare, "I want to show you what I've been doing."

She opens her laptop and while it's loading she says, "The insurance industry is worldwide as you know, but what you don't know is that they have a mutual agreement to be able to share information. Now the bigger companies have already uploaded a lot of basic data onto the Cloud. It isn't complete and it's unsophisticated, but it works if you have a lot of patience and time. The smaller insurance companies have only just started storing their data on the Cloud. So, one still must log in and out of different servers to get all the info needed. Over the past days since I got back from your place, I've been doing quite a bit of research."

"What have you found?"

"Something you said made my ears prick up. Remember you mentioned your sister-in-law was keen to buy this big catamaran, so I thought if they bought something that big, being worth a few hundred thousand, they would surely want to insure it."

"I first checked what a 'cat' that size would cost. Not new, say preowned and I got a figure of between $250/350K for a 35/40 Ft. 'cat' in good condition. Then I started to look at who had taken out insurance on a boat in that time frame, around those values. There were hundreds so I narrowed the search down to the US and the surrounding countries. I then ended up with twenty-five possibilities."

"Most of them were in the US, some in Canada, the rest were in the Caribbean Islands and Bermuda. Then I got to thinking about what Agent Cooper said when we were in the car coming back from Cape May."

"He said a few things, what in particular are you referring to?"

"Remember he said that with Bob Croning's financial experience he could have taken the money and put it in an offshore account. So, I started to look at some of our neighboring islands and places he may have accounts like Trinidad/Tobago, Cayman, Bermuda, Belize. I found two boats that had been insured in that time frame, one was a 41 Ft 'cat' called the Skipjack for $380K sold in Belize and paid for by a brokerage firm in London. The other was a smaller one 32 Ft for $185K sold in Hamilton, Bermuda. What do you think?" Clare asks.

"It sounds like the forty-one-footer called Skipjack could be a possibility," I said. "The broker in London could mean it was for anyone. Have you spoken to the Feds about this?"

"No, I've only just finished getting this all together the last few days and then you arrived, so no I haven't yet."

"When are you planning on telling them?"

"Well, you are hopefully going to get a full pardon tomorrow and I was thinking maybe we could go and do some snooping around down in Belize, what do say?"

"Belize, where the fuck is Belize?"

"You mean you don't know where Belize is Mr. Hughes, I can see you have not been living the good life, where have you been all this time man?" says Clare sarcastically, with a smile on her face.

"Maybe the reason you don't recognize the name Belize is that it was formerly known as British Honduras. The country is bordered by Mexico in the north and Guatemala to the west. It is now one

257

of the top destinations for US and European tourists. Now, do you remember?"

"Yes, thanks for the geography lesson, Ms. Gibbs. Are you seriously thinking of going down there?"

"Why not, I have been on the Belize dealership's website who sold the boat, to download pictures of the catamaran Skipjack and we have pictures of Robert Croning as Mark Edwards. As for Robert and Sylvia Croning, I'm sure you can rustle up a few pictures of them, as well as pictures of your Diane and Jason. We can go down there, play the tourist thing, snoop around, show a few pictures here and there, and see what bites. I think you deserve a little holiday after all the crap you've had to go through."

"So, we keep this to ourselves for the meantime, don't tell the Feds and we go down south to do some Dick Tracy stuff?"

"Yeah, that's the general idea."

"Okay, let's see what happens tomorrow."

I tell Clare I must call my attorney and tell him I'm in town otherwise he will be wondering if I've arrived. I promptly do and explain to him that I'm not at any hotel but staying at a friend's place in Somerville. He said no problem, I give him the address and he said he'd pick me up at 11:00 a.m.

We order a pizza for dinner and I go out and get a bottle of wine from the local store. We watch a bit of TV and then crash. The situation is much the same as the previous night, we both fall asleep and I'm the perfect gentleman.

It's funny how some dreams are more realistic than others, some are in black and white and others are in color and so vivid. In this dream it's all in color, I'm driving a late model bright red sports

258

car with the top down. Clare is sitting next to me and we are on this long straight deserted road. In the far distance, I can see this bright blue glow, sort of hovering over the road. Clare is shouting 'go, go, faster, faster.' I'm pressing down on the accelerator and we are screaming down this road and I'm enthralled. I keep pressing harder on the pedal and Clare is shouting 'yes, yes, go, go,' when suddenly I wake up.

"Oh my God, not again!" I say, "Clare what are you doing?"

She is astride me, fully naked, her beautiful breasts are inches from my nose.

"Oh, just go Grant, just go, go, lift me, lift me higher, oh my God," she cries out loud, as she moves up and down on my body.

I fall into the rhythm of this beautiful race, now I have to finish it, the blue hovering light seems only seconds away and I push down further on the accelerator and we both blast through the sound barrier with a sonic boom. We lay next to each other breathless, for at least five minutes neither of us saying anything.

Then Clare turns to me and says, "Christ, you are something! Ever since I heard your story in the courtroom, I've been fantasizing about this event, as I think a lot of women in the courthouse that day must have had similar thoughts. I never thought it could happen, especially not with you anyway. When I woke up this morning and I saw you just lying there in your sleeping shorts, I got so horny I couldn't help myself. I said to myself, 'fuck does he really sleep so soundly? My God you certainly answered my question, —— what an experience!"

She rolls over on her side and puts her leg over mine and kisses me full on the mouth.

"Thank you I needed that, it's been a long, long time," she says.

We lay like that for a while, nothing was said, and there was nothing that needed to be said. We eventually get up; I shower and dress for court.

Clare says she is going into the office and I should call her and let her know how things go in court later that morning.

Adrian picks me up at eleven outside Clare's apartment. On the way, I brief him of recent events and what the Feds found when they dug up the body.

"Christ Grant, we're going to sue those bastards fucking asses off. Do you have time after court to come to the office? I want you to meet with our civil guys unless you want to go with someone else in Philly."

"No, Adrian, I don't have anyone in mind. That would be great," I say.

We are scheduled to meet Judge Alex Harper who is the same judge assigned to my retrial in the lower district court at 11:30 a.m. The assistant district attorney is present, so is the court clerk and stenographer. The judge comes in and addresses the assistant district attorney. There are no formalities.

"I believe the assistant district attorney wishes to make a statement."

"Yes, your honor," and he picks up the charge sheet and reads from it.

"The people wish to withdraw all charges against the said defendant Grant Hughes for the murder of Mr. Robert Archer Croning, the rape and aggravated assault of Mrs. Sylvia Rebeca Croning, as well theft and robbery of sixty-five thousand US dollars from the safe in their home at 44 Willow

Grove Lane, Cambridge, Massachusetts, as well as calculatingly setting ablaze the said premises."

"What brings you to this decision?" asks the judge.

"Certain evidence has presented itself indicating that the body was not that of Mr. Robert Croning. As a result, it now appears that Mr. Hughes was a victim of a scam, and all charges have been dropped against him."

The judge looks at me and says, "Mr. Hughes, will you please stand."

I stand and the judge says, "Mr. Hughes, there are times when the justice system makes mistakes and people like you become the victims of these mistakes. We are not infallible. We apologize for your misfortune and suffering you must have had to endure during the time you were in custody. You are now free to go." The judge bangs his gavel and says, "Court adjourned."

"That's that." Adrian looks at me and says, "Well, in all my days in court, this is a first for me, congratulations Grant," and he gives me a big bear hug. "Thanks, Adrian, you have been a great attorney. What a relief, you can't believe how pleased I am that this nightmare is finally over."

We are just about to leave when the assistant district attorney comes over and says, "Mr. Hughes, we would like to get in touch with your wife and your sister-in-law, if you have any idea where they may be. I would advise you to inform us, as withholding of information relating to a crime is an obstruction of justice. I'm sure you don't want to be arrested again."

As he is about to turn and leave, Adrian says, "I was under the impression this case is now in the capable hands of the FBI."

261

"That's a matter still to be decided," says the assistant district attorney, as he turns and walks away.

Adrian calls after him, "Good luck with that Sherlock."

"Gee — what a fucking asshole, he didn't even have the decency to come and say, 'hey we fucked up —— I'm sorry.'"

"That's why they become prosecutors and don't go into practicing law. It's 'the nature of the beast'. They just can't leave it alone and can never see the fucking forest for the trees."

CHAPTER 19

I call Clare and tell her that I'm no longer a criminal, saying I'm going back to Adrian's offices to discuss the civil case against the state. She said she has discussed our Dick Tracy thing with her boss, and we should discuss it later when we see each other.

We go back to Adrian's office in the East Cambridge commercial district one block from the river. Their offices are located on the seventh to the tenth floor. I met with two of Adrian's colleagues, Keith Anderson one of the other senior attorneys, and Martin Taylor. Their specific office was on the top floor where they have a splendid uninterrupted panoramic view of the river and surrounding district. We spend an hour discussing my case while they take copious notes. It's agreed that I have ample grievance to warrant a civil lawsuit against the state. They certainly would like to take on my case and file a lawsuit with the district justice of Cambridge, against the Cambridge Police Department. They will lay the complaint out for Adrian and myself to read and approve before they actually file it.

Adrian walks me out and says, "Grant we will be seeing more of each other. These civil cases can take time and I mean years for one like this to finally come to court and fruition, because of all the political red tape that is associated with suing the state. Be patient, we will get these bastards and justice will be served."

With that, we shake hands at the elevator and as he turns to leave, Adrian says,

"Check downstairs with reception, I think there is a package for you."

Downstairs in the lobby, I walk over to the reception,

"Hi, I'm, Grant Hughes, I believe there may be a package here for me?"

"Oh, yes Mr. Hughes," she reaches under the counter with both hands and comes up with a box and places it on the counter.

"I believe this is for you," she says, and she pushes the box towards me.

It's a gift box containing three different bottles of Glenmorangie Highland Single Malt Scotch Whiskies.

"Don't drink them all at once," she says and smiles.

I call Clare and we arrange to meet at a bar just a few blocks from her apartment in an hour. She says she is just finishing up a report and would be on her way in a short while. I hail a cab and give him directions to the Red & Gold bar. I was about to take a sip from my second beer when Clare sits herself down opposite me in the booth where I was sitting.

"Whew!" she exclaimed, —— "it's been a busy day and it started that way too, didn't it?" she says smiling. "You can get me a beer too please."

I get up and get her a beer, when I return, she's examining the box of whiskey.

"Wow —— have you been on a spending spree to celebrate?" she asks. We click beer bottles, and both take a swig.

"No, it's a gift from my attorney!"

"Tell me first how your morning in court went?"

I tell Clare and she says, "I told you they are all fucking assholes, every one of them. I hope your guy sues their asses off, fucking scumbags," and she takes another long swig from her beer

264

bottle.

"What did your boss think of our trip down south?" I ask.

"He wasn't too enamored with the idea. He thought the information was a bit too sketchy to go flying down there. He put a call through to our London office to see if they could find out who this broker represented. Depending on what they come up with, I may get the go-ahead," she says.

"Okay fair enough. Did he mention anything about telling the Feds?"

"No, and I wasn't going to mention it unless he asked."

"So, I guess we just sit tight and wait to see what London comes up with."

"Yeah, the boss gave the guy in London my email, so he will contact me directly if he gets anything or needs more info. They are six hours ahead, so hopefully, by tomorrow we may have a reply."

When we finish our beers, I call my dad and tell him I'm now a free man again and we are working on some leads to find Diane and Jason and that I may be away for a while. Clare recommends a good Chinese restaurant within walking distance from where we are, and we make our way there for dinner. I ordered a bowl of Crescent dumplings to share for starters, with white pork in garlic sauce as our main course and Clare ordered the Kindling noodles. We have fun with the chopsticks and drink a bit too much rice wine. It's a good thing we can walk back to her place.

The next morning Clare is shaking me awake.

"Wake up, wake up." She has a mug of coffee in her hand and sits down on the side of the bed.

"Come on, sit up you can't drink coffee lying

down," she says.

"Okay, okay give me a chance to at least open my eyes," and I push myself up into a sitting position and take the coffee from her.

"Thanks, I don't think rice wine and I agree too well" "Not feeling your chirpy self this morning Mr. Hughes?" "Na,— I just need coffee."

"Guess what?" she says.

"This is a bit early in the morning for guessing games, I have no idea."

"I got an email from London and they have followed the money from a bank in the Caymans, National Bank & Trust Ltd. And get this,— the boat was registered in George Town, Caymans, under the name of —— wait for it —— Mark fucking Edwards. It was dated and signed there six weeks ago."

Now I was fully awake. "Whoa! —— he was there six weeks ago."

"That means he bought the boat in Belize and then sailed it to the Caymans to get it registered there. That somehow doesn't make sense," she says.

"I agree, why to sail to the Caymans just to go and get it registered, why didn't he just register the boat in Belize where he bought it?"

"I need to go into the office and discuss this with my boss and see what he has to say, it's getting complicated. Can you stick around, no I tell you what, why not come into the office with me, my boss would love to meet you."

"Are you sure, —— if it's not going to complicate things for you?"

"No of course not, he knows you were going to play Dick Tracy with me down south."

"Okay then, let me get some clothes on."

An hour later we are sitting in Clare's boss's office discussing the scenarios of the case. They decided that we needed to bring the FBI up to speed. The boss calls his contact at the FBI and he is put through to the investigating officer in charge of the case, Agent Brian Moore. Clare briefly explains to him what we have discovered, and he says he wants to discuss this with us face to face as it is becoming complicated.

Thirty-five minutes later the four of us are sitting in the boardroom. After dispensing with the introductions and the refreshments, Agent Moore takes up the discussions.

"Right, you two have done a great job of tracking this guy down, but unfortunately, we don't have any jurisdiction in the Cayman Islands, so we can't officially go snooping around down there. All contacts we make must either go via the US Embassy in London or here in Washington DC. Believe me, both are a pain in the ass, they want to know all the fucking details, the ins, and outs of the cat's backside, and then some. So, we try and avoid them as much as possible."

"What I can't understand is why would he go to all the trouble of sailing to the Caymans to register the 'cat,' why not just register it there in Belize, much easier wouldn't you think?" I ask.

"You have a point," says Agent Moore. "I think it has something to do with the fact that many boat owners choose to have their boats registered in places like the Cayman Islands to avoid the high taxes of the western world. You see, the country in which you have your boat registered and then fly their flag can have a big effect on the amount of money you will be able to save, as well as your freedom of travel."

267

"The (CSR) Cayman Island Shipping Registry is one of the world favorites because it offers so many advantages, such as full protection by the British Royal Navy in any international waters. If you are in a hurry to get a boat registered and you have the right amount of cash, then the Cayman Island Shipping Registry can process your registration immediately."

"Okay, I can now see why he would go to all that trouble to have the boat fly the Cayman flag. That means he has virtually unrestricted sailing rights around the world."

"Yes, even in and around our waters they can cruise unrestricted, they need only to report to US customs when entering the country or changing customs district. Not only that, because the Caymans is Tax Neutral, they automatically get banking facilities and directorship services, together with, of course, all the other wonderful tax benefits the Caymans offer."

"Whoa —— !" says Clare, "I think I know now where the fourteen million from the insurance went."

"I would guess you are right," says Moore, "but our hands are tied, we need strong proof that a crime has been committed before they will even investigate it. They don't want to lose their reputation as a money haven."

"Now here's my proposal," says Agent Moore. "Why don't you two go down to the Caymans as tourists and do some investigation work? You see what you can come up with and report back to me directly. What do you think, Ms. Gibbs? You have the experience being in the force long enough to know the ropes. What does the boss man say?"

Clare's boss says,

"Well, you two had better start making some travel plans then, I guess. How many days do you think it will take Clare?" he asks.

Clare looked at me and said.

"Well, Mr. Hughes, do you feel like a bit of travel?" and I sort of shrugged my shoulders.

"Sure, why not, I'm in your capable hands Sherlock Gibb," I say.

"Boss I have no idea, at least three or four days,— who knows what we find, could be longer, could be shorter."

"Okay, I'll leave it up to you Clare. Mr. Hughes I would like to say I could expense your trip but unfortunately, I can't, my CEO would have my balls for that."

"No problem, I wasn't expecting your company to do that. I will add it to the ever-growing expenses I'm going to submit when my civil case goes to Court."

"Aha! —— yes I can understand Mr. Hughes, you must be very angry."

By the late afternoon, we had booked our flights out of Philadelphia to the Caymans for the day after tomorrow and made hotel reservations at the Comfort Inn in George Town. I rebooked my return flights to Philly for tomorrow morning and Clare made a single booking.

We're flying out of Philly because I need to pack a bigger bag and to bring my folks up to speed with recent developments. It's also an opportunity for them to meet Clare and to go out for dinner together that evening to celebrate my acquittal. That evening dad and Clare, for the most part, are deep in discussion. Sometimes they look over at me and laugh. It would seem I'm the topic of most of their discussion, but if they are having fun, be it at my expense, I didn't care. I'm happy for dad and I carry on my conversation with mom.

The next day we fly six hours to George Town's Owen Robert International Airport. Fortunately, we don't have to contend with any time difference, only a temperature difference at a balmy 84°F when we walked off the plane and into the airport at 3:30 p.m. that afternoon.

Our accommodation is at the Comfort Inn on West Bay Road and we get a cab, or a taxi as they call it there. The island is sooo big that it takes us all of twelve minutes from the airport to the hotel and the driver says one can get to most places on the island within 10 to 15 minutes!

We make ourselves comfortable and recap our strategy for tomorrow. We have the family pictures we'd previously discussed, as well as the downloaded Skipjack pictures. We intend to pay the Shipping Registry offices a visit in the morning, see what information they will disclose, and take it from there. As there is nothing else, we can do, we slip into our bathing gear and make for the pool.

After a fine breakfast, the next morning we get a taxi to the government buildings on Elgin Avenue, which is, yes you guessed right, ten minutes away. The taxi drops us outside this rather large impressive building taking up most of the block. It must be five stories high with a pinkish brown façade, and the front of the building has beautifully manicured lawns with palm trees. Hedges are growing alongside the wide granite stairway leading to the four large doors at the top. We ascend the ten or twelve stairs to the top and enter through the doors into a hall more like a large bank.

I now understand, there's a lot of money in

270

shipping registration on this Island. The place is not that busy, I spot an Information sign and we head towards the counter. I greet the young lady behind the counter. "Good morning, we are trying to establish if my brother-in-law registered his boat here. Is there someone we can speak to please?"

"You will need to speak to one of our agents, I'll see if one of them can see you. Please take a seat over there," she says, indicating to several black leather couches, and tables dotted with magazines. A small trickling water-fall feature that cascades over artificial rocks into a pool with goldfish, sits to one side of the seating area.

We sit and scarcely have time to look around when a middle-aged local islander comes over to us and asks what it is we want to know. I explain to him we are looking for my brother-in-law Mark Edwards, whom we lost contact with some weeks ago. The last time we spoke to him he was in Belize and he informed us that he was in the process of sailing to the Caymans to register his boat, the Skipjack, here on the Island. We were wondering if you can tell us whether that took place as we have not heard from him since then.

"You know sir, this island here is renowned for its *con-fi-den-ti-ality,*" he says, drawing out the letters of the word as he speaks, "we ain't allowed to disclose dat sort of information, I'm really sorry sir, but de rules is de rules," he says.

"Aha!" I say, "that's sad, he's going to have a big shock when he flies home for Christmas because his mother passed away a week ago and his father asked me to try and locate him. Oh well, I guess we will have to go down to the various marinas and see if anyone down there has seen the boat. Thanks anyway."

271

"I'm really sorry sir I can't help you."

As we turned and walked out, I hear him say as he walks back to his office "Hey Jenny, I'm goin te take me a quick smoke brek."

We get outside and stand on the top of the stairs and look out over the lawns and palm trees wondering where to go next.

Clare says,

"Nice try, now what?"

"Well, I guess we'll go down to the marinas and see if anyone down there recognizes the boat, I know it's a long shot with the hundreds of boats out there but it's our only chance. Let's walk down towards the shoreline for a taxi, maybe we can spot one there."

We start to walk down the steps when I hear, "Sir, sir," and the agent with whom we spoke inside, is lighting up a cigarette and walking over to us.

"Sir, —— go check in de library for de newspaper, it will be about two weeks ago," he says.

"What's in the paper?" I ask.

"No, you check." He shrugs, turns and he walks back to the front of the office and carries on smoking.

I look at Clare, she looks at me, "What was that all about?"

"I don't know, but maybe we should go check it out, what have we got to lose."

A taxi takes us to the George Town Public Library on the corner of Fort and Edward St, if we knew it was that close, we could have walked. The Library like many of the buildings here is old but has been very well preserved. It's situated in front of a park with a fountain and the same palm trees that are growing everywhere on the Island. It's a

272

large white rendered building taking up maybe a quarter of a football field, larger than I would have thought one would have on a small island. It must be three stories high with a sort of a square tower-like structure in the center. Over the entrance of the double doors is written '1939' so I assume it was erected around that period.

Inside the building, the walls are full of shelves, packed with books and magazines, and we make our way over to an Information desk. I ask one of the female assistants behind the desk if they keep copies of past local newspapers.

"Yes," she says. "There are only two local papers, the Cayman Compass and the Times. Copies are filed on the computer and you are welcome to browse on any of the ones that are open on the desks over there." She points to tables where people are sitting working on computers.

"If you need any help, please ask," she says.

We find a table that's not occupied and start the PC. Not quite sure what we are looking for, we type in the names of the two local newspaper papers she mentioned in the search bar. We select the Times and pull up the paper for a date two weeks back. It's a Tuesday and page through it, but nothing sticks out. We do the same with the Compass, nothing. So, we check for the next day Wednesday, and bingo, front-page article! 'Visitor Mark Edwards dies in a diving accident'. A picture of the boat and the police bringing the body ashore, also pictures of Sylvia in a wet suit being interviewed, the story reads:

Mark Edwards and his wife Sylvia were diving off the reef in Bloody Bay Wall.

'They were down at about ten meters, reported Sylvia. Mark was swimming above me and to the side, looking at some reef fish in the coral. I went around the other side of a large coral outcrop and watched various fish. I lost sight of my husband for several minutes.'

'When I came around the coral again and looked up, I could see him to my left. He was upside down and sinking slowly into the reef. I thought that was strange and no air bubbles were escaping from his demand valve. I immediately finned-up to him, turned him the right way up, and looked at his eyes inside his mask, they were closed. His mouthpiece was still in his mouth, but he wasn't breathing.'

'I ditched his weight belt and slowly inflated his life vest. We surfaced a few minutes later. My sister was on the yacht. I shouted for her to bring the dingy and we pulled Mark on board. I pulled off his mask and tried to revive him but on the dingy it was impossible. We got him back on the boat and both took turns performing CPR while we motored back to port.'

The coroner's prognosis was Mark Edwards had died of a heart attack while underwater. It was a tragedy. He, his wife, and sister-in-law had been vacationing on the island for some weeks.

"Whoa! —— **can you fucking believe it**," I say out loud, forgetting where I am. Everybody suddenly stops looking at their screens and looks over at me. "Sorry, sorry," I say, raising my hand in apology.

Clare looks at me, pulls an ugly face, says, "oops," and whispers, "You look like you're ready to blow your top."

While reading this newspaper report, I'm imagining Jason witnessing his uncle lying dead with his mother giving him CPR? The vision in my mind is just horrific. I'm so mad. I'm beside myself.

"I need to get some fresh air, let's finish up here ASAP," I whisper back.

After looking through the papers, we also find the obituary giving the date of the funeral which was a private cremation ceremony. Well, my sister-in-law wasn't about to make the same mistake twice, this time she's burning the evidence. We make several copies of the newspaper articles and leave the library.

After several deep breaths of fresh air, I say, "Another dead body, is it really Bob this time? What's been going on here, this adds a whole new twist to the saga?"

"Clare, just think,—— Jason saw all that on the boat."

"Oh my God yes, I forgot about Jason being there to witness all that, poor kid it will no doubt haunt him the rest of his life."

"If I could get hold of Diane now, I'd throttle her."

"Okay so what now," says Clare, "where do we go from here?"

"I have an idea, let's head back to the hotel for lunch. We can use the internet there and let's look up diving shops in the area. I bet they bought some of their dive gear here on the island and even if they didn't, the diving fraternity would be familiar with this dive accident. They just may be able to tell us where the boat is moored."

We head back to the hotel, Clare gets her laptop from the room and we sit out by the pool, ordering some beers and a light lunch. Clare pulls up the dive shops on Google, there must have been forty. So, we eliminate all the resort ones, concentrating on the ones specializing in supply, sales, and service of dive equipment. We make a list of phone numbers.

I call the first diving shop and speak to an assistant.

'Yes, they heard about the accident, very tragic, such a freak accident. No, they didn't know where the Skipjack was moored, but could they interest me in a dive course, it's really very safe, blah, blah, blah.'

On my fourth call, I hit pay dirt.

'Yes, they supplied them with a portable compressor, four scuba tanks, and some other gear. Yes, they delivered the stuff to them at Mainstay Sailing Marina.'

After lunch, we head out to Mainstay Marina and have a look around. There were several 'cats' moored there but none that fit the description of the Skipjack. We go into the office and speak to the manager and ask him when Skipjack left. He gives us the normal 'who are you, why do you want to know, we like to keep things confidential,' speech. I tell him that my wife Diane was aboard the Skipjack with her sister Sylvia, when my brother-in-law died in the freak diving accident two weeks ago. After the funeral, which unfortunately I couldn't attend being in Europe on business, I received their message that they were still determined to sail home to the US, much to everyone's concern. As no one has heard from them since that message, we flew down here yesterday looking for them. I show the manager pictures of us, the Skipjack, and fortunately, he buys our story.

He says it's a terrible thing that my brother-in-law had a heart attack while driving. The two ladies were beside themselves when they got back here from their dive. He called the police for them, so tragic. They paid up and sailed out a week later, but he did not know which US port was to be their destination.

I ask him, besides the two ladies, was there anyone else on board and he says they had taken on a young crew member, but nobody else. When they first arrived at the marina, there were only three people on board.

We thanked the manager and he said, "I sure hope you find your family soon."

That's extremely worrying I thought, for sure Jason would be with Diane. Where the hell was Jason if he wasn't on the boat with them? There could only be one other explanation, she had left him with her Aunt Joan in Florida. Why didn't I think of that before? I just assumed she would have taken him with her wherever she went.

We go back to the hotel and call Agent Brian Moore and give him all the details. He commends us on a great piece of detective work. He says they already have an APB out for the three fugitives, and they will remove the one for Robert Croning alias Mark Edwards. They will now alert the coast guard and Customs and Immigration at all ports of entry into the US. The noose was tightening slowly and surely.

I call dad, giving him all the news and ask him to go to my house to look in the phone book next to the telephone, for the number of Diane's Aunt Joan. An hour later my dad calls back with her number. I call her.

"Aunt Joan, it's Grant,——Jason's dad, can I speak to him please." I was purposefully abrupt, to throw her off guard and make her believe I knew Jason was there just in case Diane had told her not to tell anyone where Jason was.

"Grant is that really you, you're not in jail?" she asks.

"No, Aunt Joan I was found not guilty. Can I now please speak to Jason?"

"But of course, you can," she says, "he's outback running around."

I can hear her calling in the background, "Jason, —— Jason, —— phone, it's your daddy."

A minute later I can hear a scramble for the phone,

"Daddy, daddy, where are you?"

"Hi — how's my buddy doing, you been okay while I've been away huh?"

"Where are you daddy, when are you coming to take me home?" I can hear the anxiety in his little voice.

"I'm not too far away son, I'll be there to pick you up tomorrow, you just hang in there okay, let me speak to Auntie Joan again, I love you lots and lots, see you tomorrow."

"Okay daddy byeee —— Auntie Joan, daddy wants to speak to you."

"Hello Grant, if he could have climbed down the telephone line he would have, he had it pressed so hard against his little ear, it's all red," she says.

"Aunt Joan I don't know what you have been told, but whatever it was, it's a pack of lies, I was framed. Maybe the newspapers down your way never carried the news, but my release was in the press up here last week. I only found out today that Jason was not with Diane, so I assumed she had left him with you."

"Oh, Grant I'm so glad you called, I've been worried sick, I haven't heard from Diane in weeks, she normally calls at least once a week to speak to Jason, but lately nothing. He is so sad; he misses

278

you terribly and asks about you constantly."

"Look Aunt Joan, I don't know where Diane is, so I'm flying down there tomorrow to come and get him. I'd like to spend a day with you and explain things if that's okay."

"That will be lovely Grant, I look forward to seeing you again, what time should I expect you?"

"Aunt Joan it will be late afternoon I expect, but I'll call you and keep you informed. Please give me your address as I'm not at home now." She does so and we hang up.

I call my dad and mom, tell them I have found and spoken to Jason and that I'm going to get him tomorrow. They were over the moon with joy.

"You come straight here from the airport, don't even dare go home first," dad says.

I tell him I would spend a day with Joan sorting things out with her, then we will fly back.

We contact Agent Moore again and inform him that I have found my son and there's a big possibility that his mother is going to call her Aunt sometime. Maybe they could trace the cell phone when Diane does call and get her location. Moore said he'd get the necessary people onto it immediately.

CHAPTER 20

Clare flew back to Boston the next day from the Cayman Islands and I flew into Tampa. I rented a car and drove to Aunt Joan's place in St Petersburg. Well, as you can imagine seeing Jason again after so long is just overwhelming. I had tears in my eyes as I swirl him around and around in my arms. We played catch with the baseball until it's too dark to see. Jason wanted to know where his mommy is and why she hasn't called, like she said she would every day.

Now how do you tell your six-year-old son that his mother is a felon? I must tell a lot of white lies and hope that they will not come back and bite me later. I know I will eventually have to tell him more when she is arrested one day and goes to jail. But at this moment, all I wanted was to see him happy.

That night when Jason is in bed. I explained to Aunt Joan as best I could what Diane and her sister have been up to, without being too realistic and hard on Diane. I explained that there's a warrant out for both sisters' arrest and that if she in any way assists Diane, it will be classified as assisting a felon and seen as a serious crime. She should please bear this in mind before making any rash decisions to help the two sisters. There is also the possibility that the authorities will be coming along to tap her phone in due course.

The next day I squared up financially with Aunt Joan for taking care of Jason. That afternoon two plainclothes cops and a technician came to Aunt Joan's door with a court order to allow them to tap into her telephone line. They explained the procedure and informed her of the big possibility Jason's mother would try to call before Christmas, and what she was to do if this happened.

The next day Jason and I drove to Tampa International Airport and flew into Philly. My folks could not wait to see Jason, so they were at the airport to meet us. It's an exciting and emotional family reunion. Jason and Grammy sat in the back and they never stopped talking for one minute on the way to my folk's home.

The next couple of days I'm busy sorting Jason out and shopping for Christmas.

We are going to have Christmas dinner at my folk's house and mom has invited Clare to come down and join us. She delightfully accepts the invitation and flies down the day before Christmas. Jason and I pick her up at the airport after I explain to Jason that Clare is an old family friend and that she's a detective, and that sealed the bond. Poor Clare never got five minutes peace, she is peppered with questions left, right, and center.

I tell Clare she will have to sleep in the guest room, but to please come and wake me in the morning, and if she can be quick and quiet, it can be 'unconventional' if she likes, I say with a sly grin, she shakes her head and just gives me that evil eye look.

Christmas is wonderful, Jason almost forgot about his mom, as we keep him preoccupied with his gifts and play games with him. It snows the day before Christmas, and Clare and I help him build a snowman in the front garden and mom gives us an old shirt of dads, together with a floppy hat to dress the snowman. We take lots of pictures of Jason and the snowman to show his mom when she gets back.

That night with Jason in bed, I shared a theory with Clare.

"Mmmm, —— and what's your theory?" she asks.

"Maybe the reason Diane and Sylvia haven't been in touch with their aunt is because they have been delayed somewhere by a storm. I'll check the internet and see what the weather has been like down in the Caribbean."

Sure enough, my assumptions are right, a tropical storm had been brewing there for the past three weeks and it is only now making its way out of the Gulf of Mexico. So that would more than likely have delayed them from reaching the US coast.

Clare returns to Boston the second day after Christmas. A week later I get a call from Agent Brian Moore who informs me that they had arrested both Sylvia and Diane trying to enter Tampa Bay. Diane called her aunt as predicted when they got within cellphone range and their location was immediately picked up via the local cell phone towers. Coordinates were quickly calculated and the boat's approximate location out at sea was radioed through to the local coast guard. They had no trouble locating it in the early hours of the morning. Two officers boarded the yacht and escorted it into the Port of St Petersburg.

CHAPTER 21

Eight months have passed, and the trial of Diane and Sylvia was a long, drawn-out four-week affair. I was called as a witness and so was Clare. Diane decided to turn state witness in a plea bargain for a lesser sentence.

This is how the story unfolded in Court.
Both Sylvia and Diane in their teens had developed a lesbian relationship with each other. They had always fantasized about owning a yacht and sailing around the world together. They also wanted to have a child, so Diane was elected to be the mother. Although unsure of how all this was going to come about, they would just follow the course of time and take what opportunities came their way and put their plans in motion. I was dumbfounded and could hardly believe what I was hearing, coming from the woman I had been with for over ten years.

Sylvia had convinced Bob it would be a cinch to pull off the scam and claim all the insurance. Bob being the materialistic person he was and having got away with one insurance fraud claim, was all in to make the big-time money. After all, who cares about a tramp that has been missing for years?

When the prosecution asked Diane, 'what about your husband, surely you must have felt some remorse or guilt with what you were planning,' she said, 'no, not really, this was like a business. He was just a casualty in the whole scheme of things.'

That really got to me, 'just a casualty' — that's all I was to her.

I sat in Court with Clare and we looked at one

another and shook our heads, it was unbelievable.

Sylvia knew that Bob had no scruples and once he got his filthy paws on the money, Sylvia and Diane could kiss it all goodbye. Unbeknownst to Bob, Sylvia had taken a video of Bob shooting Mark Edwards, and later copied it onto a memory stick and put it in a safety deposit box at a bank. The key she sent to her good friend Dr. Ann Madison in Los Angeles, with instructions that if anything should happen to her, she should go to the bank, open the box, and give the memory stick to the police. Bob was later informed of this. That was their insurance.

They still had a problem though. Bob was also no fool and wasn't about to hand over $14 million to the girls just like that. He had, like we suspected, invested the monies offshore in the Caymans. All his banking details and encrypted accounts were on his PC and there was no way to access it. He apparently changed his password to his PC regularly and this was stored on his cellphone, with access via his phone's thumbprint. His phone seldom left his pocket.

So, Sylvia came up with a unique way of doing away with Bob and making it look like an accidental death. Sylvia had remembered an experiment they had done in high school where the science teacher was demonstrating the different types of gasses. They were using (SF6) Hexafluoride gas in this particular experiment. This gas is five times heavier than air. It's non-flammable, odorless, and contains less than 12% oxygen, compared to the normal atmosphere. If one breathes this gas for several minutes you will die of suffocation. The teacher put ping-pong balls in a long glass beaker and then filled the beaker with SF6 gas. The balls all rose to the top and some fell out, showing how much heavier SF6 gas is than normal air.

Her idea was to insert a quantity of SF6 gas into Bob's blue colored dive tank. The small amount of SF6 gas would drop to the bottom of the tank being five times heavier than air. If the tank was in the upright position, normal air could be received from the tank via the demand valve in one's mouth. However, as soon as one descends forwards down through the water, the dive tank is now inverted and the heavier SF6 gas drops and collects at the other end of the tank where the air intake valve is situated and the SF6 gas would then be inhaled through the demand valve and into the lungs. One would not be conscious of this, assuming one was still breathing oxygen-enriched air. Asphyxiation will occur within minutes. This was the plan, all they had to do was wait for their opportunity for Bob to leave the boat and go ashore for some length of time.

They didn't have long to wait. Bob needed to do some banking, so they sailed back to port in George Town, and while he was away, they did the dirty deed.

Silvia hooked up one of Bob's 10-liter dive tanks to a pressure gauge, it still had 2.3 bars pressure left in the tank. That was fine. She only needed to insert a small amount of the SF6 gas into the tank and under pressure, it would take up little space. She took the cover off the compressor, removed the air filter, and attached a length of rubber hose to the air intake pipe. The tank was then connected to the compressor which Sylvia started. Once it was running smoothly, she opened the valve to allow the tank to receive compressed air. Then she inflated a small balloon and placed it

285

in a five-gallon bucket. She then filled the bucket with SF6 gas from the 2.3-liter SF6 gas canister she had previously bought and had hidden in the locker with the fire extinguishers.

As the gas went into the bucket, the balloon lifted to the top. She then turned the gas off, inserted the end of the rubber hose into the bucket, and almost immediately the compressor sucked up the gas and the balloon dropped back to the bottom of the bucket. She did this three times. Then switched tanks and did the same procedure with his other blue dive tank. Within thirty minutes they had everything back where it belonged.

It was fascinating listening to Diane explaining all this. I could not believe that these two women could come up with something like this, it was mind-blowing. I think the whole Court was flabbergasted with what they had done. But it got more macabre.

Once they had the body back on board the boat, they were able to use Bob's thumbprint to open his cell phone and get the latest password to open his PC. They inverted the two blue dive tanks and discharged most of the air in each tank making sure that all the SF6 gas had been discharged.

Mission accomplished, they sailed back from the dive site and reported it as a dive accident, just as we read in the newspaper.

When the FBI searched the boat, they found the cylinder of SF6 gas still tucked away in the fire extinguisher locker. They also found Robert's PC which the police went through, like they did mine, and guess what! They found the very same cell phone trigger device on his laptop. The FBI suspected he had used it to blow up his folk's yacht while they had been cruising in the Gulf of Main, so he could collect the insurance. Also, on his PC were dozens of pictures of tramps, vagabonds, drifters, guys at AA meetings, the Salvation Army, food banks, and soup stalls, among which was a picture of Mark Edwards. For months Bob had been looking for a suitable candidate to use as a look-like of himself and someone who would not be missed.

I was correct in my assumption that someone had been staying in the studio before I arrived. That person had been Mark Edwards. Apparently, according to Diane's testimony, Bob had selected three other hobos also to be the victim of their scam but ended up choosing Mark Edwards as he and Bob bore the best resemblance.

They had already heavily drugged Mark Edwards before I arrived at the Croning's house and moved him from the studio where he had been staying for a week, to a spare back bedroom upstairs. On the day I was to leave, sometime in the early hours of that morning, Bob came downstairs, checked to see that I was sound asleep. They had already moved the drugged Mark Edwards to their bed. Bob put on gloves and removed the gun from the drawer in the sideboard and collected the knife I had used to cut cheese, which Sylvia had hidden in the kitchen. He then went back upstairs, shooting Mark Edwards point-blank through the pillow to muffle the sound. Unbeknown to him, Sylvia was in the background secretly filming him on her cell phone. She then excused herself saying she wanted to be sick and went to the bathroom and quickly emailed the video clip to her sister, then immediately deleted it. She came back and put the cell phone in the bedside drawer.

Bob then took the gun, went back downstairs, and placed it in the trash bag with the empty wine bottle and other vegetable trash. Later, that morning Sylvia came and woke me up, made me coffee before I left for my conference, giving me the trash bag with the gun to dump in the main trash as I left the premises.

Diane also pointed out that the sixty-five thousand dollars in the Massey's plastic bag did originally come from her. She had drawn the money out of her 401K account and given a check to Bob to cash. Bob said the $65K showed that Diane was committed. He said he wasn't about to fork out that sort of cash to have it just sitting in the evidence room collecting dust.

Bob and Sylvia then cut some strips from the bed sheet using a different knife, Bob then threw the knife I cut the cheese with under the bed. When Sylvia was inserting some of my sperm she had saved from our sexual encounter into her vagina, she and Bob got into an argument as he accused her of enjoying sex with me. When she denied it, he said he had been downstairs at the studio door listening, he called her a liar, a slut and a bitch, slapping her around. Although Sylvia's battered face and bloody nose was not part of the original plan, it added authenticity to the scam. He then tied her feet tightly to the bed, her hands in a noose, and left her.

In the garage, he took a can of gasoline splashing it all over the three cars and around the walls of the garage, opened the garage door with the remote, went out, and closed it again. Just before it closed, he threw a burning match under the door, then walked out the back yard and across the grove of woods into the next neighborhood. He stood there for several minutes until he could see the flames on the roof. He then called 911 from one of his burner cell phones and reported the fire. He had all he needed with him in his backpack. He had been growing his beard and hair for two months. With his long black dyed hair, he looked very much like the now-dead Mark Edwards.

He caught two separate cabs to the Marina Bay where we had moored the boat the day before at the restaurant and it took him four easy days cruising down to Cape May. He had already contacted the Manager at Bluefin Marina Sales & Service who said they would be interested in buying the boat, which Bob had registered into Mark Edwards's name the previous week. Having sold the boat, Bob flew to Belize where he and Sylvia had seen a catamaran for sale on the internet.

In Belize Bob negotiated a deal with the sales guy. Having sold his boat, he had cash to put down as a deposit on the catamaran and they allowed him to live on the boat, although he couldn't sail it until it was fully paid for. Six weeks later the first of the insurances paid out, when he was then able to pay the balance owing on the 'cat'. He hired two young guys who were keen to go to the Caymans as crew and they sailed to the Grand Cayman Islands soon thereafter. Several weeks later the two girls arrived, they then registered the 'cat' and started to live the good life.

Sylvia was sentenced to life with no parole for being an accomplice to the murder of Mark Edwards and for the murder of her husband Robert Croning. Diane got fifteen years for being an accomplice to both murders, but because she became a state witness, she would be allowed to apply for parole at some stage.

Clare and I wondered why Diane turned state witness against her sister after all they had gone through together, but as it so often happens, there was a fallout among thieves.

After tying up all the loose ends on the Caymans such as change of banking details into the joint names of Sylvia and Diane, appointing an attorney to take care of the estate and the Will of the late Mark Edwards, they could finally set sail for Florida to pick up Jason. Sylvia hired the Club's part-time bartender as a crew member. With this British, young, good looking guy with a great physique, Sylvia started partying as soon as they left the Caymans and she spent more time in his cabin than her own. When they had to make for the nearest port on the way to the US to avoid the tropical storm, they ended up in Porte de Chiquita on the southeastern tip of Mexico.

Here more partying took place. Drugs were plentiful in Mexico if you had the cash and Sylvia being flush with cash, and in her inebriated state, was spreading it around like candy. This pissed Diane off big time, as she was not a party girl and wanted to get to the US to pick up her son. It would now appear blood is thicker than stepsister's love. They were already weeks late in getting to the US and now more delays. Diane had one hell of a job getting Sylvia to sober up and agree to set sail again, as all she wanted to do now was to party.

It got to the stage where Diane was having second thoughts about this sailing into the blue yonder thing. The idea was that they would anchor about a mile off of the US shore and in the early hours of the morning just before light, the new crew hand was going to drop Diane ashore in the dingy and then return to the boat. He and Sylvia would then sail back out into international waters, waiting for Diane and Jason to join them. As we know the Coast Guard put a stop to that plan.

Unbeknownst to Sylvia at the time, Diane was the downfall of them getting caught, all because of the one call she made. Sylvia had told Diane she could not risk calling, as the call could possibly be traced. Diane thought that just a quick call of a few seconds just to check if Jason were fine, would be okay but unfortunately for them, she was wrong.

CHAPTER 22

I divorced Diane which went through without any hitches. My life changed from being a married man to a single parent dad. We were allowed visitation rights in jail for Diane to see Jason once a month. Explaining to Jason why his mother was in jail was the most difficult job I think I ever had to do. Somehow with the help of my folks and friends, we managed to soften the shock to him and although he did not fully understand the circumstances, he understood that if someone does something wrong, they get punished, even your mother. Jason and I spent a lot of our spare time with Jim and Emma, whose friendship helped me tremendously adapting to being a single parent.

Clare as a result of her success had moved up on the ladder and was doing quite a bit of international investigation. Initially, the insurance companies had one hell of a time getting the bank on the Grand Cayman Island to release the monies that had been deposited there by Bob Croning, alias Mark Edwards.

Lloyds of London eventually stepped in being one of the reinsurers. They threatened to withhold all their insurance taken out on the Island unless the bank agreed to release the funds to the FBI. According to Clare, the process of sorting out how much cash was still available, and the insurance allocations to the various insurance companies, was an absolute accounting nightmare. Once everything was settled, her company would get a percentage of the recovered funds and Clare would be in for a nice bonus.

The Skipjack was sold on auction. Interestingly, on the CSR form, all three names appeared as owners, Mark Edwards, Sylvia Croning, and Catherine Hughes.   It looked like there was no trust amongst thieves. The FBI confiscated Croning's first boat called Taimen and that went back to the insurance company. It also went up for auction and the people from whom it was confiscated, bought it back for less than what their insurance paid them out for it. So, everyone was reasonably happy.

Two years later I was back in court and without boring you again with Court proceedings, allegations, disputes, and so forth, the State finally agreed to settle for one million, three hundred thousand dollars, which was somewhat of a record payout.

Mayor Vernon Lance didn't get re-elected. District attorney Melvin Benmin moved to another state. The new mayor appointed a new chief superintendent at Robert W. Healy Precinct and as a result, many heads rolled.

I was able to pay my dad back the hundred thousand dollars he lent me to pay the Bail Bondsman. I added another hundred thousand to it and told him to take mom on that 'Around the World' cruise they have been talking about for years.

Clare and I became an Item. It was a long-distance relationship as she was away on business a lot. Now it seems to work for both of us. Maybe later when she gets tired of the travel and investigation work, we could settle down together somewhere, who knows, time will tell.

Jason and I grow closer and although I try to be there for him twenty-four seven, it's not always possible with my type of job. He spends a lot of time with my parents and my mom tries to be the mother to him he misses. Once a month we drive up to Boston and visit his mother at the MCI Framingham Correctional Institution. We initially flew to Boston a couple of times but despite the little time we saved, I decided driving there was certainly a lot less expensive, especially with the added car rental cost.

Leaving West Chester just after school on a Friday, we'd arrive at Clare's place sometime in the early evening depending on the traffic, and spend the weekend with her. On Saturday morning we'd visit Diane at the prison just outside Worcester, MA for an hour. One had to make an appointment with the authorities at least a week in advance. The visit would practically take up the best part of the morning with all the protocol one has to follow, from visitors' approval process, children's rules, dress code, parking permits, searches and then it depends on the number of visitors they have on that particular day as to what time slot you get to visit.

It was great on the one hand for Jason to see Diane at least once a month, but on the other hand, emotionally challenging for me to sit with Jason in front of his mother for an hour and have truly little to say. I didn't particularly want to be there, but it was important for Jason who wants to see his mother. There are plenty of questions I want to ask Diane, but the opportunity never came up until much later. For now, it was Jason's time with his mother and I was content to sit back and watch them talk or play board games, look at a book Jason had brought her, or some school project he had been working on.

After the first year, Jason was getting tired of playing board games with his mother as she always won and I could never understand why she never gave the kid a chance to win and give him some confidence and a desire to continue wanting to play. The facility had a play area for the children with games and a TV with children's programs running continuously. Jason decided that after visiting for fifteen minutes with his mother and having nothing more to say, he would go to the play area and watch TV. Now with Jason in the playroom, it gave me the opportunity of asking Diane a few pertinent questions I'd been waiting to ask.

"Diane, now that Jason isn't here, I must ask you, because it's been bothering me for a long time, have you and Sylvia always been lesbian partners?"

"Do you really want to know now, it's not going to make any difference whatever I say, does it?"

"No, but I think at least you owe me the truth. I never did anything to deserve what the two of you put me through."

"Yes, you're right, but now the tables are turned, instead of you being in jail, I am."

"Yes, it's funny how life is, it has a way of coming back and biting you in the butt, so are you going to tell me or not?"

"As little kids Sylvia and I played doctor and nurse, we bathed together, we explored each other. We never thought anything of it. I think my dad must also take the blame for bonding the two of us together as he was always lecturing us about how evil men were, that they would hurt us, take advantage of us, and all that crap, he was just so paranoid, obsessed and overprotective of the two of us. He taught us how to play board games like Chess and Mahjongg to keep us housebound and remember when we were eight, he sent us to the sailing academy in Toms River. All to keep us away from the boys."

"Sylvia and I, we sort of built this fantasy world around us where we would wipe out all the men and it would be just a world of women. We played Chess and the pieces were men and we would play to eliminate as many of the men as we could, in the shortest possible time. When we were kids we didn't know, but dad had a brain tumor. It was a big shock to us as he kept it a secret from us all that time and that's why he had to sell the house at the shore to finance his treatment. You may remember he passed away when I was at college and Sylvia was still completing her final year at high school. My mom took it very badly and went into a depression and never really recovered, and today she is in an assisted living facility and has advanced Alzheimer's disease."

"I'm sorry to hear your mom had to move into a special care facility."

"Well, with the two of us here, it's the best, and there is no other family to care for her."

"To answer your question, —— yes Sylvia and I were lovers when you and I were dating."

"You're joking, you mean the two of you were screwing each other all the time I was dating you?"

"Yes, and you don't have to be so crude. If you must know we were lovers even after you and I were married. Whenever we got the chance to be together, we made love."

"Christ, I can't believe it. My dad always said there was something funny going on between the two of you and I just pooh-poohed it. How the hell could I be so blind?"

"As you heard in court, we planned as kids

growing up that one day, we would be together, but we wanted a child and it was decided that I was to marry first and have the child. Then Sylvia would become a famous film star and we would elope with our child to some far away and obscure country and live happily ever after. Our first plan went to shit when Sylvia's first husband John Ellsworth didn't work out and she divorced him, the two million she got from him as an out of court settlement was hardly enough for us to elope with."

"And then Bob came along, and we waited and waited for the opportunity to do away with him and collect all the insurance money and skip the country with Jason. You didn't really come into the picture or weren't part of the initial plan, but when the conference came up, we got this bright idea that we could kill two birds with one stone so to speak, and just so you know, I never had any idea Silvia was going to wake you the way she did. I was upset about that and I was pissed at you for letting it happen. The rape was a last-minute thing that she and Bob came up with to add authenticity to the crime." "Whoa! You were pissed at me —— that's a bit rich coming from you, seeing I was only business to you. But for your information, immediately after that incident I did feel guilty having cheated on you, but that guilt soon changed to a feeling of contempt, but it's all water under the bridge now. I still can't believe the two of you thought you could pull something off like that."

"Well, we nearly did."

"Yes, but as they say in the classics 'A miss is as good as a mile' —— oops here comes Jason. Just a quick one, do you see much of your sister?"

"No, she's in a separate cell block but we are working on it."

Good luck with that, I thought and with that, the bell rings indicating that in five minutes the visiting time would end, and we need to pack up to leave.

On the way back to Clare's place that Saturday afternoon Jason asks, "Dad, can we get a puppy?"

"A puppy, you want a puppy?" I ask.

"Yes, daddy please can we get one, I always wanted a dog, but mommy doesn't like dogs, so can we get one now?"

"Sure, we can get a dog. When we get home, we will go down to the local SPCA shelter and see if they have one you like."

"Gee dad honest, can we really, that's so cool?!"

He is so excited when we get back to Clare's place all he can talk about is getting a dog.

The drive back from Boston that Sunday afternoon seems to fly by, we are speaking about nothing else but dogs. Jason wants to know everything there is to know about the dogs I had growing up: their names, male or female, what they ate and where they slept, could they swim, did they run fast, and did they play catch? It's almost as if a new world has opened to him and he is getting his first glimpse of it.

Normally Jason gets the bus to my parents' home after school and I pick him up on my way home from work. But today is special, I leave work early to collect Jason from school, as I promised we were going to the local West Chester Shelter to see if they have a dog he likes.

At the shelter, we were overwhelmed with the number of dogs that were up for adoption but what pulled on the strings of Jason's heart is a little puppy that had been rescued a week ago with a broken tail. It was a Beagle/Terrier mix of some

298

sort, maybe four months old. There were four of these pups in the litter, but one came over to Jason, and bites on his sleeve and pulls, trying to play tug-of-war with him. Jason picks him up and says,

"This is the one dad,— this is the one I want please."

"Don't you want one that has a straight tail? What about that one over there?" I say, pointing to one of the other puppies.

"No dad, this is the one I want, can I please have him?"

A few hours later and a few hundred dollars to a good cause, we were on our way home with a puppy, a chip implant, and all the inoculations he needed for a puppy of his age.

"So, son, — I asked on the way home as Jason cradled his new friend in his arms, "what are you going to call him?"

"I don't know dad, — he's got a kind of cute *twist in his tail*,—— maybe I'll call him Twister."

"Yeah —'Twister'— I kind of like that name too."

END

If you enjoyed reading this book, you will want to read another of author T F Grill's books: **'The Marriage Fee. (Ilobola)'** It is completely unrelated to **'A Twist in the Tale,'** and you will definitely enjoy the historical novel which takes place in Mozambique, Rhodesia, and South Africa. You can find the book on Amazon.

www.ingramcontent.com/pod-product-compliance
Lightning Source LLC
Chambersburg PA
CBHW070808180626
46818CB00001B/156